Secrets of the Soul

Facilitated Communication with
Special Children Reveals
Startling Spiritual Messages

of the Soul

Facilitated Communication with
Special Children Reveals
Startling Spiritual Messages

RABBI YEHUDA SREVNIK

Copyright © 2000 by Rabbi Yehuda Srevnik
ISBN 0-9670705-1-1

All rights reserved. No part of this book may be reproduced or transmitted in any form or by any means (electronic, photocopying, recording or otherwise) without prior written permission of the copyright holder.

Distributed by:
Israel Book Shop
501 Prospect Street
Lakewood, NJ 08701
Tel: (732) 901-3009
Fax: (732) 901-4012
Email: isrbkshp@aol.com

Author's address:
24 Agasi Street
Jerusalem, Israel

Printed in Israel

address for questions and comments:
email:ysitzman@barak-online.net

בס"ד

לעילוי נשמת
אבי אדוני מורי ורבי
ר' נחמן דוד ב"ר משה יוסף ז"ל
שנלב"ע ג' תשרי תשמ"ו
ת.נ.צ.ב.ה.

לעילוי נשמות
ר' שמואל ב"ר מרדכי נייר ז"ל
ואשתו מרת רבקה נחמה ב"ר שלמה אשר ז"ל
ת.נ.צ.ב.ה.

לעילוי נשמות
ר' יעקב ב"ר מאיר הלוי סגל הי"ד
ואשתו מרת חנה בת ר' אברהם יוסף הי"ד
ויוצאי חלציהם הרכים
שנרצחו בידי הצורר הנאצי ימ"ש.
ת.נ.צ.ב.ה.

יבלחט"א ויזכו לברכות ר' אבא בן זאב וולף
ודינה בת דוד שלמה עבור תרומתן הנכבדה

בס"ד

שמואל קמנצקי
Rabbi S. Kamenetsky

2018 Upland Way
Philadelphia, Pa 19131

Home: 215-473-2798
Study: 215-473-1212

יום א' דר"ח מנ"א דפ"ק בשנת וימלא ה' שלום

לכן נא הלוי' פקח גדול את לב ונשמה ורוח הטוב
לתקן את מסקפיידה תחת לולב קציצה ולחזק לחנך ולהראות
את להגיר ה' יתברך בעת נחת וגילולות ולחגור גדלו לאולם
נעין לקין את רבו ולותו לגלות על הקודם בבית
מקו אומות ולחחת לגלות את ריגעה לו לכולם.
אלה ושלום פאר יבן גלה כך להדר אחרים על הלוה
פתח ותמא גבה הוא. והאשם שבו לגעל נתב אתה פה
אקן ולי אש הלך הא את שלח הגעל לגם לה הגע ולגם ...
הם נולה ולגלות הפה.

ולכן כאן להגאים סיד פה הגגא אלגבות שועל הקהל
ואלוה הזה. ורב כשת אלוני אתה רבה, לעיל לתקן
להוזרא בהלות לא הלא רשות.
                    בברכת כהם

                    שמואל קמנצקי

שמואל קמנצקי
Rabbi S. Kamenetsky

2018 Upland Way
Philadelphia, Pa 19131

Home: 215-473-2798
Study: 215-473-1212

Erev Rosh Chodesh Menachem Av 5760

Some time ago I saw this thought written by a great person:

Every soul enters this world in order to accomplish its mission in life. Most people are sent into this world to complete their own life's purpose and also to influence others, according to their ability. However, there are lofty souls who are unable and do not require a personal tikun, but are sent to this world strictly to teach others.

Perhaps these souls are sent to point out to us man's great strengths and what lies within us. These souls who spent their time in utero studying Torah, and achieved such greatness that they saw from one end of the world to the other with unlimited clarity, were brought into the world to make us understand man's great knowledge and abilities.

Therefore, it is worthwhile to print this book in English, so that people may understand the secrets and greatness of the human being. One must not forget the directive, "You shall be wholeheartedly faithful to Hashem, your G-d," and not use these abilities to predict the future.

With best wishes for hatzlacha,

[Rabbi] Shmuel Kamenetsky

The Recommendation of
HaRav Hagaon Rav Nosson M. Wachtfogel *shlita*

Mashgiach of Beth Medrash Govoha of America, Lakewood, New Jersey

25 Sivan 5757

"The nation which walks in the darkness, saw great light." We are currently living in an era in which immense darkness and confusion prevail. Many Jews are not even familiar with their Father in Heaven, while many [in Torah observant circles] are still far from perfection. The Creator Blessed be He pitied His Nation, and in His vast kindness sent us a means for arousing people from their deep slumber, in the form of a new mode of communication with the mentally disabled. This form of communication demonstrates to us that the spiritual world is revealed to the disabled. Even though in the eyes of the world, these people are regarded as lacking in understanding and in cognizance of their surroundings, this new form of communication called Communication by Support [or Facilitated Communication], shows us that their knowledge of the spiritual aspects of the world, and their perception of their Creator, and of [the workings of] Divine Providence, as well as their knowledge of *mussar* is on a very high level. [This phenomenon] has already greatly strengthened many Jews, causing them to return to their roots or to strengthen their link with Torah and *mitzvos*. Therefore, I feel that it is very important to publicize the book, *Ve'Nafshi Yodaat Me'od* (the Hebrew version of *Secrets of the Soul*) and the messages of the mentally disabled, which result in the drawing of the hearts closer to our Father in Heaven.

Due to my many commitments, I was unable to read through this book, and asked a *talmid chacham*, whom I trust implicitly, to review it. He indeed reviewed a large part of the book, and conveyed its content to me. In addition his first hand observations of this form of communication caused him to conclude that it is authentic and highly valuable.

Alongside this, we must stress that while the messages conveyed to us by means of the disabled are worthy of strengthening and drawing close the hearts, one may not practically implement their advice without consulting a Rav, since as it is known, the Jewish Nation is led only by the Torah sages.

May all those disseminating these important messages, with the purpose of sanctifying Heaven's Name and magnifying His Blessed Name in the world, be blessed. May *Hashem Yisborach* help them, and may they succeed.

[Rabbi] Nosson Wachtfogel

Comments of Harav Hagaon Rav Aharon Yehuda Leib Steinman *shlita*

The great gaon, HaRav Aharon Leib Steinman has personally[1] told me that he regards this new form of communication with the mentally disabled as a manifestation of profuse Divine compassion meant to arouse the slumbering who, due to the vanities of our time, have forgotten the truth, and their entire lives immerse themselves in empty and futile pursuits. He also regards it as a means for strengthening *bnei Torah* in all those areas which require strengthening in our time.

Their words of *mussar* are like searing flames of fire, which greatly arouse all those who examine them. Therefore it is befitting to disseminate and publicize them.

Harav Steinman was personally present at FC sessions with the mentally disabled, and marveled at their answers to his questions. According to HaRav Steinman, it is very

---

1 HaRav Steinman saw this letter, and authorized its insertion in the book.

important to examine their words of *mussar*, in order to take stock of one's ways. These messages should not be disregarded.

Hakodosh Boruch Hu is sending us an illumination from Above, which many people overlook or deprecate. Therefore Harav Hagaon Rav Steinman greatly encouraged me to publish this book which conveys these messages to the public at large. However, he also asked me to caution that one may not use these messages in order to derive practical advice or for halachic guidance. He also warned not to ask the mentally disabled questions about the future. We have merited the revelation of this remarkable phenomenon only for the purpose of drawing the hearts of the Jewish People closer to their Father in Heaven.

Comments of Harav Hagaon Rav Gavriel Krausz Regarding FC

Listen, and Your Soul Will be Revived, a recently published pamphlet by Harav Hagaon Rav Gavriel Krausz the Raavad of Manchester, contains many transcripts of FC sessions with mentally disabled children. Following is an excerpt from its introduction:

> [Many] of the mentally disabled children in Israel who communicate by means of FC have asked that some of their essays be published, along with citations of the sources of their ideas from *Chazal* and other sacred *seforim*. I feel that abiding by their wishes, to the extent that this is possible, will strengthen our readers and prove how deeply the children's words are rooted in our sacred sources. Due to my limited expertise, I am certain that I have overlooked many sources. However, the few which I did locate demonstrate that we cannot disregard the words of these children. For thousands of years,

autistic people, as well as those with Down syndrome and cerebral palsy, were considered *shotim*. Now it has become clear that they are very intelligent, and by means of FC often capable of expressing themselves far more articulately than we who employ regular speech. For many, this is not easy to accept. However, that does not alter the veracity of the phenomenon whose authenticity has often been proven

Two *talmidei chachamim* showed my pamphlet to one of the *gedolei hador*. Even though he didn't read it himself, he warmly endorsed our promulgating it, and said that the publishing of this material is a rectification for the souls of the disabled, and, if it arouses people to do *teshuva*, a merit for us. That *gadol* cautioned about the various obstacles liable to ensue from FC. From his comments, it seems that we must not ask them questions which involve decision making, in particular on halachic or medical issues. This is because disabled children cannot serve as alternatives for *gedolim, rabbonim* or doctors. He added that the disabled do not always formulate their messages and answers precisely, and said that when they foresee tragedies or calamities, *Rachmono litzlan* are often incapable of determining precisely what they see."

Comments of One of the Gedolei Hador in Israel Regarding FC[1]

A very rare phenomenon has recently been revealed to our generation (one in whose unfolding I had the *zechus* to be involved). By means of this phenomenon, it is possible to understand the inner and true essence of individuals who until now were defined as delayed in all aspects of life, due to their brain damage which prevents them from engaging in even the most minimal activities of which regular human beings are capable. After dwelling on the essential characteristics of these individuals, it has become clear to me that there exists a different type of person whose subliminal grasp is phenomenal, and who lives a life of rich inner content, but in a different framework linked to the World of Truth, where the matter of reward and punishment is revealed to all. After learning this information, we approached the core of the problem itself, and *boruch Hashem* managed to uplift the spirits of these children in general, as well as to make them feel important

---

1 The *gadol* who wrote these remarks asked that his name not be mentioned.

and to include them, to a certain degree, in communal life. This helped to rid them of many of their inferiority complexes as well as of the loneliness in which they lived until this discovery (factors which produce terrible emotional suffering), and also to make their parents and siblings aware of the remarkable, although different type of child in their midst, one who should occupy a main place in all family experiences.

We live in a generation which denies the main principles of faith. We live in an era in which chaos and abandon prevail in all areas, an era in which the leadership of the *klal*, has been wickedly taken away from the luminaries of the People by a regime which controls all means of communication with the Nation, and strews heresy and wreaks havoc on the hallowed edifice of the community, sometimes directly, and sometimes indirectly, foisting false ideas into the Torah observant community too — and there is no need to prove what is well known. Basically, they have caused belief in reward and punishment to be uprooted, and have promulgated the idea that the events of this world occur by "chance," a belief, which, as the Chofetz Chaim says, comes from the seed of Amalek. To a great extent, they have succeeded in dulling the belief in Divine Providence, and in inculcating the notion that the world is a jungle in which only the powerful succeed, and that all that occurs depends on might.

In reference to the *dybuk* which was manifest in his time, Rav Chaim of Volozhin once said: The time will come when people will long to see a *dybuk* (in order to strengthen their faith, and to illustrate it in a most tangible manner) but won't find one, because drawing people out of the snake and scorpion pit in which they wallow, and arousing them from their slumber and from their immersion in false illusion, can only be done by Hashem, in His kindness. It is a Heavenly secret. We do not know the reason for this open revelation of the Divine method of the Judge. But what we do know is that Divine conduct has been revealed [in this case] to teach that there is justice and a Judge, and that overt punishment is dependent on this justice, and is inescapable. This reality shocks man. It is as if someone has awakened him from his deep and sweet slumber, and has confronted him with the truth, which is the opposite of his sweet dreams. However, this shock still does not constitute one's deliverance, because if one lets habit prevail over this arousal, it will wane, and nothing will remain of it. This arousal will be effective only if one decides that he is prepared to modify his habit, and to adapt himself to a new course in his life, and adhere to the true reality, which is good for him in this world and in the World to Come. After he stops marveling over the phenomenon his resolve to change his ways should continue as the Ramban says. Since the merit to arouse us has come about through these children, it might be the very factor which will liberate them from their terrible suffering.

Even though the children have extensive knowledge, this knowledge has no bearing on any public problem, because Hashem entrusted the leadership of our Nation solely to our great luminaries with whom *Hashem Yisborach's* views coincide. We thus are not permitted to utilize the messages conveyed by these children for the solving of any communal problem. However, we may derive lessons from the manner in which they live in our world and from the life of punishment which belongs to the World of Truth. But they have no power to express opinions, since they lack freedom of choice, and live in a clear world which has taken away their ability to change by means of the power of free choice.

Contents

Introduction xix
Reader's Guide xxiii

Windows to the Soul

1. Open Wide the Gates 5
2. Unique Capacities 11
3. Is it True? 31
4. Seeing With the Eyes of the Soul 59

Heart to Heart — Soul to Soul

5. Previous Lives 71
6. Sound the Trumpets 85
7. The Three Pillars 97
8. Who Am I? 109

Our Heroes

9. Ima, I Love You 129
10. Beila Holds Her Own 171
11. Rivkie Triumphs 187

12	"My Soul Thirsts" — A Visit to Pisgat Yehuda...	193

Appendix

I	Inspiring Interviews	203
II	Golden Strands: Essays by Ben Golden (verbatim)	217
III	The Religious Viewpoint	253
IV	The Startling Implications of Facilitated Communication	257

Glossary

Glossary 269

Introduction

This book is about the power of the soul.

Secrets of the Soul focuses on the amazing phenomenon of Facilitated Communication, a unique means for communicating with the nonverbal. The discovery of this phenomenon has startled the world. Disabled people have broken through their prisons of loneliness, darkness and non-communication. The messages they convey enable us to peek into the remarkable domain of the soul, that pure and untainted Divine entity which G-d has placed into each and every one of us.

The title of the Hebrew version of this book, *Nafshi Yodaat Me'od*, is taken from a verse in Tehillim (132:14) and means, "My soul knows much." The soul of an ordinary person, immersed as it is in the world of the physical, is virtually undetectable. Disabled people, as we shall see, are more soul than body. It is they who provide us with a glimpse into the wondrous spiritual world of man.

You will find the episodes related within this book to be remarkable — even awesome. It is the intent of the author that you should find them inspiring. In the opinion of HaRav Aaron Leib Steinman, shlita, the discovery of this new form of communication is an "illumination from Above" — a wake-up call to arouse us from our slumber.

All of the interviews and essays in this book are authentic. In many cases the authors of the essays or the children being interviewed are given fictitious names, in order to protect their privacy. I do, however, have precise information for each and every transcript presented in the book, as well as the names and particulars of the individuals who participated.

It is important to note that our rabbinical leaders, while they marvel over the discovery of Facilitated Communication, also warn us not to approach the disabled for solutions to personal, matrimonial or medical problems and surely not on halachic issues. For medical guidance, one should consult a doctor. For guidance in life or on halachic issues, one should speak to a Torah sage. The words these special individuals express, stress our rabbis, should serve as a source of inspiration capable of drawing hearts closer to our Father in Heaven — both the hearts of those who are already Torah observant, and those who still have not savored the sweetness of Torah.

I pray that no stumbling blocks will arise from my efforts, and that the book will serve as a means to draw both the distant and the near closer to their Father in Heaven — because we all are in need of His closeness.

*   *   *

It gives me great pleasure to thank those who made this book possible. First and foremost, I wish to thank the precious children who shared their profound thoughts and

Introduction

feelings with us, as well as their dedicated parents, who were very helpful to us. Much credit is due to the devoted and tireless facilitators who help these children emerge from their dark prisons of loneliness.

My wife is to be thanked for her endless dedication to this effort, as well as for her wise comments, her proofreading of the Hebrew version, and her having released me of all my other obligations so that I could devote myself to this book.

I owe a deep debt of gratitude to Harav Yechiel Sitzman of the Dvar Yerushalayim Yeshiva, who unstintingly helped in every aspect of the publication of both the Hebrew and English versions of this book. Utilizing his extensive knowledge of the entire subject, and his vast Torah knowledge, he guided us in every stage of our work. The assistance of Mr. Moshe Kaufman of the Israel Book Shop in this effort defies description. Thank you Reb Moshe for everything. Without you, there wouldn't have been a book.

Our dedicated translators, Rabbi Pinchos Rohr and Mrs. Devora Friedman, did a truly phenomenal job. Thank you for your patience and efforts, and for sharing your remarkable skills with us. The advice and comments of Mrs. Zelda Goldfield, our talented editor, were invaluable. Thank you, Mrs. Chana Dowek, for your expertise in correcting the manuscript. The painstaking proofreading of Mrs. Debrah Ismailof was highly appreciated.

If this book will achieve its aim of raising the spiritual level of its readers, we will feel duly recompensed.

Rabbi Yehuda Srevnik

Reader's Guide

Although the majority of FC users quoted in this book are children, a few are adults. Nonetheless, we did not refrain from affectionately referring to them as "special children" because indeed we are all referred to as Hashem's "children."

Some of the messages of our special children take the form of essays. Others are transcripts of interviews, conducted by facilitators. In these interviews, we generally used the letter "F" to refer to the facilitator, and the initial of the child's name to refer to the FC user. When a mother was the facilitator, we used the letter "M."

At times we had access to the original transcripts of the interviews and essays of English speaking children. In such cases, we presented them verbatim (i.e. without changing or editing the wording of the children). Whenever an essay or interview is verbatim, we have cited this at its beginning. Those which were transmitted to us in Hebrew were translated into English, and are thus not verbatim.

All of the dialogues, essays and stories presented in this book are authentic and documented and we possess precise information regarding the FC users, their families and the facilitators who communicated with them.

Section I

Windows to the Soul

- The Impossible
- Open Wide the Gates
- Unique Capacities
- Is it True?
- Seeing With the Eyes of the Soul

He brought them out of darkness and the shadow of death.

Tehillim 107:14

Introduction to Section I

The Impossible

Everyone knows my name. I am the sadness of your soul. I am the broken heart which brings you closer to the Redemption. I am the embodiment of Hashem's *rachmanus* toward you. You need me. Our generation needs Menachem. You need many like me to mitigate the terrible sentence which hovers over our heads. A broken person with a broken heart searches for Hashem.

Menachem, an autistic child

Love can be defined as one's need for social contact, the need to feel that others are concerned for him. Love is a haven in our grim world....Love, for the believing Jew, must be for Heaven's sake. It must be based upon the Torah's laws. Hashem's love is the paragon of genuine love. He loves us unconditionally.

Galia, a CP child

Impossible, you are probably thinking, as you read Menachem's and Galia's touching words. *I don't believe it. How can non-verbal, non-literate children who are so detached from everyday life convey such ideas?*

Yet, thanks to Facilitated Communication, the "impossible" has become a reality.

In this section, we will explain this remarkable technique which has freed mentally disabled chidlren from their loneliness, their prisons, their agony. We will also explore its early beginnings, discuss the views of its opponents and proponents, and present the crystal clear insights of *Chazal* which clarify the entire phenomenon of FC.

1

Open Wide the Gates

> Countless people the world over are unable to communicate adequately through speech. They may have cerebral palsy, head injury or Down syndrome, or may have been diagnosed as having an intellectual disability or autism...Their thoughts, ideas, needs and desires go unspoken. They are trapped in a wordless prison...Communication partners, using Facilitated Communication, provide these people with physical support in order to help them overcome their neuro-motor problems and develop functional movement patterns that will allow them to use communication aids.
>
> quoted from *Teachers College Press* (1994, p.1) by *American Psychologist* (Sept. '95)

How Does it Work?

Facilitated Communication is currently being successfully used in thirty-eight states in the United States, as well as in many countries all over the world. It is a method whereby nonverbal, disabled people construct words, phrases and sentences by striking the keys of a typewriter or a computer, or by pointing to the letters on a language board. A person called a facilitator gently supports their hands or wrists, enabling them to reach the letters to which they wish to point. In many cases, this support is only necessary in the early stages of communicating. Once the person becomes familiar with the technique, he quite often "graduates" to needing only the touch of the facilitator on his shoulder or merely the presence of the facilitator in the room. Generally, the facilitator launches the FC session by asking questions, while the user types out his answer on the computer or typewriter.

How Did it Begin?

The early beginnings of this remarkable technique are described by Professor Douglas Biklin in a scientific article published in the 1990 edition of the prestigious *Harvard Educational Review*. Professor Biklin, the Director of the Unit for Special Education and Rehabilitation at Syracuse University has developed many practical methods for implementing this technique and the special children with whom he works have displayed marked scholastic and social progress. The article is entitled "Communication Unbound: Autism and Praxis." In it Professor Biklin interviews Ms. Rosemary Crossley, the woman who first observed FC's ability to release autistic children from their prisons. The interview took place at the D.E.A.L Communication Center in Melbourne, Australia where she serves as a program coordinator. This center advocates the use of FC.

Dr. Biklen writes: "During the 1970's, when Ms. Crossley worked at the St. Nicholas Institution, she used hand support or arm support to help people with cerebral palsy achieve greater control over their movements, to slow them down, and to give them more likelihood of hitting an intended target (for example, a switch, key, button, letter or picture on a board).

"The first autistic child with whom she used this method was Jonothan. He was a handsome but challenging child. He was not toilet trained. He fidgeted. To get things, he simply grabbed them. He did not look people in the eye. He nearly skipped when walking on the balls of his feet. He had a history of fits of screaming, regurgitating, scratching, and running away from people. In March of 1985, when Jonothan was seven, Rosemary Crossley invited his mother to leave him with her for an afternoon. That afternoon, after watching Jonothan's stereotyped, repetitive play with a squeeze mop, Crossley managed to settle Jonothan on her sofa, first interesting him in a speech synthesizer and then in a Canon Communicator. With wrist support, he pressed buttons that she touched. Occasionally he pressed buttons without any assistance. She typed 'Jonathan' followed by 'Mum,' and then asked him to type out 'Dad.' He went straight to the 'd,' without wrist support and then to 'a,' where he hesitated.

" 'I think he completed 'Dad' with no prompting, but with wrist support,' she wrote in her notes that day. If she had "prompted" him, she would have actually moved his wrist toward the letter or letters; instead she merely supported his wrist as he moved his hand toward the letters.

She typed 'Jonathan,' whereupon he typed 'Jonothan.' Crossley later checked the spelling with his mother. Jonothan had been correct. Crossley asked him if the mop was a plane when he was playing with it. He typed 'mop.'

"She guided him through the entire alphabet on the keyboard, then asked him with what letter the word 'good' starts. He pressed 'g.' She asked him how many fingers she had on one hand. He pressed '5.' She asked how many on two hands. He pressed '10.' She asked if he had anything else he wanted to say. He spelled 'stop.'

"Coincidentally, on the afternoon I interviewed Crossley about how she had discovered that this method worked with Jonothan, he came to visit DEAL. Crossley told him that we had just been talking about the first time he had typed on the Canon. She asked him if he remembered what his first word had been. As she asked the question, she held out a Canon Communicator. Independently, he typed 'Dad.' Then he typed, 'Jonothan, not Jonathan.' This is one child who remembers his first words!"

At nearly the same time, a communication disorders specialist named Carol Lee Berger, who was unaware of Rosemary Crossley's work, made similar observations in the United States. She describes her findings in the 1992 fall issue of *Communication Outlook*. Her description further enhances our understanding of how FC works.

"In 1987, I made a startling discovery," she writes. "I found that my autistic students could type out intelligent thoughts on a computer. Although I had been a therapist for 18 months, my first encounter with autistic children occurred when I began teaching developmentally disabled children in Eugene, Oregon. Many of these students were nonverbal. They are generally unsociable, make little eye contact, and recoil from human touch.

"Autistic children are prone to violent outbursts. They are strongly affected by changes in their routines, and any deviation may trigger a violent reaction. They don't seem to notice people in their vicinity, shift constantly and often find it difficult to grasp objects.

"One day, I seated a nonverbal, autistic seven-year-old boy in front of a computer. I decided that he deserved to learn how to type his name. This child was totally uncommunicative, yet his gaze seemed intelligent, and I felt that he was trying to get through to me.

"Fearful that the child might throw the computer to the floor or that I might be hit, I placed a chair in front of the computer for him and a second chair behind him for myself. This enabled me not only to control his arm movements by placing my arms around him, but also to take his hand and guide his index fingers across the keyboard. In this manner, we spelled his name, and even touched all of the letters on the keyboard.

"A few days later, I again took him to the computer lab. Following the same procedures, I placed my chair behind his, took his hand, and guided his index finger. I told him: 'Let's type your name.'

"However, this time, he moved his hand himself, without my help, and typed 'Richard.' I was amazed that he had remembered the patterning I had taught him. Nervously, I asked him a question that required a cognitive answer: 'What is you mother's name?' He typed 'Mary.'"

Ms. Berger further relates that she showed him a picture of a dog on the computer screen, and told him: "Touch the dog." Richard, who had never learned to read, moved his hand toward the word "dog," one out of three words which appeared at the bottom of the screen. She tried the same experiment with "pumpkin" and eighteen more pictures, and he succeeded in pointing to the correct word nineteen times. She taught all of the other autistic children in the class the very same method in no more then two lessons. The technique worked without any snags. All of the children (aged five through twenty-one) succeeded in communicating.

In addition to teaching, Ms. Berger delivers lectures on FC and trains other facilitators all over the world. She has also written books and articles on the subject.

2

Unique Capacities

Aided by thousands of facilitators, Professor Biklen developed many practical methods for implementing the technique. As it became more widespread, many amazing capacities of these children were revealed. In time, a team of researchers from Syracuse University further probed the phenomenon and documented their findings on film.

What are these capacities?

- **Fluent Command of Language:** Although many FC users are nonverbal and have not been taught to read, their responses to the questions of their communication partners are generally articulate and fluent, and the thoughts they convey profound and incommensurate with their maturational levels. Educators and parents who have seen transcripts of these responses affirm that intellectually able children of corresponding age groups are incapable of expressing such deep ideas.

- **Command of Many Languages:** Special children are able to communicate in every language known to the facilitator, even though they may never have heard that language before. Sometimes, even when asked questions in a language totally unfamiliar to their facilitator, they are still able to respond by means of FC.

- **The Ability to Convey Messages Sightlessly:** Such children don't always look at the language board or the computer keyboard while communicating, and can even convey messages while blindfolded. The blind, the comatose and the deaf are also capable of expressing themselves through FC.

- **Advanced Literacy and Arithmetic Skills:** The reading comprehension rate of many special children far exceeds that of their able counterparts. Some special children can scan an entire page in a split-second, and recall its content in full, conveying the knowledge they have absorbed not verbally, of course, but through FC. The above-mentioned researchers from Syracuse University videotaped a session between a facilitator and a number of two and three-year-olds who reported on the content of books they had skimmed before going to sleep. Special children were also recorded as they solved complex arithmetic exercises.

Keen Insight and Perception

Unlike regular people, special children also possess keen perception and are able to see through many of the veils which cover reality, even those separating this world and the World of Truth. These abilities can be categorized in the following manner:

- The ability to perceive events which occur beyond the

range of regular vision.

- The ability to discern the spiritual implications of the behavior of others, to assess their spiritual levels and see their hidden and former deeds.
- The ability to sense future events.
- The ability to understand the workings of metaphysical phenomena.
- The ability to recall their past lives.
- The ability to explain the spiritual aspects of events.

The following accounts illustrate some of these abilities. They were culled from a broad spectrum of cases, which took place in Israel, the United States and England, and included children from various types of homes. The facilitators involved in these cases also came from varied backgrounds. (Examples of children describing earlier lives are found in Part Two, in the chapter called "Previous Lives.")

Many more dialogues and essays illustrating these points will be presented throughout the book within other frameworks.

Beyond the Range of Regular Vision

Quite a number of parents and teachers report that special children know when certain relatives are about to pay them unexpected visits. Parents have noticed that prior to these visits, their children become unusually excited for no apparent reason. Moments later the unexpected guest arrives.

Mrs. Simon began to prepare light refreshments, because she knew that if her son, Aviad, was bouncing up and down on the sofa with unusual exuberance, guests were probably coming.

When the guests indeed arrived, one of them asked, "Aviad, who told you we were coming?"

"No one, but I knew anyway, and have a special message for you," he replied.

*   *   *

A woman once approached an FC consultant and said, "It's true! Those children really know."

"I've been saying that all along," the consultant replied, not completely understanding what the woman meant. "What happened?"

"My daughter is a teacher in a school for special children. A few weeks ago, one of the children began to prance around her. My daughter asked the child why she was so excited and the child replied, 'You're expecting twins.' My daughter laughed and said that she wasn't pregnant. A number of days later, she went for a routine checkup, and believe it or not, the tests showed that she was indeed expecting twins."

*   *   *

Spiritual Implications

Beila T., an eight-year-old CP child, offered spiritual guidance to the distraught parents of Ari Levi. After his military service, Ari Levi set off for the Far East. In the beginning, he wrote his parents, but after a few months they lost all contact with him. Ari's parents knew that Beila was special, and asked Mrs. T. whether they could ask her, by means of FC, if Ari was safe and sound, and whether they should search for him.

"Right now, he's in a daze," Beila replied. "I don't know what happened to him. But I do know that he's not the same happy-go-lucky boy you once knew. The truth is that he was lost even before he set off on his trip, dead even before he left home. You killed him. He is lost to Judaism. He has disappeared in a strange country, under bizarre circumstances and for silly reasons. He's a victim of our depraved society. Of course you should search for him. But know that if you find him, both you and he will have to make a comeback. It'll be a miracle if you find him — one which will obligate you to acknowledge Hashem's existence. This tragedy occurred for a specific reason. Nothing occurs without a cause.

"You come from a family of *tzaddikim*. Your grandfather was a rabbi. Your father lost his faith during the Holocaust. Your grandparents are weeping over you in Heaven. The only way to bring you to your senses was to take Ari away from you. Ari is your family's offering. Hashem wants you, but you reject Him. You don't dress like Jews. You don't behave like Jews. You worship the Golden Calf. Ari went to the Far East in search of a bit of truth and some fun too. You cry. But why did you let him leave home in the first place? Find him. It's worth all the money in the world to bring him back. I don't know where he is. But I'm certain that he is alive. May Hashem help you."

Assessing the Spiritual Levels of Others

Many special children are capable of assessing the spiritual levels of others. When asked how the soul of a person who has sinned appears, one child answered, "His sins deface his soul, which looks like a garment which has been decomposed by mold and decay."

Mrs. Goldman was very interested in FC, and asked permission to observe a session in a certain school. Surprisingly, Beila, the CP child she was observing, told the facilitator that she wanted to speak with Mrs. Goldman's son, Dovid. Mrs. Goldman was startled, and couldn't imagine what Beila wanted from her son, whom she had never met. Mrs. Goldman called Dovid and asked him to come to the residential facility. Dovid was a yeshiva student who had begun to associate with undesirable friends. When Dovid arrived, Beila asked everyone, except the facilitator, to leave the room.

"Dovid, I know everything you do — even your most secret deeds. Did you read books which are unsuitable for yeshiva students?" Beila wrote by means of FC

Dovid remained silent.

"Answer 'yes' or 'no,' " Beila insisted.

"Yes," Dovid replied.

Beila went on to describe all of Dovid's misdeeds. Then she told him, "Hashem knows everything you do. Get a grip on yourself before it's too late."

The shocked boy later told his mother, "Ima, that girl told me things that no one in the world knows about, except me."

Counselors who work in facilities for special children relate that the children are extremely selective in their relationships with people. When certain people enter the facility, the children flee in terror. When others enter, they grab their hands or cling to them, refusing to let go of them. Such extreme and selective behavior toward people is unnatural. In general, sociable people are friendly toward everyone, while the unsociable withdraw from everyone. The extreme behavior of special children is highly irregular, and suggests that they are capable of seeing beyond surfaces. Ordinary people generally assess others on the basis of external characteristics, as it is written, "A person sees into the eyes, while Hashem sees into the heart"

(*Samuel I*, 16:7). Special children see the inner essence of people and relate to them accordingly. If a person is compassionate, they are drawn toward him. If he is base, they are repelled by him.

> A girl with cerebral palsy once broke into terrifying cries. She explained by means of FC: "A man in the room is reading a secular newspaper. When he reaches sections which contain indecent material which cause him to have sinful thoughts, terrifying and threatening destructive angels are formed. These angels horrify me."

*   *   *

Yossi, a seven-year-old autistic child perceived that Reuven was degenerating. In the following "conversation," he even points to the cause of the problem:

> Q: Why did Reuven degenerate and stop observing *mitzvos*?
>
> Y: He became friendly with someone who had a very bad influence on him. One day they went to a restaurant in Tel Aviv and Reuven ate non-kosher food which contained transmigrated sparks of the soul of a very base person. This had a very negative effect on him and he continued to degenerate and even to doubt his faith.
>
> Q: How can I help him?

Y: *Daven.* Arouse *rachmei Shamayim.* At this point, talking with him won't help."

Q: Will Reuven become Torah observant again?

Y: He'll undergo a crisis, and will realize his mistake. Afterwards, he'll become Torah observant again.

Q: When will this happen?

Y: I don't know. But if we *daven,* we can speed up the process and prevent him from reaching a situation from which it will be difficult to extricate himself.

*   *   *

Galia's father did not join her mother in her spiritual progress. Galia discusses this point in a conversation with her mother:

M: Do you want to tell Abba anything?

G: Yes. Tell him that I forgive him, and that he is in spiritual danger. He's a person who hasn't found his place in this world because he thinks that falsehood is truth. He has to search for the truth. Now he's unfortunate, and I pity him very much. I'm happy that I could finally tell you this.

M: Are you angry at him?

G: One who knows the truth can't be angry. Abba forgot me, that's all. (Galia's father hadn't visited her for a long time.)

> M: Do you want to tell your brothers anything? (She has two older brothers.)
>
> G: They won't understand what I want to say. They're too immersed in this world, and at this point I have nothing to say to them because we have no common language.

Premonitions

Nearly all the special children tell us that they foresee the future, but are forbidden to reveal it. Nonetheless, the premonitions of some children were confirmed.[1]

> Yossi, a ten-year-old with Down syndrome, awoke one morning and began to shout, "Hospital, ambulance! Hospital, ambulance!" His parents were surprised, but sent him to school nevertheless. Later that morning, Yossi's mother visited her elderly father, only to discover that he was in a critical situation. She summoned an ambulance, and the medic determined that Yossi's grandfather indeed had to be hospitalized.

>   *   *   *

> Sari, a facilitator from Jerusalem, relates that in the beginning of Adar 5755, Shimon, a

---

[1] Asking such children to foretell the future may violate the injunction, "You shall be straightforward with Hashem, your G-d," (*Devarim* 18:13). In the following instances, the children volunteered the information on their own initiatives, in order to arouse *klal Yisrael* to do *teshuva*.

ten-year-old autistic child conveyed the following message: "One of the *gedolei hador* will soon go up to Heaven where he will avert an impending disaster." Upon reading this message, the startled facilitator told two people about her experience. A week later, HaRav Shlomo Zalman Auerbach, *zt"l*, passed away. As is known, his demise was unexpected.

* * *

It was a dreary day, shortly after the passing of the Admor of Gur. Galia's mother saw that her daughter was in an unhappy mood, and asked:

> M: Every time I tried to put you to sleep yesterday afternoon, your body became rigid and you seemed terrified. Was anything wrong?
>
> G: A great soul has left our world and I am very upset.

* * *

In September 1995, many special children warned about an impending Arab attack and urged *klal Yisrael* to *daven* with great intent on Rosh Hashana and Yom Kippur. During that period, the Palestinians attacked Jews at Joseph's Tomb in Shechem and in Kfar Darom in southern Israel. At the same time it was feared that the Syrians might join the fray, and that a large-scale war might erupt. Miraculously, a lack of accord between the Syrians and the Palestinians stalled this effort and the situation improved.

* * *

In 1996, certain children sensed the imminence of an earthquake and, after it occurred, related that if not for some righteous women who had organized *Tehillim* shifts, it would have been far more severe.

* * *

A few days before a terrible helicopter collision which resulted in the deaths of seventy-three people, Galia, who predicted HaRav Shlomo Zalman Auerbach's passing, told her mother that she had seen a fire in the sky which seemed to spell impending disaster.

* * *

Before every terrorist attack, a CP child named Chaya bursts out into uncontrollable tears. One time she conveyed a rather startling message to her mother, which read: "A lot of people are going to weep now. *Klal Yisrael* suffers so much misfortune, because we aren't unified, and because *lashon hara* is so widespread."

Metaphysical Insights

Some special children possess vision which transcends the limits of our material world. One young man writes: "I am autistic and I see the world much differently than the vast majority of [human beings]. I see the Adam that is G-d's creation. I see clearly body and soul and their connection with the higher worlds."

The following dialogues with various autistic children illustrate their links to supernal sources, and their ability to sense the *Shechina*'s presence:

A Sweet Light
Chananya

> Q: Do you see the *Shechina*?
>
> C: Yes.
>
> Q: Do you see it directly?
>
> C: No. It is covered by a strong and sweet light!
>
> Q: Does the *Shechina* rest on me?
>
> C: Yes!
>
> Q: Why don't I see it?
>
> C: Your body interferes with your ability to see it.
>
> Q: Can you describe the Heavenly Court?
>
> C: There are angels on the left and angels on the right.
>
> Q: What can I do to help you complete your *tikun*?
>
> C: Study *mishnayos*.

Q: How can I help my father, *z"l*?

C: By doing *chessed*. That helps him more than anything else.

Q: When will Moshiach come?

C: I can't answer that question.

Q: Do my *chiddushim* go up to the Heavenly *mesivta*?

C: With your *chiddushim* you create worlds.

Hashem is One
Shraga

Q: Do you like going to the Kosel?

S: Yes.

Q: What do you see there?

S: The *Shechina*.

Q: Whenever we go to the Kosel you shout "IHinei" (here). What do you mean?

S: Hashem is One.

Q: Is Hashem's existence clear to you?

S: It's as clear to me as daylight is to you.

Q: Can you describe the manner in which you sense the lShechina?

S: It's like the sun's warmth.

Avigdor is a twelve-year-old autistic child who used to cry and shake a lot. The following conversations took place between him and his mother:

I'm Frightened

>M: Why are you crying?
>
>A: Because he's frightening me.
>
>M: Who?
>
>A: The S. M. (a term used for negative spiritual entities).
>
>M: What can we do to help you?
>
>A: If I study Torah I won't be afraid anymore.

I'm Not Afraid Anymore

>M: Avigdor, now that Chaim studies Torah with you, do you feel better?
>
>A: Yes.
>
>M: Do you enjoy studying with Chaim?
>
>A: Yes.
>
>M: Why do you look at the ceiling during the *shiur*?
>
>A: Because I enjoy watching the angels created by our Torah study.

* * *

Ima You're Beaming
Ziva

>M: Why are you so happy?
>
>Z: I'm happy because you did a big *mitzvah*.
>
>M: How do you know that? I didn't tell you that I was going to a *bris*.

Z: I see a light radiating from you, the same light I see when you say *Tehillim*.

Explaining the Spiritual Aspects of Events

When communicating with a parent who lost a child, twenty-two-year-old Ben, an autistic young man, makes insightful comments:

Q: Why do small children die?

B: There are many reasons why this occurs.

Q: Why did my daughter die?

B: Her soul had to finish a mission which it began in a previous reincarnation. But now she's closed her account. She's completed her task. She's gone to a better world.

Q: Why did this happen to me?

B: In order to draw you closer to Hashem. You tend to believe only what you understand. But mortals don't understand how Hashem conducts His world. We must have faith under all circumstances.

Q: Will writing a *sefer Torah* in her memory help her?

B: She's in a good place. But writing a *sefer Torah* is always beneficial for the souls of the deceased. It will help you too.

Q: How do you know all this? How do you know more than we do?

B: My brain doesn't restrict my body. My soul knows everything.

* * *

Reena discussed her brother's physical condition with Chaim, an autistic child:

R: Why is my brother totally paralyzed?

C: In a past life he used his body in order to defy Hashem's will, and was sent back to this world as a cripple. He repented but for his final *tikun* he still has to suffer.

R: Will there be peace in Eretz Yisrael?

C: Yes, when Moshiach comes.

R: When will he come?

C: Soon.

* * *

Galia and her mother discussed the topic of human suffering:

M: Why must we suffer? Does suffering purify us?

G: Hashem inflicts suffering on us when we don't listen to Him. In His great love for us He teaches us — sometimes by means of rewards, and at other times by means of blows. If we learn our lesson, then we merit eternal life. Hashem causes us to suffer because He loves us. He tries to save us; yet we are stubborn.

M: Is suffering a punishment?

G: It is the *chinuch* of a loving Father.

M: Can't a *tzaddik* be compared to a good child who

has but one fault? Why can't he be forgiven?

G: The *tzaddik* accepts with love what is given to him with love.

M: What is the purpose of suffering in life?

G: To bring man to recognize the truth. Without suffering, you would never have reached Hashem.

M: True, very true. But it hurts me to have a daughter like you — a daughter who suffers so much. Why do I deserve such suffering? I am certain that I deserve it due to my behavior in a former life, or perhaps in this life.

G: Ima, Hashem causes you to suffer because He loves you and wants you to reach a high level. You should be as trusting as your relatives who died a number of generations ago and are already in *Shamayim*. They had genuine *bitachon*.

M: What relatives? To whom are you referring?

G: To your grandparents and great-grandparents.

M: On whose side? My mother's side? My father's side? Both sides?

G: Both sides. Those generations were closer to Hashem. Your suffering and efforts to reach Hashem will raise you to their level.

* * *

A woman with two developmentally disabled daughters asked Ben, an autistic young man:

Q: Why were they born that way?

B: In their previous lives, they didn't study the laws of family purity carefully, and as a result committed many sins. For you, they are a *nisayon*, whose purpose is to help you perfect your faith and trust in Hashem.

Q: What should I do for their sake?

B: Do *teshuva*, and when beseeching Hashem to help you with your problems, ask Him to pity *klal Yisrael* too.

3

Is it True?

FC soon aroused a storm of controversy in the scientific world. While there are many supporters of FC, there are also staunch opponents to the method, which cannot be fully explained scientifically.

Before presenting the various points of contention regarding FC, it is significant to know the position of current *rabbonim* and *gedolei Yisroel* on the issue. Many *gedolim* are actively involved and fully supportive of the use of FC.[1]

HaRav Aharon Leib Steinman, *shlita*, examined the FC method and the entire phenomenon. He personally witnessed a number of sessions with autistic children, and even interviewed them himself. Enthused by the children's responses, he encourages facilitators who approach him for advice, and tells them to continue with their work. He feels that the discovery of this new form of communication is an

---

[1] While not denying the validity of FC, some *rabbonim*, for various reasons, expressed reservations regarding its use. These are discussed in "The Religious Viewpoint" which appears in the appendix.

"illumination from Above" which should serve as a wake-up call in order to arouse us from our slumber. HaRav Steinman regards the entire phenomenon as an expression of Hashem's deep compassion for us, and considers the messages these children convey to be *mussar* thoughts worthy of our attention and contemplation.

HaRav Nosson Wachtfogel *zt"l* said: "The Creator, Blessed be He, has pitied His People and in His great compassion has sent us a means to awaken us from our deep slumber. This form of communication, shows us that the spiritual world is laid open to [the mentally disabled]. The world at large regards such people as lacking cognitive abilities and as oblivious to their surroundings. Facilitated Communication enables us to affirm that such individuals' knowledge in spiritual matters and *mussar*, as well as their understanding of the workings of Divine providence, are on a very high level. Many have been strengthened by their messages. Many have returned to their roots after reading samples of the dialogues and essays of these children."

HaRav G. Kraus *shlita* the Raavad of Manchester wrote a pamphlet called *Listen, and Revive Your Soul*. In it he cites interviews with many mentally incapacitated children, some of which he personally conducted. He writes: "For thousands of years, those suffering from autism, Down syndrome and cerebral palsy have been considered mentally disabled. Now it has become clear that they are very bright, and by means of FC often express themselves far better than [regular people]. Many find it difficult to accept this fact. But [their reservations] do not alter the truth, which has been proven beyond a doubt many times."

The Controversy

Why are people skeptical about FC? It is often very difficult to believe that autistic children, who have never been taught to read or write, and who are characterized by the entire medical world as extremely antisocial and totally alienated from their surroundings, can suddenly communicate in an articulate manner, and even display deep concern for their beloved ones. How could dialogues like the following have taken place?

> F: Why can't you fall asleep at night?
>
> M: Ever since my little brother died, I remain awake at night, and count the members of my family in order to make sure that they are all here. Divine Justice begins with the *tzaddikim*, and works mainly at night.
>
> Motty, a six-year-old autistic child

*   *   *

> F: Do you have anything special to tell Ima?
>
> Y: Ima, I know how much you love me. You don't have to feel guilty about my situation. I am happy that I have two *tzaddikim* for parents. Tell that to Abba, because he feels very bad about my situation.
>
> Yechezkel, a ten-year-old autistic child

Upon reading dialogues like these, many people think that the facilitator has moved the child's hand, and has written the answers. Another claim people make is that the mentally disabled "merely" read the thoughts of facilitators,[2] and that the messages do not originate with the children. They also attempt to corroborate these beliefs by noting that the children do not look at the language board or the computer during FC sessions. It is impossible, these opponents say, to compose answers, or even write single words without seeing the letters to which one is pointing.

The first suspicion has been proven totally groundless,[3] because with the development and expansion of the technique, often all that is needed in order to stimulate a child to respond is to touch his shoulder.[4]

---

2 There have been many reports of the uncanny ability of some autistic children to known the thoughts of others.

3 Currently there are a few thousand trained facilitators in the world, and it is highly improbable that every single one of them deliberately moves the hands of the children, and fabricates responses.
   Those who have attempted to apply this method definitely feel that their hands are being moved by the children, and not the opposite. I personally witnessed a session at which someone vehemently rejected the validity of FC, claiming that it was the facilitator who was moving the child's hand. This man was asked to attempt to facilitate himself and asked the child which form of Torah study is preferable, *bekiyus* (extensive Talmud study) or *iyun*, (in-depth study). The man himself advocated the *iyun* approach, and attempted to push the child's finger so that the letters of the word *iyun* would appear. But the child proved stronger than the questioner and spelled out the word *bekiyus*!
   When FC was in its incipient stages, the claims that the facilitator was moving the child's hand might have seemed plausible. However, currently, the technique has been developed to the point that the facilitator merely has to touch the child's shoulder in order to receive responses. Sometimes, as videotapes produced at Syracuse University show, the child answers questions without being touched at all. All this demonstrates that this is not a valid reason for doubting FC's authenticity.

Regarding the other claims, the reason psychological researchers find it difficult to validate FC and to prove that the thoughts proceed from the children is that science has no genuine tool with which to test the phenomenon. It certainly can't be evaluated by neurological tests or brain scans, nor discerned by means of ultrasound or x-rays. Professor Howard Shane of Boston Children's Hospital, conducted a series of tests in which all scientific attempts to ascertain FC's validity failed. Similarly, his studies seemed to indicate that children cannot answer questions whose subject matter is unknown to the facilitator, something they in fact do.

The test used by Professor Shane and other researchers involved controlled experiments in which the facilitator is asked a question which the child does not hear, and the child a question which the facilitator does not hear. If the child answers the question posed to the facilitator, this indicates either that the child is not the one composing the answer or that the child is mind-reading. If he answers the questions posed to him, this indicates that the answers have originated with him.

Although Professor Shane's tests failed to validate FC, other psychological researchers conducted similar tests which in many cases produced corroborating results. When such tests were conducted in Australia, the children

---

4 Ben Golden, an autistic young man who has contributed extensively to this book, explained that the physical contact with the facilitator activates him to write. One mother described the technique, saying that the act of touching the child is similar to placing the plug of an electrical appliance in a socket. Without plugging in the appliance it cannot work.

responded to the questions asked them, as they did in recent tests conducted in the United States. This test is described in an article called "Investigation of Authorship in Facilitated Communication," which appeared in the August 1996 edition of the distinguished scientific journal *Mental Retardation*. It describes how researchers showed randomly chosen words to forty-three brain damaged children who were placed in ten different classrooms, while their facilitator stood outside. When the facilitator entered the various classrooms, he asked each student to type out the word exactly as it had been recorded. Afterward, the results were examined. 3800 such tests were conducted over a period of six weeks. The results indicated that under controlled conditions, certain FC users can convey precise and correct information. The article also explains why previous studies did not succeed in validating the phenomenon, and pointed to ways of improving its assessment and evaluation.[5]

Professor Biklen Replies

Basing themselves on a series of studies, Professor Biklen and his colleagues answer these claims (primarily those of Professor Shane), and maintain:

- Each of the children who participated in the studies

---

[5] Another article appeared in the very same edition of *Mental Retardation*. It is called, "A Validated Case Study of Facilitated Communication" by Professors Michael Solomon Weiss, Sheldon Wagner and Margeret Bauman and describes how three separate tests conducted with a severely disabled thirteen-year-old validated FC.

displayed a uniform style which did not vary even when he communicated with various facilitators, whose writing styles differed.

- The spelling and grammar mistakes which the children made recurred in all of their communications, no matter with whom they facilitated. If their communications had been totally influenced by the facilitator, the mistakes would have varied with each facilitator or would not have been made at all.

- Certain children conveyed information unknown to the facilitator. This information was later verified.

- Certain children conveyed personal information about other people present during the session. Such information was unknown to the facilitator and known only to the person to whom it pertained.

- The children sometimes disclosed information about third parties who had either passed away, or did not live near the children.

Explaining why Professor Shane's tests failed to validate FC, the proponents of the phenomenon say:

- Children who communicate by means of FC are sometimes unwilling to cooperate once they realize that they are being tested.

- The facilitators involved in Professor Shane's study were not sufficiently proficient in the use of technique, and as a result were unable to effect adequate responses.

- The accouterments used in the studies, such as

earphones, partitions, etc., produced a contrived environment which lowered the self-confidence of the children, and impeded optimal communication.

Dr. Stephen Calculator is also a well known expert on FC. At a lecture which he delivered at the Shaarei Zedek hospital in Jerusalem, he pointed to the amazing calming effect FC has on various autistic and mentally disabled children, and concluded that it stems from FC's having enabled them to relate to their social surroundings. Many children have said that FC has liberated them from their solitude or their intolerable existence, which is the result of their lack of communication. He cited the case of one extremely violent autistic child who severely injured some of the staff members of his residential facility, and was finally put under lock and key. After being taught to communicate through FC, he became calm and relaxed and even began to pursue a gainful occupation in a regular place of work. Hearing that there was oppositon to this method, his parents stopped the FC sessions, and his violent behavior recurred. Having no recourse, his parents resumed the sessions. Today, he functions like a regular person.

In his lecture, Dr. Calculator cited other proofs which support the authenticity of FC. He stated that the positive results of this method, such as improvements in the motoric functioning and concentration capacities of the children, have not been achieved by any other technique. Some mentally delayed children, he said, are unable to concentrate or even sit quietly for more than a few seconds. However, when taught to communicate by means of FC, many of these same children are able to sit still for a number of hours without tiring or growing restless. By the same token, many of their hyper-sensitivities disappear, such as their extreme aversion to noise.

Dr. Calculator admitted that although from a scientific standpoint he tended to support the view that there is no substance to FC, he could not deny the outstanding effectiveness of this method, and its great benefit for mentally delayed children. With emotion filled words, he said: "If I had such a child, I would sharply oppose anyone who tried to prevent me from depriving him of the benefits of FC."

Indeed, attempts to discredit FC seem senseless, for if FC has no substance, how could its application result in such striking achievements with children whom conventional science regards as totally unreceptive and non-functional? All admit that considerable progress has been made with special children by means of FC. Indeed, parents who reap the immense benefits of communicating with their children via FC feel no need to prove what for them is obvious.

Dr. Sue Lehr, the Assistant Director of the Institute of Facilitated Communication at Syracuse University, presents the reactions of parents of special children who communicate with them by means of FC. She quotes from the pamphlet, *If You Look in Their Eyes, You Know*, written by a group of parents in 1992:

> We totally reject the claims of FC's opponents. We know that our children are capable. We know that they have feelings and thoughts like ordinary children, and we are aware of their

ability to communicate. What surprised us was the high level of the interchanges which take place by means of FC.

We can only tell you the truth which we as parents know. We must brave many difficult days. We do not have the surplus energy it takes to support our children's hands, as they convey their feelings of anger over their disabilities, or relate unpleasant stories about offenses to their feelings or descriptions of the painful and sometimes horrible experiences they have undergone. We surely have not forced our children to express such thoughts. They choose the words, and we as parents are obligated to listen. We would not be writing this booklet for other parents, if we did not believe in this method of communication

Drs. Arthur and Orleah Schawlow are a very special couple. Dr. Schawlow, a physicist, is a Nobel Peace Prize winner. Their autistic son Arty was born in 1956. For many years, his parents searched for ways of helping him. In 1981, when Arty was 27, they went to Stockholm for the Nobel Peace Prize ceremony, and met Dr. Karen Stensland Junker, a psychologist and a parent of an autistic child. She told them about FC, and the enthused parents began to use it with Arty. Encouraged by their success, they wrote about the phenomenon in various newspapers in the United States, and even discussed the topic at the Worldwide Conference on Autism which took place in Los Angeles in 1985.

When Dr. Schawlow speaks about the first time Arty communicated with them by means of FC, he says: "His first movement was far more important to me than my winning the Nobel Prize."

The opponents of FC, among them Professor Shane, cannot explain FC from a rational vantage point, and therefore they refuse to accept it. If a rational explanation were to be found for the phenomenon, ostensible reality, coupled with logic would mandate its validation.

The Court Verdict

Testimony obtained from autistic children by means of FC has been accepted as evidence in courts in several American states, including Kansas and New York. In one case, the court conducted a battery of tests involving information unavailable to the facilitator, and ruled that the responses of the autistic witness originated from him and not the facilitator. In several other instances, the refusals of certain courts to accept testimony obtained through FC were overturned by an appeals court. In a certain case, a court agreed to accept testimony obtained through FC on the condition that the facilitator wear headphones which prevented her from hearing the questions being asked the autistic witness. Rosemary Crossley's findings were investigated by the Supreme Court of Victoria. It, too, ruled that FC involves no deceit and that the responses were not influenced by the facilitator. These examples indicate that FC has been proven as reflecting the thoughts of autistic children even by rigorous criminal court standards.

The Content Speaks for Itself

Following are many proofs based on the content of messages obtained through FC. These proofs indicate beyond a doubt that the messages originate from the children, and not from the facilitators.

The Child's Needs

Many parents use FC in order to determine their disabled child's physical needs, such as thirst, hunger or discomfort. These parents relate that crying children who have told their parents, via FC, what they want, stop crying once their needs are fulfilled. If the facilitator had originated the message, why would the child have stopped crying when he received what he wanted? This author witnessed a session at which a child suddenly started crying. When the facilitator asked what was wrong, the child said that he was upset because his father had left the house. This proved to be true, although no one present was aware of the father's departure.

Following are a number of interesting accounts which illustrate this point:

> Itzik, an autistic child who lives in a facility, was home for Pesach. When his parents began to prepare for an excursion, he started to cry. Lonnie, a volunteer facilitator asked him what was wrong, and he replied: "I don't want to go on a silly trip. I have plenty to do at home."
>
> When Lonnie told him that he could stay at home if he pleased, he calmed down a bit. A

short while later, he began crying again.

"Why are you crying again?" Lonnie asked.

"I don't want to stay home alone."

Lonnie told him that his father and older sisters would remain at home. Placated, the boy lay down to rest. The mother left on the excursion and when they came back, the father related that their autistic son had behaved amazingly well and had even gone to *shul* with him.

* * *

Shemaryahu, a Down syndrome child, told his facilitator that he wanted his father to respect him and not to belittle him so much. When the facilitator met with the father, she told him that his son had a lofty soul, and had access to much information unknown to regular people. The father was very pleased to hear this. At Shemaryahu's next FC session, he ran over to the facilitator, grabbed her arm and cried out: "Write! Write!" The facilitator sat him down, and he wrote: "I just want to say thank you for telling my father that I have a high soul." Then he refused to continue with the session, and happily sat down to play.

* * *

Motty is an eight-year-old Down syndrome

child whose brother died from a sudden illness. Following the misfortune, Motty remained awake until very late every night. A facilitator was invited to investigate the cause of Motty's behavior. When she asked why he refused to go to sleep earlier like other children his age, he replied: "I'm counting the members of my family to make the sure that their bodies and souls are in one place. At night I can feel Divine Judgment, [which is known to be operative at night] and I am *davening* for the welfare of my entire family.

"Why did you begin behaving this way only after your brother's death?" the facilitator asked.

"At that time, I didn't know that they were going to take him. Now I watch over the family and hope that my prayers will save them. Hashem always begins His warnings by taking *tzaddikim*. Hashem is just in all His ways."

The facilitator explained: "You can't change Hashem's will by staying awake. Your behavior is upsetting the whole family. You can *daven* early in the evening."

Persuaded by her words, Motty began to go to sleep early.

*   *   *

Tami, a seven-year-old CP child had suffered

from night-time wakefulness since birth. Her behavior severely disrupted the household, since her mother was forced to remain up all night. When asked why she didn't sleep at night, Tami replied: "I *daven* then, because nighttime prayers are the best ones".

The facilitator told Tami that that her behavior was disrupting the family's daily life, and that she should *daven* earlier. Tami took the facilitator's words to heart, and began to go to sleep early, sleeping the entire night.

*   *   *

Effy had dropped out of yeshiva. He was severely injured in a car accident, and was in a deep coma for a long time. The following conversation took place while Effy was unconscious:

F: Do you want to regain your consciousness?

E: I don't want to return as the clown I once was.

F: We'll help you and study with you.

E: I know that you'll help me, and really want to regain my consciousness. But I'm afraid.

F: Can you describe your experiences in the Heavenly Court?

E: They said that I hadn't studied, *davened* or done *chessed*. They called me a disgrace to *Am Yisroel*. They decided to give me time to correct my shortcomings. I desperately want another chance, but am afraid of failure.

The facilitator tried to persuade him to make an attempt to regain his consciousness, and said, "When you return, we'll remind you of your experiences in the Heavenly Court. This will help you improve your character traits, and pass the test successfully Are you willing to try?"

"Yes," he replied.

"Give me a sign that you mean what you say. Open your hand," the facilitator said.

Effy opened his hand.

"Open it twice."

He opened it twice.

"Open your eyes."

He opened them, and slowly began to return to himself.

These cases show that the messages elicited by means of FC express the thoughts of the children and not those of the facilitators. The disorders described in these examples are serious ones. When the roots of the disorders were discovered, it was possible to find ways of alleviating them. But how could the measures taken have solved the problems if the communications originated with the facilitator? Surely Tami wouldn't have stopped crying at night if the entire conversation had been the product of the facilitator's mind, nor would Effy have regained his consciousness. Although we have changed the names of the involved parties, all of the cases are authentic. We possess complete and detailed data for each and every case, including affirmations made by family members and other relevant sides.

Scientific Theory is Toppled by an Infant

The following amazing account not only unequivocally proves the authenticity of FC, but also overturns the widely-accepted scientific theory that the ability to communicate by means of FC is acquired by "environmental absorption."[6]

> On 3 Iyar 5754, Yael was asked to assist a family in Tiberias, whose severely ill three-month-old daughter had been in the hospital since birth. This was the third time the family had undergone such experiences with infants. Two of its other daughters had died from precisely the same illness, both at the age of three months. Yael was summoned to the hospital to facilitate with the baby. On the surface, the parents appeared totally non-religious. The facilitator held the baby's hand and the baby pointed to letters on the alphabet chart. The parents asked the questions.
>
> Q: Why did you come to the world in such a form?

---

6 The term "environmental absorption " may be defined as unstructured learning, in which a person acquires knowledge informally by absorbing it from his surroundings.

A: I lack the merit of honoring my parents. I didn't honor them properly in my past life.

Q: Why do we suffer so much?

A: This is the third time I've returned to this world, but you still haven't changed your ways.

Q: What must we do?

A: *Teshuva*.

Q: But we *are* good Jews![7]

A: If you go to Rav L. in the north, he will help you see the light.

Q: What is his first name?

A: Yehuda.

Q: Why do we have so many other problems?

A: They stem from the same root.

Q: Should we move?

A: Yes. Move to a Torah community.

Q: Is it urgent to do so now?

A: Yes. Life is short and much must be accomplished.

Q: Will that help you?

A: Yes!

Q: Will it help you physically?

---

[7] The facilitator relates that the parents' external appearance indicated that they were secular. However, every person believes that his lifestyle is correct, as it is written, "A man's way is righteous in his eyes." (*Mishlei* 21:2)

A: No!

Q: Will we have additional children like you?

A: No.

Q: If we do *teshuva*, will you live?

A: I'll merit eternal life in the World of Truth, and you, with Hashem's help, will have other healthy children.

Q: Why have we merited such revelations, while many other families also require guidance?

A: You have *zechus avos*. You stem from *tzaddikim*. [The family was astounded to hear this. After investigating their roots, they learned that both the husband and wife descended from *tzaddikim*.]

Q: Whose soul do you bear?

A: Your great grandmother's.

Q: On whose side?

A: Ima's.

Q: What was her name?

A: Rivka *bas* Beila. [The mother did not recognize the name, but when she asked her father it turned out that the infant had indeed specified the correct one.]

The parents asked their daughter many other questions. She replied: "Do what I say, and stop asking so many questions."

Later on, the parents searched the country's

north for a rabbi named Yehuda L. and located a Nissim with the same family name. When they approached him for spiritual guidance, he said that he was too old to become involved in their case. However, he referred them to his grandson, Yehuda, who was also a rabbi.

They visited Yehuda, and embarked on their path to *teshuva*. At his advice, they began to pray for their daughter's recovery, even though she had told them she would not get better. They also related that for a long time after this conversation, their daughter stopped having convulsions.

Astounding! A three-month-old infant provided accurate information, totally unknown to her parents and the facilitator. No one present at the FC session knew Rav Yehuda L., but the infant's statements were totally accurate. Her mother didn't know the name of the great-grandmother, which was later on confirmed by the mother's father. The parents had no idea that they were descended from *tzaddikim*, a fact which was confirmed only after they investigated their family's genealogy. Obviously, the three-month-old baby hadn't acquired her linguistic skills by means of "environmental absorption." Obviously, the facilitator had not made up the answers herself.

Profound Thoughts

The deep thoughts conveyed by certain special children surely could not have been the products of the facilitators' minds:

Belgian parents of an autistic child wrote the *rosh yeshiva* of the Chidushei HaRim yeshiva that their son had said that he wanted to write Torah innovations currently being studied in Heaven. By means of FC, he then wrote the innovations of two great Admorim of the Chassidic dynasty of Gur, the Sfas Emes (who passed away in 1905) and the Beis Yisrael, (who passed away in 1978). The family wasn't Chassidic, so that the child had certainly not heard these ideas at home. The facilitator was also not Chassidic. The parents sent the transcript to the *rosh yeshiva* to verify the authenticity of the innovations. The *rosh yeshiva* replied: "The innovations cited in the name of the Sfas Emes are accurate, and may be found in his published writings. Those in the name of the Beis Yisrael do not appear in print. But I was very close to the Beis Yisrael and heard them directly from him."

*   *   *

One child was asked which judges presided in the Heavenly Court. She answered, "Either the *Shechina* or the *Ze'eir Anpin*." The facilitator, who had no knowledge of Kabbalah, surely hadn't provided this answer.

*   *   *

During a visit to a school for the mentally

delayed, we spoke to a Samaritan (*Shomroni*). The Samaritans belong to a sect which adopted some Jewish customs, however, they are not considered Jews. The child was asked: "What is the difference between a Samaritan and a gentile?"

"We're closer to the Jews than the gentiles, but our sin is greater than theirs, since we had the opportunity to know the truth, but squandered it."

After receiving this answer, the facilitator innocently asked: "Is a *Shomroni* someone who lives in the Shomron region?" This question indicates that the answer could only have emanated from the child, and not the facilitator.

Yet another proof is the fact that the children are often asked questions in a language which the facilitator doesn't understand, proving beyond a doubt that the answers could not have originated with the facilitator. One woman relates that the mind of her elderly father, who had once been a prominent *rav* had ceased to function normally. The family hired a Sephardic facilitator, while they speak to him in Yiddish, which the facilitator doesn't understand. The responses of the father are amazing, and he offers each one of the members of the family guidance as in better days.

Many of the essays and messages of the children convey profound ideas which were certainly not written by the facilitators, most of whom have no knowledge of such deep philosophical ideas. In one conversation, Galia discusses the nature of the soul. Her mother asked: "Does the soul receive another body in Heaven?" Galia replied: "Ima, there is no such thing as a soul without a body. For every world there is an appropriate type of body which suits that world and its purpose. So, my dear Ima, in the World of Truth, which is a spiritual world, there are spiritual garments which suit one's deeds and one's *tikun* in this world. It is very important then to observe the *mitzvos* and to do good deeds, because every *mitzvah* fashions our exquisite spiritual garments and decorates them with countless numbers of adornments. Those who do not perform *mitzvos* will be unfortunate in the World of Truth, because they won't be able dress themselves. They will remain unclothed, without garments, and will no longer be able to prepare clothes. The opportunity to prepare clothing exists only in this world. In the World to Come one is dependent on the kind acts performed on his behalf by those in this world [such as the lighting of *yahrzeit* candles, the reciting of *Yizkor* and the studying of *Mishnayos* for the benefit of the souls of the deceased.]

Beila's mother asked, by means of a facilitator, how the Holocaust could be understood. Beila replied: "Complacency and comfort are far more difficult trials than the Holocaust." This answer could not have originated in the mind of the facilitator, since she herself did not understand the answer until receiving a detailed explanation of it.

When asked such a question, most people would try to explain why the Holocaust occurred. Beila, though, not only does not offer reasons for its occurrence, but also rejects the common assumption that the Holocaust was a negative phenomenon, adding the surprising idea that our situation is far worse than that of the Jews during the Holocaust.

What did Beila mean? Believing Jews evaluate situations not by means of temporal yardsticks, but rather through absolute ones. Can a comfortable lifestyle which causes its pursuer to lose his share in the World to Come be considered good? Can transitory suffering which atones for one's sins and enables one to acquire a share in the World to Come be considered bad? The wicked prosper in this world so that their share in the World to Come will be withheld, while the righteous suffer in this world, so that they will merit a share in the World to Come. Thus although those who suffered and even perished during the Holocaust endured untold torment, they have assuredly entered the World of Truth, while those who enjoy the comforts of our current era run the risk of losing their share in the World to Come, since Man is more prone to rebel against Hashem when he is content, as it is written: "And Yeshurun grew fat, and he [rebelled]" (*Devarim*, 32:15).

Confrontations

Throughout the conversations with Galia, Rivkie, Beila and many of the other children who appear in this book, we are keenly aware of disagreements between them and their relatives. Beila "had it out" with her mother, who didn't want her to appear at a public rally. Rivkie often chastised the members of her family and insisted that her sister Miriam take her to visit a teacher, the last thing on earth

Miriam felt like doing. Every now and then Galia tells her mother: "Ima, take my advice!"

One of the most cogent examples of a dialogue in which the views expressed by the child certainly could not have been the products of the facilitator's mind took place between a brain damaged four-year-old and a non-Jewish facilitator. The child's parents had asked Syracuse University to provide them with a facilitator to communicate with him, and Syracuse sent a non-Jewish one. In his conversation with her, the child used the word *goy*, which he had never heard in his non-Orthodox home Following is a verbatim transcript of that session as recorded by the facilitator:

F: Hello. What have you to tell me today?

C: Why do you wear that cross? Fry it! Why do you believe in that *goy*?

F: What is a *goy*?

C: A non-Jew.

Several days later, when the facilitator returned, the following exchange took place:

C: You're still wearing that cross. I told you to burn it.

F: Why does my wearing this cross bother you so much?

C: Because it talks false about G-d! I write about G-d to teach you the truth.

F: Why are you crying?

C: I told you, don't believe Jesus is the son of G-d. I

repeat: Believe what I tell you for it is the truth. I love G-d to talk to you too because He could tell you the truth. Then you might believe the truth people have been denied for years. They were misled by that man called Jesus.

F: Why do you keep getting up and then returning to type more?

C: It's hard to be focused enough to listen to G-d and type.

F: Is there anything else you would like to say?

C: He told you to worship him, but you should only worship G-d Himself, for there is only one true G-d. You talk about Jesus as the savior of the world but this is a lie for Jesus is not the son of G-d.

F: I have never spoken to you about Jesus, from where have you gotten this information?

C: From G-d. He tells me.

F: Is there anything else you would like to say?

C: Truth is what I speak to you. The truth shall be known to you soon.

F: What truth?

C: The truth about G-d.

F: What would you like to say?

C: G-d has asked me to convey my thoughts to you.

F: Why me?

C: So that more might believe the truth about G-d for

He is the way, the truth and the light.

F: Is there anything else you would like to say?

C: The true word is from G-d Himself. Teach the truth to everyone.

In this case, the boy obviously could not have been reading the facilitator's mind, since his remarks contradicted her beliefs. Could there be more compelling proof than this that the messages children convey by means of FC originate with them?

4

Seeing With the Eyes of the Soul

Not all scientists invalidate FC. However, many of those scientists who give credence to FC still miss the point when trying to validate it, and the explanations they offer for it are so inadequate, that they actually contribute to and even heighten the disbelief. A number of them maintain that disabled children acquire their writing skills by means of "environmental absorption," a process which does not work with regular children who must be taught how to read and write. According to these scientists, ordinary children are so busy forming human relations, that they can't devote their energies to the environmental absorption of language skills, while children who are detached from their surroundings can focus on such learning, even independently.

This explanation is obviously insufficient and unconvincing. It does not explain how children can communicate in every language, even those they don't know. It does not explain how children, who grew up in homes which were totally devoid of Jewish content, can express deep religious thoughts of which their parents have absolutely no knowledge, nor does it explain how an infant whose story is presented in this book can "write" like an adult, and convey information totally unknown to the facilitators who conducted the sessions with him. Indeed, a prominent *rav* in the United States, the father of an autistic child said: "My son would not have heard in my home in a thousand years the information he conveys to me by means of FC."

Scientists cannot explain how such children can read so rapidly, nor can they explain how they can compose words and sentences without looking at the keyboards of their computers. Some scientists maintain that the children actually look at the keyboards from the corners of their eyes. But this does not clarify how the comatose, the blindfolded and the blind can also communicate by means of FC.

By offering flimsy explanations, these scientists are actually paving the way for denial and disbelief.

How then can the phenomenon be explained?

The Crystal Clear Eyes of *Chazal*

Chazal are called *"eini ha'eidah,"* the eyes of the Jewish Nation, and it is by means of their crystal-clear perspective that Torah Jews view the world. But before bringing those of their insights offered by the *Gedolei Yisrael* which shed light on FC, it is worthwhile to explain the basic difference between *Chazal's* view and science's.

Torah's Light Burns Forever

Writing in *Ye'aros Dvash*, which contains discussions on the limitations of science, Rabbi Yonasan Eibeshitz explains that science, which analyzes reality with man-made tools, finite parameters and corporeal eyes, eventually reaches an insurmountable barrier, a veil which it cannot pierce. Torah, on the other hand, which is the expression of the infinite wisdom of the living G-d, breaks through these barriers and discloses the truth.

Rabbi Eibeshitz illustrates this idea through the Menorah which stood in the *Beis Hamikdash*. The Menorah's six outer stems, he explains, represent general branches of wisdom, while its middle one represents Torah wisdom. The fact that the six stems incline toward the middle one, implies that all of the other branches of wisdom are merely Torah's handmaids, who serve it and glorify it.

The miracle which occurred when the Kohen prepared the wicks of the Menorah, further illustrates this idea. Every evening, the Kohen would fill the Menorah's lamps with the amount of pure olive oil needed to sustain its flames until the subsequent morning. The flames of the outer lamps would die out by dawn. However, the middle lamp, which represented Torah, would continue to burn until evening even though the Kohen had not replenished its oil supply. This miracle suggests that, even in areas where the other branches of knowledge become ineffectual, Torah's light continues to burn and to enlighten the world.

Rabbi Eibeshitz's observation may be applied to our issue too. Although science has reached a stalemate in its efforts to explain FC, the Torah provides us with insights which seem to cast light on the phenomenon of FC.

The Powers of the Unborn

The Talmud conveys fascinating information about the extraordinary capacities and potentials of entities and people commonly assumed to have no abilities at all. In *Bava Basra* (12b), *Chazal* describes the unique capacities of the human fetus, which is able to view the entire world "from one end to the other," even though it is confined into its mother's womb. It also depicts the remarkable learning process the fetus undergoes before it is born, stating that while it is still in the womb, an angel teaches it the entire Torah. (See *Nidah* 30b.)

These two Talmudic statements give rise to a number of questions. How can a fetus whose eyes are closed and whose view of the world is supposedly obstructed by its mother's body, see what occurs in the world, and even more so from one end of the world to the other? How can so tiny an entity grasp the entire Torah in so brief a span of time?

Once we understand the true essence of man and his potential, the answers to these questions will become clear.

Body and Soul

Man is composed of two parts — body and soul. However, the soul is man's essence, while the body is merely a vestment which enables the soul to manifest itself in a physical world. When Iyov declares, "In skin and flesh You dress me; with bones and sinews You cover me," (*Iyov*

10:11), he is alluding to this idea, which the *Zohar* explicitly states, when it says: "What is man? He is a soul, while [his] flesh, bones and sinews are garments" (*Parshas Yisro*, 77a).

The fact that human life ends when the soul departs from the body, while the soul lives on and achieves even more of its potential after its bearer dies, further underscores this point.

It is commonly assumed that learning and information assimilation take place via the brain, and that the mentally impaired lack this ability. Surprisingly, though, this assessment is not precise. Writing in *Michtav M'Eliyahu* (Volume Four, p. 163) Rabbi Eliyahu Dessler explains:

> Before the soul enters the body, it receives an unlimited quantity of metaphysical knowledge. Internal perceptions regularly flow into the soul, unlimited by time and place, and without intermediaries. These perceptions emanate from upper worlds and from the Divine Source of knowledge, Blessed be He. Thus the soul is not bound by restrictions in its vision and hearing, and has unlimited learning capacities. Such restrictions take effect only when the soul enters the body, and are outcomes of the body's limitations.
>
> The organ which links the soul to the body is the brain. As long as the soul is constrained by the body, its spiritual powers are limited by the brain. The brain acts as a screen and filter for the soul, and ensures that no information reaches it,

except that which conforms to the body's limitations, as well as the era and the place in which the bearer of the soul lives, and his behavior in the world of activity and free choice. The screens of those with cerebral impairments aren't as strong as those of the mentally able.

Now the Talmud's statement that the fetus studies the entire Torah during its nine-month stay in its mother's womb becomes clear. It does not study with its tiny and limited mind, but rather by means of the soul, whose powers of absorption are not bound by time restrictions. By the same token, it does not see from one end of the world to the other, with its physical eyes, which are closed, but rather with its spiritual eyes — the eyes of the soul which is not yet bound by the restrictions of the body.

Chazal say: "A candle burns over [the fetus'] head." To what candle were they referring? *Chazal* are using "candle" as a metaphor for the soul, and by saying that the candle burns *over* the fetus' head, they were intimating that the soul can see "from one end of the world to the other" because it is not confined within the fetus' body. This also explains the fetus' ability to learn the entire Torah so very quickly, in spite of its small size and undeveloped state.

Immediately before the infant is born, an angel strikes its mouth, causing it to forget all the Torah it has learned in the womb. What does this blow represent? The Maharal explains (*Gevuras Hashem*, Chap. 28): "Before the infant is born, its soul is linked only to the spiritual world. Once the infant's formation is completed, it emerges into the world, and the soul which then connects to the body via the brain, situates itself within the newborn's body.

The angel strikes the infant, when the mouth — the seat of the power of speech — is completed. But once the soul unites with the body, the infant, whose brain now restricts its soul, forgets all of the Torah it was taught in the womb."

Although the act of forgetting the Torah occurs only in the body, the soul never forgets it. The soul's capacity to recall is apparent in the mentally impaired, who, as we shall soon see, may also recall their past lives.

This lucid insight helps us understand the extraordinary capacities of special children, which we have described in Chapter Two.

- Special children convey messages without looking at their language boards or computer keyboards. *How is that possible?* Their souls are their eyes:

> I see the keyboard with the eyes of my spirit, a kind of imaginary keyboard, and that's what I point to.
>
> a child filmed at Syracuse University

*   *   *

> I don't have to look with my eyes in order to see. Ordinary people need eyes in order to see, because their brains prevent them from seeing. I see with my soul.
>
> a young girl with CP

- Special children absorb reading material at an incredible rate, which far exceeds that of regular people. *Why?*

Regular people read with their corporeal eyes, and all physical feats involve many complex steps, such as the processing of each letter and word. Cerebrally impaired children, though, read with the eyes of their souls, which do not have to process each unit, but assimilate an overall entity and transfer it directly to their soul's memory in an instant. (They are also mathematical whizzes for the very same reason.)

Their knowledge of languages and their heightened spiritual understanding can be explained similarly. Since these special children interact with their souls, and not only with their brains, they are not limited by normal restrictions and barriers to understanding. Therefore, it is not surprising that they have access to knowledge unavailable to us, or which would at least require many hours of studying for us to master.

In Brief

> My soul isn't wrapped in a healthy body, and as a result can sense the *Shechina*.
>
> a thirteen-year-old CP child

> I see the world differently than most people. The developmentally disabled are more soul than body.
>
> a ten-year-old autistic child.

Section II

Heart to Heart — Soul to Soul

- "Let Us Go Out to the Field"
- Previous Lives
- Sound the Trumpets
- Three Pillars
- Who Am I?

"My Lord, the soul You have placed within me is pure"

from our morning prayers

Introduction to Section II

"Let Us Go Out to the Field"

In this section we will take a fascinating journey into the rich inner world of the mentally disabled, which, as we shall soon see is a veritable rose garden, filled with lovely thoughts and replete with love of one's fellow, love of Hashem, love of Torah and deep concern for the Jewish Nation (or as our precious Galia likes to call it "our precious Jewish Nation") — a pure world in which the weeds of *loshon hora,* egoism and vain pursuits are non-existent, a world which is all soul.

The dictionary defines autism as detachment from reality. Most children with other types of mental disabilities also display that characteristic. We know that there is no such thing in this world as a void or a vacuum, and that the moment one is created, it is automatically filled. Although such children seem to be living in a void, FC has shown that their external detachment has been well compensated by an inner world of spirituality.

"Let us go out to the field ... sleep in the vineyards" (*Shir Hashirim* 7:12) of the beautiful thoughts of the mentally disabled.

5

Previous Lives

Even though the Arizal states that the majority of us have returned to this world in order to rectify sins we committed in previous incarnations, most people have no recollection of their previous lives.[1] Hashem deliberately causes us to forget our former lives, in order not to inhibit our free choice in our present ones.

According to Torah sources, disabled children are reincarnated souls. Writing in *Sefer HaPardes*, "*Shaar Eser ve'lo Teisha*," Rabbi Moshe Kordovero says:

> The reason certain people lack various limbs is that they defiled them...restricting, thereby, the *neshama* from spreading to those parts of the body. Birth defects are the consequences of spiritual damage inflicted in previous incarnations.

In *Shefa Tal* (p. 7), he writes:

> Apparent bodily deformities point to hidden

---

[1] Some people return to fulfill a mission, or to help relatives fuflill a *tikun*.

defects of the soul, which were caused by [the violation of or the failure to perform] one of the 613 mitzvos...When one transgresses, the Heavenly light, which is consequently marred, ceases to shed the light of life on some of his spiritual limbs. When these spiritual limbs fail to receive such light, their parallel physical limbs become maimed. *Kohanim* with physical deformities were considered unfit to perform the Divine Service, because overt deformities are indicative of hidden spiritual defects caused by sin...Those born with deformities had marred their souls in previous lives.

Unlike regular people, the disabled generally possess precise knowledge of their previous lives, often saying that they are incarnations of people, as a rule grandparents, uncles or other relatives known to their contemporaries. They are also conscious of the sins for which they were returned to our world. However, since they lack free choice, this knowledge does not impede their efforts to rectify themselves.

Following are a number of accounts in which special children describe their past lives:

Hashem's Great Compassion
Chaim C., a twelve-year-old autistic child

As a base sinner who has undergone the sublime process of Divine purification and who has been granted the power of self-expression, I consider sharing my experiences with others a sacred duty.

In my past life, I sinned in secret. On the surface I was an upstanding, devout member of my community. I *davened*, gave charity and was a good husband. My behavior, though, was entirely superficial. Underneath all those lies was the dismal truth. During my youth I attended yeshiva and succeeded in my studies. When I married, I left yeshiva and went into business with a friend who had studied with me.

Soon I began to lead a double life. My friend's familiarity with life's pleasures and vanities far surpassed mine. He was an enthusiastic teacher, and I was an eager student. We went into business together, at first deceiving only non-Jews. But quite rapidly we began to deceive our own brethren.

Our business expanded and I became a prominent member of the community, whom the poor regarded as a *tzaddik*. I tried to quiet my conscience by giving large sums of charity to the needy. My family grew and I prospered. My appetite for sensual pleasures increased. Cuisine became important to me, and I imported delicacies from all over the world. This disturbed my conscience, and as a result I made large feasts in order to share my hidden passions with others. My Shabbos and holiday tables were a delight to the eye and to the palate. I became famous for my hospitality, but in reality I was only an inflated rascal.

Soon I sank to greater depths, and stopped studying Torah altogether. Although I went to shul, I merely pretended to be *davening*, and drew further and further away from my Maker.

On the surface, I was a perfect husband. But I soon

betrayed my pious wife, as I did Hashem. Eventually, I reached rock-bottom.

At that point Hashem, in His great mercy, saved His wayward son. My deceit was discovered. I was disgraced, and found guilty of an even greater sin, that of *chilul Hashem*. I was cast into prison. I felt that my life had ended and was futile. I was lonely and forlorn.

Then, I started to *daven*. It was difficult to approach Hashem after having been so distant from Him, and after having so sullied the pure soul that He had given me. I bemoaned my wasted life, and was overcome by dreadful shame. I did genuine *teshuva* and Hashem commiserated with me. I was like a child who had found his way back home. I died that night in prison.

When I reached the Heavenly court, my sins were placed on a scale. The heap was so enormous that I thought I would be sent to the most fiery place in *Gehennom*. However, a defending angel piled my remorse on the other side of the scale, and a perfect balance was achieved. I was told that I could tip the scales in my favor if I returned to the world as an autistic child, unable to enjoy the pleasures of life.

I was also given the capacity to relate my story. If this tale of woe helps others to do *teshuva*, I will be credited with a *chessed shel emmes*, because I derive no worldly pleasure from telling it. This *chessed* will help tip the scales in my favor, and propel me into *Gan Eden*. How can I express my deep love for Hashem? How can I thank Him? He lifts the basest sinner and gives him life. How can I praise such great kindness? Because I was saved from spiritual death, I must try to save others. Return wayward children to your loving

Father because if not, you will be destroyed together with your iniquities.

* * *

A Warning
Yossi, a ten-year-old autistic child

I am *ploni ben almoni*. I was sent to this world as a punishment for the sins I committed in a past life. I suffer greatly from my predicament, but fully understand the great wisdom of Divine retribution, which enables the basest sinners to attain their portion in *Gan Eden*. The message I am about to convey constitutes a warning to everyone.

I suffer a thousand pangs of grief a minute in this empty world. I am a stranger in a world which regards me as deviant. I am angry at myself for not having understood, while there was still time. My sins forced Hashem to show me how repulsive I really was. He sent me back to the world as an autistic child — a wretched, helpless youngster who disturbs his surroundings, and causes much heartbreak to his parents.

I want to warn everyone who reads this essay: examine your behavior and determine where it is inadequate. Then repent before your time is up. Do your utmost to forestall the prospect of being sent back to this world for rectification. Returning to this world as a reincarnated soul is a dreadful punishment, perhaps even worse than *Gehennom*.

* * *

I Returned to this World Against my Will
Yerachmiel, an autistic young man

I was a *talmid chacham* and a *tzaddik*. I toiled in Torah day and night, and made great efforts to improve my character. However, I had one shortcoming: my love for Hashem wasn't greater than my love for His Torah. I loved the depth and sweetness of the Torah and sincerely tried to change my negative traits. But when I *davened*, I didn't sense Hashem's presence. I didn't feel Him in my heart.

I wasn't aware of this failing because the *gedolei ha'dor* held me in high esteem. I believed that I was a genuine *tzaddik*. As I was about to leave the world, I realized that my faith had been lacking, and I was overcome by trembling and dreadful fear.

The Heavenly Court tried me and found that, although I had studied Torah day and night, I hadn't served Hashem but rather my body which wanted to study Torah in order to be acclaimed by eminent people. I wanted to be a *gadol ha'dor* and not an *eved Hashem*. The Heavenly Court decided to send me to *Gehennom*. But the Torah I had studied saved me, because someone who studies Torah necessarily loves Hashem.

I was offered the chance to return as a disturbed person who is incapable of studying. However, I couldn't reconcile myself to such a punishment, and pleaded for mercy, crying out: "Anything but that! Life without Torah is not life. It's *Gehennom*." But they didn't ask me and here I am, undergoing terrible suffering. Nonetheless, Hashem pitied me, and placed me in a yeshiva for the mentally disabled. For my soul, even such Torah is sweet music.

* * *

I Wanted to be a *Talmid Chacham*
Gadi, an eight-year-old Down syndrome child

I wanted to be a *talmid chachcam*. I pored over my studies, but didn't develop the trait of kindness. As a result, my Torah was incomplete. Toward the end of my life, I realized my mistake. But by then it was too late. I had lost the ability to commiserate with the suffering of other Jews and didn't realize how lacking I was in compassion. Although I did *teshuva*, my penance wasn't sufficient because I didn't know how to repent properly.

* * *

I Didn't Believe
Yaakov, a fifteen-year-old CP child

I was born in Iraq, and in my previous life was called Binyamin HaKohen. I am the soul of someone who didn't believe that the universe has a Master. As a youngster I studied in yeshiva, but was attracted by this world. My mother came from a family of *tzaddikim*. But I didn't want to study Torah, and forsook the World of Truth for one of falsehood. I mingled with intellectuals and was accepted by them.

It hurts me to speak about my past. I behaved like a

non-Jew. Nonetheless, Hashem showed me the truth. He sent a group of non-Jews to murder me. One of them — a Jew who imitated the gentiles — killed me. But I had already realized the truth before I died, and had done *teshuva* with all my heart.

As one who attempted to pursue a false lifestyle, I want to warn all Jews who think that they can flee the truth — those who think that they can live like non-Jews: You can't escape! Hashem won't let His holy people immerse themselves in *tum'ah* (impurity). He will wipe out those who don't accept the yoke of Heaven. Ima, tell Rav S. what I have said. That's part of my *tikun*.

Ima, you and I have a very strong bond, because you have always been with me. You are part of my soul. You can't understand that. In a former incarnation, you were my mother. You cried because I left the true path — Hashem's path. You shed bitter tears over my fate. Now Heaven has given you the opportunity to attend to my needs again in this world. Ima! Don't cry anymore. I'm an *eved Hashem* (servant of G-d).

Ima, you're not alone. Hashem is with you! Deep down, you know this. Hashem gives you strength. Don't be afraid. Your reward is great.

*   *   *

The Same Soul
Beila and Her Mother "Speak"

> M: Do you know whether your soul was previously in a different body?

B: Yes. I was one of your relatives. She was a very kind person. But her motives were not always altruistic. I have returned to earth also in order to reveal Hashem's greatness to a blind society. Although I helped others in my previous life, I sometimes had ulterior motives. I had other failings too. The Heavenly Court gave me the opportunity to rectify my character flaws by letting me return in a form in which all my behavior is totally selfless.

M: Why did I give birth to a child like you?

B: In order to help you overcome your lack of trust in Hashem.

Other Interviews:

I Wasn't Humble Enough
Nissim, a seventeen-year-old- young man with CP

F: Can you tell me about your past?

N: Yes. I lived 230 years ago in Poland.

F: Was that your first time in the world?

N: No.

F: Why did you return this time?

N: Although I was a *talmid chochom* I wasn't humble enough. I had a place in Gan Eden but wanted a higher place, closer to the hallowed light. I wasn't willing to accept the verdict of the Heavenly Court and they offered me a choice of accepting the place reserved for me, or returning to this world as an incarnated soul. They told me what I would have to undergo when I returned. I consented, and am not sorry about it. I waited between *Gan Eden* and this world.

F: What do you mean?

N: You can't understand.

F: Can you tell me about your previous lives?

N: I don't remember all of them. But I can tell you about the most recent one.

*　　　*　　　*

Do as Much as Possible
Yehoshua, a seven-year-old brain damaged child

F: What were you in your previous incarnation?

Y: I was a *talmid chacham*. I was so engrossed in my studies, that I didn't always *daven* with a *minyan*. When I reached the Heavenly Court they claimed that, even though I was a *tzaddik*, I couldn't receive the place reserved for me in Gan Eden. Since I refused to accept a lower place I was sent back to earth to rectify my failing.

F: How can one avoid returning to earth as a reincarnation?

Y: Do as much as possible *l'shem Shamayim* (for the sake of Heaven).

F: Do the *tikunim* done according to the Ben Ish Chai help avert affliction?

A: Yes, provided that one helps himself.

* * *

I Didn't Do Enough *Chessed*
Beila, a brain-damaged girl of eight

F: Why did you come to the world in this form?

B: I was a good woman who kept the *mitzvos*. But I didn't do enough *chessed*. It's difficult to do *teshuva* for insufficient *chessed*. Nonetheless, because I was basically good they let me rectify my past by returning to the world in this form. Now I can perform the genuine *chessed* of helping people discover the truth. I am speaking the truth. I know that you are good, and that you are seeking the truth. Keep searching, and you'll find it.

F: How can we help you?

B: Help the mentally disabled find places to study Torah, to be among G-d fearing people and to be able to continue with their sacred work.

* * *

Only the Fool Doesn't Accept Heaven's Dominion
Miriam, a brain damaged child

F: Why have you returned to earth in this form?

M: I didn't accept the dominion of Heaven.

F: Did you commit other sins too?

M: My failure to accept the dominion of Heaven was enough of a sin to cause me to be reincarnated.

F: Do you remember the Heavenly Court?

M: I prefer not to think about it.

F: Were you in *Gehennom*?

M: Yes.

F: What was it was like?

M: You are incapable of understanding how terrifying it is.

F: How does being an autistic child constitute a *tikun* for the refusal to accept the sovereignty of Heaven?

M: It is a fitting punishment. Anyone who doesn't accept the sovereignty of Heaven is a fool.

*   *   *

Never Leave Me
Esther, a brain damaged child

F: What have you to say?

E: I *daven* all day to Hashem, and ask Him never to leave me. I know which *mitzvos* I failed to do. I didn't fulfill my obligations.

F: Is this the end of your punishment?

E: Yes. Do *mitzvos* properly. Don't reach a situation like mine.

* * *

I Spoke *Lashon Hara*
Yoav, a seventeen-year-old autistic boy

Yoav's noble appearance gave him the aura of a holy person, attracting the attention of all. Another autistic child told a facilitator: "Yoav is not like the rest. He was already in Gan Eden, but in order to attain a higher level, he opted to come back down to earth to correct minor deficiencies." The following exchange took place between Yoav and the facilitator:

F: Do you remember your past incarnation?

Y: Yes.

F: Why have you returned this world?

Y: I spoke *lashon hara* against someone and did not beg his forgiveness, although he forgave me in his heart. This occurred ninety-six-and-a-half years ago. It involved an argument between two *talmidei chachamim*, and I spoke wrongly about it.

* * *

Please Study the Laws of *Lashon Hara*
Refoel, a seven-year-old CP child

F: Why were you born paralyzed?

R: I was a *tzaddik* in a previous life, but spoke *lashon hara* against someone.

F: Why didn't you ask forgiveness?

R: I asked, but the person didn't want to forgive me.

F: How can we ease your *tikun*?

R: By studying the laws of *lashon hara* at your Shabbos table.

(The child's mother related that on two occasions, after Shabbos was over, the boy cried intensely for most of the night. When asked what was wrong, he replied; "You forgot to study the laws of *lashon hara* at the table.")

6

Sound the Trumpets

Hurricane Mitch Takes the Lives of 20,000

Thousands Perish in an Earthquake in Turkey

Serious Drought in Israel

When such calamities take place, penetrating questions pierce the air. Why? What can we do? Are such occurrences chance?

Rambam (*Hilchos Ta'anis,* Chapter One) explains the Torah approach to calamity:

> It is a positive *mitzvah* of the Torah to cry out and to sound the trumpets when disaster befalls a community, as it is written: "Because of the enemy that besieges you, you shall sound the trumpets" (*Bamidbar* 10:9). This *mitzvah* pertains to all calamities that oppress [the Nation]: drought, pestilence, locusts, and other natural disasters. Whenever these occur, one must cry out and sound trumpets. This response is one of the ways to *teshuva,* for when tragedy

strikes and [the people] cry out, all will reach the understanding that the tragedy is the result of their misdeeds, as it is written: "Your sins have caused these [evils] and your misdeeds prevented the good from reaching you" (*Yirmiyahu* 5:25). This [reaction] will cause the misfortune to be eliminated.

But when a community does not cry out and does not sound the trumpets, but rather feels: *This calamity is a natural disaster, a chance occurrence,* this is the path of indifference and will cause [the community] to become more attached to its evil deeds [resulting then] in the occurrence of more tragedies.

Many of the messages which special children convey help us perceive the inner meaning of calamities and disasters.

Galia Looks at Life

Hurricane Mitch

M: Galia, what can you tell us about Hurricane Mitch, which in 1998 caused the deaths of nearly 20,000 people in Central America and left more than a million without roofs over their heads?

G: Ima, everything is from Hashem. Such disasters are signs that the Redemption is imminent. Natural catastrophes will shortly begin to occur more frequently and with greater force. This was a minor one in comparison to what lies ahead for all humanity. Soon, more tornadoes and hurricanes will shake the United States and the world and will wreak much havoc. They will claim many lives, and inflict much damage. Wind, which is intangible, can in half an hour destroy and obliterate people's homes and worldly possessions. If wind is only G-d's agent, how much more is G-d Himself capable of? Only the Jewish Nation has the capacity to prevent or soften the effects of the great anger against those wallowing in folly, materialism and fantasy.

Heat Wave

Dear Ima. The current heat wave suggests that we are living in erratic times. It is rare and its purpose is to arouse us and to cause us to ask "Why?" If we begin by asking "Why," then we will eventually reach the truth.

What is that truth? Hashem is the King of the entire universe. He is One and the only One. He is the ruler of entire universe and of all the worlds. There is no power greater than Hashem. There is none above Him. He alone can deliver us, not only from the heat, but from all the difficult times destined for us. Holy and pure Jews who do *teshuva*, soften the imminent blows. These blows are being mitigated, but not canceled. It's sad that the decree still hasn't been annulled.

Unseasonable Rain (Av, 5757)

Dearest Ima, rain falls out of season, when Heaven is sad and worried about us, the beloved Jewish Nation. A war will soon break out, and we will suffer. It hurts to think of this. Apparently, such a war can't be prevented, because a large section of the Nation is still in deep slumber and must wake up, so that when Mashiach comes, someone will be here to greet him. Every blow the Jewish Nation suffers is for its benefit.

Drought

Dear Ima, Hashem sends us drought in order to open our eyes. If people violate the commands cited in *Shma Yisroel* the first punishment to befall us is drought. If we do not do as Hashem commands, "He seals the Heavens and there [is] no rain, and the earth [does not] give its produce." The danger is very real. All of the bizarre disasters which occur, and which will occur more frequently, are meant to highlight our irregular situation. Hashem is waiting for us to return. He wants us to ask, "Why?" He wants us to ask, "How?" He wants us to examine and investigate and to see that many questions cannot be answered by science. If we probe deeply we will see that that man has no control over the world even though he thinks he does. He has no control over natural catastrophes and death and cannot cope with them. Ima, my precious Ima, how do people, who regard themselves as intelligent, fail to open their eyes? How do they fail to look about and to perceive that all that transpires is from Hashem, and that we control nothing? Ima, I have already said this, but must repeat it again and again, because very shortly terrible tremors will shake the world. The earth will begin to tremble, to quake, to erupt. The current calm will cease and a series of events, which are meant to precede the Redemption, which is so near, will ensue one after the other.

Israel, and the entire world, are in danger. Nonetheless, Israel will be the safest place. Of course, that doesn't mean that all of Israel's Jews will survive.

Natural Catastrophes

Warnings
Moshe, an eight-year-old autistic child

Times have changed. Hashem is telling us very clearly that He intends to purify the world so that Mashiach can come. Now is the time in which we must save chareidi Jewry because they are the key to the world's deliverance. They are the summit of the mountain and the reason for the creation of the world. When they do true *teshuva*, the world will be saved. Therefore, Rabbi K., I ask you to publicize what I have said. Hashem warns us by taking away so many people from our community at such frequent intervals. He warns us by means of the many mentally incompetent children who are born, the bizarre calamities and accidents which occur too often, the many terrible problems in *shalom bayis* which seem insoluble and the numerous natural calamities which occur, they are all warnings. All these happen for a reason.

Open the Eyes of the Sleeping

So Many Messages
Yosef, an eighteen-year-old mentally disabled boy

It strikes me as funny that precisely autistic children have to tell regular people something that is so clear. It's really a shame. Hashem sends so many messages. But who listens? We hold rallies to protest the incitement of the secular government. But we must also hold rallies to spur ourselves to improve. Hashem clearly informs the religious that they are also impeding the Redemption. The religious Jews receive messages on a daily basis. Every day young people die. Every day more children are orphaned. How many sick people must there be? How many widows? How many widowers? How many children have strayed from the Torah way of life? How many bizarre tragedies? How many? How many? How many?

How many young people take drugs? How many? How many couples suffer from *shalom bayis* problems? How many? The numbers are incredible. Yet we don't understand that these are messages. Clear messages.

We must scrutinize ourselves, and not point to others. Everyone must examine himself and his social circle because something is wrong.

The Powers of Impurity are Intensifying
Galia

Dear Ima, you have to understand that the powers of impurity know for certain that their end is drawing near.

Like an injured animal, they are making last minute efforts to lead as many people as possible astray and provoke even the nations of the world to fight with each other. We must safeguard our sanctity, do Heaven's will, and not respond to the Evil Inclination, which comes on the part of the *tumah*, in order to provoke us to sin. The more Torah we study and the more *mitzvos* we observe, the less *tumah* there will be. Only a chaste and clean soul can be a receptacle for the tremendous amount of purity which descends to the world. When the number of people who have prepared themselves as receptacles to receive lights from above increases, holiness will prevail in the world. This constitutes the Redemption of the Jewish Nation. Holiness spreads and strengthens us constantly. But it isn't sufficient and we must increase this holiness and open the eyes of the sleeping. Ima, understand: People who haven't prepared themselves are not capable of absorbing holiness and supernal lights. The souls of such people are clogged and are impervious to holiness. But *boruch Hashem*, there are people who are receptacles. They receive such lights and retain them. Hashem, in His kindness, will bring down holiness from Above. It will prevail here and spread, increasing and growing. This will prepare the background for the coming of the Mashiach, in full view of all the world.

It's Not Easy
Beila, an eight-year-old CP child

Now I will explain something very simple. Everything good comes with difficulty. It's not easy. I know. Only the strong will survive this war. Those who do not trust Hashem will not be able to withstand the difficult tribulations meant to try them and curb them. Always recall Avraham Avinu and that will strengthen you.

It won't be easy. The enemy is on the verge of death and knows that its days are numbered. He is trying to fell as many as possible. He doesn't want to disappear alone. He wants to take as many as possible with him. This is a cruel and very difficult war. Even if the situation doesn't seem so grim, know that moments later hard blows may follow. But don't be afraid and don't stop. *Am Yisrael chai*. But for how long? How many will remain? In what situation?

Peace Process
Mordechai, a seven-year-old brain damaged child

It's nothing new that Esav hates Jacob. Therefore the peace process is an illusion of the mixed multitude, which, with its false views has swept up many straying souls. If they continue to be swept away, they will bring a catastrophe upon the Jewish State and to the Jews all over the world.

An Arab is an Arab
Chezki, a mentally disabled boy

The efforts of the government to prevent terrorist attacks are foolish. Hamas, PLO — there is no difference. An Arab is an Arab, and in a moment he can change the color of his skin. We need mercy from Heaven. But their end is near.

We Are Our Own Enemies
Ben Golden

I'm not worried about the Arabs, I am worried about the Jews. The Arabs aren't our enemies. We are our own enemies. Do *teshuva*, and you won't have any worries. Neither will I.

The Simple Truth
Galia

It's a difficult time for Jewish Nation. The Jews are blind. They don't see the simple truth, which is that the *Ribbono shel Olam* is the One who determines everything. It is not the Palestinians nor the Jews in the government, nor the Hamas, nor any one else — only Hashem.

Return
Ronit (a comatose patient)

We are living in a crucial era. It is very important to know that the end is near and that it is urgent for all of us to return to Torah's way. We have to work at drawing our fellow Jews closer to Hashem. People in my state are witnesses to the fact that there is a supernatural world and that Hashem is all-powerful. Make haste. There's no time. Even the religious have to do *teshuva*. They are also in danger. This world confuses everyone.

The Threefold Strand
Shalom, a twelve-year-old CP child (written 2 Elul 5757, after the terrorist attack on Ben Yehuda Street in Jerusalem)

Jews, stop pitying Ishmael, and have pity on your souls which are wallowing in your blood. How long will you close your eyes; how long will you close your hearts? As long as the Jewish Nation doesn't observe at least the threefold strand which is Shabbos, family purity and kashrus, the letter *yud* remains removed from the word *Yehudim*, and only the letters of the expression *ho dam* [which means "ho blood"] remain. Hashem demands: Do *teshuva*! Hashem knows that you are tired of hearing the word, *teshuva*. But Hashem also knows that you are even more tired of wallowing in blood.

Think! Which is harder: wallowing in blood or doing *teshuva*? Life or death?

It is impossible, and unnatural to dwell in peace without observing Torah and mitzvos. Shabbos can't remain silent, and demands: "Observe me and I will protect you and, if not, your fate will be bitter!"

Hashem is the Prime Minster. Hashem is the Security Minster. Hashem causes one to die, and revives the dead, and is the just Judge. Do *teshuva* now, it's still not late. Fellow Jews, if you don't want to find yourselves wallowing in your blood, seek Hashem now. Accept the three *mitzvos* on whose merit the Jewish Nation has survived. Shabbos observance, the observance of the laws of family purity and kashrus are the fences which protect us against the punishment. Remember, tears and sorrow without *mitzvah* observance do not exempt one from punishment.

Remember, you were warned by someone whose soul is impaired yet whose soul sees everything, even future calamities, which are liable to occur, G-d forbid, if you don't follow His ways.

7

The Three Pillars

Three main themes, interwoven throughout the messages of these children like golden strands, are: the urgency of doing *teshuva*, the significance of *achdus* (unity) between the Jewish People and Hashem and among themselves, and the potency of *Tehillim*. In their unique way, these children point to the deep relationship between unity and *Tehillim*. Persuasively, cogently and in a most original and bracing manner, they urge us focus on these three points.

On the Wings of Prayer and *Tehillim*

With a Broken Heart
Shlomo, a twelve-year-old autistic child

The only *tikun* for this generation is to pray with a broken heart which yearns to repent. Everyone must repent, even the religious. We shouldn't pray only for individuals, but for the entire Jewish Nation, because we are judged as one nation. Our greatest sin is disunity.

No Time
Yossi, a twenty-seven-year-old autistic young man

I have a direct message for the Jewish Nation. There's no time to waste on futile or sinful pursuits, no time for empty prattle, no time for materialistic ties to this world. This is a time for decision making and prayer. Only prayer and *Tehillim,* and all of us together, can bring the Redemption. If you think you're smart, and that you have time, woe to you. If we don't search for the truth ourselves, Hashem will force us to see it. The Jewish Nation will be shown the truth first. Therefore, we must begin *right now* to truly *daven* and to recite *Tehillim* with fear and trepidation and out of love for Hashem. Then goodness will descend onto this world and this transformation will take place peacefully and tranquilly.

I didn't make up this message. It comes from under the Throne of Glory. Hashem wants His people very much and wants to bring the Mashiach through peace and joy. Only prayer and *Tehillim* together can save the world.

Many think that there is time. But whoever takes a good look at life sees the dangers and the pitfalls. We must *daven* and recite *Tehillim* together, not only alone, but rather *together!* We are in great danger, not only in Eretz Yisrael.

The Most Potent Medicine
Beila

Tehillim is the most potent medicine on earth. There's nothing stronger than it. *Tehillim,* recited by large groups have the capacity to save the world and bring about the

Redemption with ease. Only *achdus* — unity — can save us. Reciting *Tehillim* together in groups is the ultimate manifestation of *achdus*.

The problem is that many Jews are egoistic. There are *bnei Torah* who don't know the meaning of oneness with Hashem or with the Jewish Nation. They think they are righteous. They eat only food with special *kashrus* certifications. They don't eat in restaurants or at celebrations or in other people's homes. Nonetheless, they lack *ahavas Yisrael*, and don't even love Hashem. A person must emerge from his four cubits, and enter the four cubits of his fellows and together with them reach Hashem.

Small children also should also recite *Tehillim*. They too should form *Tehillim* groups. The *Tehillim* of children make a great impression Above. The boys can recite *Tehillim* after *davening* and the girls can also recite *Tehillim* in school, as well as in their after-school clubs.

In brief: *Tehillim* is the most potent weapon against the strongest enemy of all. Its impact is greatest when Jews recite it together. Women should try and meet twice a week in order to recite *Tehillim*. They should divide up the all of the chapters among themselves. Such a procedure teaches us to function not as individuals, but as a part of a complete unit. Men should do this too. It is harder for men to want to participate in something in which each one will only be a part of the complete unit. Inasmuch as the natural spiritual level of women is higher than that of men, if all women recite *Tehillim* together this will effect a change in Heaven even though the men don't participate. The method of dividing *Tehillim* among a number of people in a group has the capacity to bring about the Redemption. Even if we don't succeed in accomplishing this; we will be prepared for the great day when we will need to know how to use this weapon to its fullest potential.

Teshuva

Tell Bnei Torah
Azriel, a seven-year old brain damaged child:

Examine your deeds because the end is near. Soon it will be so difficult that you won't have time or the presence of mind to do *teshuva*. Tell *bnei Torah* that the Redemption is in their own hands, and can only be brought about by means of genuine *teshuva*. *Bnei Torah* should be closest to Torah. But so many still haven't embarked on the correct path. I am very frightened because they aren't doing *teshuva*.

Wake Up!
Benny, an eleven-year-old CP child

Jews of the world, wake up. There is no time to waste. To believing Jews I say: "Love your neighbor as yourself." To those who don't believe I say, "I am the Lord your G-d Who took you out of Egypt." That's the message. If you don't understand you won't endure.

The Wandering is Nearly Over
Beila

I have this message for those Jewish souls who stood on

Mount Sinai, yet are still wandering about in the desert. We received the Torah at the foot of the mountain. We heard Hashem's voice, and said: "We will do and listen". However, from that moment on, every soul has been wandering through eternity in an attempt to achieve the perfection which prevailed at Sinai, an attempt to acquire their share in the sacred Torah. Now this wandering is nearly over. Every soul that wishes to endure must genuinely accept the dominion of Hashem and the Torah. The ordeal will soon end. Souls will be measured and judged in order to ascertain which have, indeed, left the desert and acquired the merits to enter Eretz Yisrael, and which haven't.

A Letter to a *Gadol b'Yisrael*
Ben Golden

I, Binyomin Golden, communicated personally with the Rav a few years ago, and today I have a message to transmit to the Rav. The Rav is well aware that *Am Yisrael* is currently on a low level. There are many yeshivos, much Torah, much *chessed*. The shuls are filled with people. What's lacking is heart, and when there is no heart an alien atmosphere fills the void. It is this alien atmosphere which causes a great descent in *ruchniyus*, and is what distances religious Jews from Hashem. In Eretz Yisrael the situation is very grave, but abroad, and especially in America, the spiritual decay is far worse and very disconcerting. This is very worrying, for how long can we expect that Hashem will not respond? How long? How long? The Rav knows that because of this we are in very great danger. So many

Jews are ailing. So many die young. There are so many orphans, so many divorces, so many young people stray from the proper path, so many foreign things in the holiest places. Now we must do something to return the heart to the Jewish People. One began in America. One has to start here. One needs strong rabbis who will show the truth without fear. We have to react because time is ending and we have few merits, for a Jew without his heart, without love of Hashem is not a proper Jew. I request from the Rav a blessing for us and for all the nation.

Lippy: a Message to America

My message to the religious Jews of America is: You are in the greatest danger. *Olam Hazeh* is taking Hashem's place little by little in every aspect of our lives — from the yeshivos, to the kollels, to the Rebbe's courtyard...This illness slowly seeps in, and we must stop it immediately, otherwise it will the engulf us all.

In order to combat it, we must learn to love Hashem. Hashem and His will and word must be the sole focus of our lives - not vanities, not foolish pursuits, not non-Jewish ideas. We must not let the Golden Calf gain control of us. Only Hashem and His word. We must cleanse our hearts, our minds and our lives, purify them, and reach a state of holiness. The Rav and others have to tell the truth to the Jewish world. Hashem will not tolerate the persistence of the present situation for more than a limited time. Then He will purify us if we will not have done so ourselves. We are guilty of committing many sins individually and as a community. True, we also do many acts of kindness and have so many *yeshivos*, but look closely and see into the hearts of the people and you will find that the love of Hashem is lacking there.

Divine Love
Beila

Hashem is love. His entire Creation is filled with love. Everything in Creation was fashioned with love. *Adam Harishon* was created perfect because he was the consummation of Hashem's love. Hashem, in His infinite wisdom, gave man free choice and this too was an act of love. Free choice renders man a partner in Creation. Man should have willingly accepted the fact that it is not he, but Hashem Who is the Creator and the Ruler of the universe. In His immense humility, Hashem accepted man as a partner in the Divine plan and wanted him to achieve perfection by means of his own powers. But man was deceived by the Snake — the Evil Inclination- which taught him to think that he can rebel against Hashem's will and rule the universe.

From the moment he sinned, man lost his intrinsic ability to recognize and to feel Divine love. Since that time, humankind has had to search for that love and reveal it in Creation and in itself. The greater our awareness of Divine love the closer we are to perfection. We achieve perfection by performing acts of *chessed*. When we emulate Hashem's form of *chessed* toward us, we grow spiritually. If we toil in Torah and *chessed* we will achieve perfection. The search for Divine love in the form of *chessed*, and truly for Heaven's sake, constitutes *teshuva*.

When a person decides to embark on the struggle to emulate the attributes of his Creator, he may be said to have accepted His dominion. Once we, Hashem's chosen, have launched this search, we will be enveloped by Hashem's love.

A warning must be added to the above. Time is ending. If we do not search for perfection, Hashem will perfect us through His great wisdom. That will not be an easy way. All I can say is that it would be infinitely better if we individuals initiate repentance.

Unity

Hashem Loves Unity
Menachem, a Down syndrome child

Achieving unity is crucial for us today. All those who believe in the dominion of Heaven must unite. Even though we disagree on many points, unity must prevail amidst us, for when there is unity all else will fall into place. Hashem loves unity. During the period of the Tower of Babel, the people nearly succeeded in rebelling against Hashem because they were united. Their efforts were thwarted, though, because Hashem confounded their tongue and forcibly prevented their unity.

Whoever is concerned only for himself and for those close to him affirms that he is distant from Hashem. Today's Left might one day be considered Right. Let us all pray that we speedily witness the days in which the earth is filled with wisdom of Hashem.

The Chanukah Miracle
Ben Golden

During the time of the Second *Beis Hamikdash*, all of the Jews were dedicated to Hashem and to observing the Torah's laws. A few, though, mingled with the non-Jews and began to assimilate. The Chanukah miracle constituted a warning to the Jews to beware. It hinted to them: "There is a danger in your midst. If you do not stamp it out it now, it will contaminate other G-d fearing Jews". The High Priest was charged with solving the problem. First he had to pinpoint and eradicate it. Only after achieving that, could he triumph in the war against the Greeks and find the pure cruse of oil with which to kindle the Menorah. The miracle in which oil sufficient for one day lasted eight days occurred on his merit. He didn't say, "What can I do?" He went out and dealt with the problem. Don't push anything aside. If it comes your way it's for you to do. Go to wherever and whomever needs you.

Today the Chanuka light glows strongly, as it did many years ago during the time of Mattisyahu. Its light will combat the darkness and the war will be colossal. Currently, the darkness is greater than in any generation. For the light to penetrate, a huge struggle must ensue. The great upheaval is soon. Prepare yourselves to receive that light by purifying yourselves, perfecting your character traits and your closeness to Hashem. Act now. Trials and tribulations are on the threshold.

The Trials of the Month of Teves
Beila

Today is *rosh chodesh* Teves. Historically, it has always been a month of trials for Jewish Nation — trials in faith. This Teves, as in every year, the Jews must demonstrate their love for Hashem. They must prove their dedication to Him. There isn't much time. We must act quickly. There is no time to stall, no time to hesitate. It is time to act.

My convulsions come when the fear in me becomes overwhelming. It grows to the point of explosion and then it happens. It is the fear of the unknown, not knowing what will happen to us. Only Hashem knows, but we can effect a turnabout if we improve our deeds. We must change. We have no choice. The entire Jewish Nation is in danger: everyone, no matter where he resides. No place has a claim to security. Jews all over the world must do *teshuva*. It is collective *teshuva* that will help.

It's Coming
Arela, a twelve-year-old autistic child

A terrible calamity is in store for all the Jewish Nation. Yes. It is a reality. It is coming. Every perceptive and intelligent Jew should feel that black clouds are overcastting the skies. No one can deny this. *Am Yisrael*, this is your last chance. When our warnings stop coming, that will signify that the end is near, the end of our empty lives. The truth will begin to unfold bit by bit, until those destined to survive are ready to receive the full light. *Am Yisrael*, enough with your foolish escapades. Love your fellow Jew. Return to the Torah in purity. Draw closer to your Creator. *Am Yisrael*, why perish without reason? Return. Hashem will forgive you. Don't commit suicide. *Am Yisrael*, live! Live! Live!

Warning Before a War
Nissim, an eight-year-old autistic child

Ima, I want to tell you something. We, the mentally disabled, the unfortunate of the world, have come to convey the truth to an even more unfortunate world. Ima, the Jewish Nation is in great danger. Ima, I'm terrified. There will be a war soon. Ima don't be afraid, because people who do chessed will live. Ima, you did a great *chessed* with me, and that is credited to you. I am a *tzaddik*, and you are my *tzaddekes*. Ima, I am always with you, even when I am physically far away from you. When I was born you didn't understand that I would eventually give you so much. You thought that I had come down to earth to destroy your life. But truth is learned the hard way. The Jewish Nation will be flailed by a hard blow which will save them from an even harsher one. Whoever understands the truth will remain intact. However, he who sees only lies will undergo a calamity. Ima, it's coming quickly. Hurry up. Immerse yourself in outreach work both for the religious and the non-religious, for that is the required *chessed*. To those who don't understand what I have said, I repeat: There will be huge war. Whoever wants to save himself and his family must return to the truth, which is the Torah. Hashem will cancel the decrees if the Jews return to Him, but right now that doesn't look likely.

The Purging Process Has Begun
Shmulik, a fourteen-year-old CP child

The purging process will begin soon. I beseech my fellow Jews to do *teshuva*, but very few listen. Instead they argue with us, the mentally disabled , wondering whether we really do convey these messages on our own initiative. Fools won't ever see the truth. The wise have already begun to do *teshuva* because all who seek the truth understand that we speak the truth. The war is liable to begin shortly — the final wars against the Evil Inclination. Prepare yourselves quickly, because there is no time. Only *Hakodosh Boruch Hu* can save us.

Ima, I'm terrified. Pray! Your kindness with me will protect you against all evil. Ima, pray, because the supplications of Jewish mothers have a great impact.

8

Who Am I?

"Who am I?" is a question which is at the core of human existence. It has been asked and answered in many forms by man, since time immemorial. The Patriarch Abraham knew clearly that he was *Avraham HaIvri* who stood on one side (*aiver*) of the Euphrates River, while the entire world stood on its other side. When Joseph was in Egypt, he did not forget his identity nor that of his father, Jacob. Every agonizing moment in the palace of King Ahasverus, Esther knew that she was a member of the royal Jewish Nation. Jews in the Holocaust proudly went to their deaths knowing that they were unlike the cursed fiends who persecuted them. It wasn't the yellow badge on their garments which testified to their identities, but the Jewish spark which glowed within them.

Awareness of one's core and essence includes knowing both one's strengths and one's weaknesses. "A person who does not know his weaknesses, does not know what he must rectify. However, a person who does not know his strengths isn't even aware of his work tools," (R' Yerucham of Mir, as quoted in HaRav Shlomo Wolbe's *Alei Shur, p. 169*).

How do special children regard themselves? Let's listen to them:

Galia relates: "Tell everyone that special children are like everyone else. We have needs and feelings and want to be respected and loved. People should change their attitudes toward us. They should stop regarding us as simpletons. We understand *everything* and know *everything*. We don't grasp this knowledge by means of our minds, but rather by means of our souls. We are very hurt when people don't treat us the way they should. We suffer enough from our limitations. We feel terrible about being totally dependent on other people."

*   *   *

Ben Golden wrote the following to a group of people who came to "hear" him: "I want to tell everyone here that we are like you and not so different. We are pure souls, and you also. But we can't ruin our souls any more. Your situation is much more difficult. We also have to study Torah. We can't fulfill the *mitzvos*. But we can study! Why treat us as if we are mentally retarded? You are more retarded than us. We know the truth, but you bring yourselves into a world of lies. We need a framework that is suitable for dealing with problems and souls like ours. Our test in this world is over. You have a long and hard way to go.

"I am autistic, and I see the world much differently than the vast majority of homo-sapiens. I see the Adam that is G-d's creation. I see clearly body and soul and their connection with the higher worlds.

"All mentally handicapped people are more soul than body, depending on the severity of their handicaps. It is a ridiculous notion that prevails in this world of lies that handicapped individuals have less understanding of this world and its dwellers than so called normal people do. Let's make things quite clear by realizing the true anatomy, physical and spiritual, of all Jewish mentally handicapped *Bnei Adam*.

"We are sent into this world for a reason, as are all of G-d's children. Our purpose here is manifold, partially of an individual nature and in part to serve the *Klall*. This is a natural notion for those who sincerely follow Hashem's Torah. The individual purpose is to be *metaken* past *aveirot*. This is a very difficult and painful task for unfortunate souls to achieve. It involves much emotional pain. Handicapped people are *Goy Ba'aretz*. Every individual that is autistic, retarded, C.P., etc. is forever being scorned by adults and children. Their lives are lonely and always they are treated as inferiors. A mentally handicapped person is a joke to society or a fearful image to be avoided. We move through life being loved as infants even though we may be adults. Most of the time we are resented as a destructive element in the normal parents' lives. All members of the handicapped person's family may feel strong embarrassment when facing the negative reactions of society.

"Then there are those parents that cannot cope, and so their handicapped children are given away to not *frum* families, or worse to *goyim*. A Jewish soul that is given to a *goy* suffers indescribable tortures. Even if the gentile family are kind-hearted people and take care of all the child's physical needs, still the Jewish soul in their hands is doomed to unfathomable misery. Their souls can never find a moment of peace. It is harder for those unfortunate souls to achieve their *tikun* because a *treif* place devoid of *kodesh* can only bring a Jewish soul to disaster.

"I am tired of inconsiderate people who are forever finding reasons to prove we are different than they are. To them I say, "Woe to you." They talk about us in an unfriendly and degrading manner right in our presence. They feel no shame because we are, after all, mentally disabled and cannot understand, and even if we do understand, we will never tell, and if we do tell, no one will take us seriously. Then there are those people that are not bothered by the fact that what they say to us and about us in our presence and behind our backs, just might be *loshon horah*. I suppose that they feel that in *Shamayim* we cannot testify either. Woe to those unfortunate misguided souls.

"Families that are sensitive to their special child will certainly be able to tell the world that their special child has a tendency towards *Kodesh*. They will attest to the fact that their child is sensitive to what is happening in the house, that there is a special bond and communication with at least one of the parents and maybe one or more of the normal brothers and sisters. To be able to recognize these special attributes of the special individual the family or teacher must be close to Hashem, living according to His Torah. The normal person's vision is enhanced by intelligence, sharpened by sensitivity, but sees the truth only through Torah.

"To summarize: We are souls sent to this world to rectify

past sins. For *Klall Yisroel*, we are another opportunity to do *Chessed*. For the parents and siblings, we are a test of their *bitachon* and love of Hashem. Remember what I have written and take it to heart, for time is running out. In our poor, lowly generation whose *bitachon* is in material things, we, the mentally handicapped Jewish souls, show to all willing Jews a glimpse of G-d's Truth."

* * *

Yossi, a ten-year-old autistic child tells us his feelings: "When I saw that I could express myself by means of this new form of communication, I couldn't believe that I had been released from my prison. I felt that Hashem had pitied me. I felt very relieved. Now I understand that this isn't only for my good, but also an obligation. I am obligated to tell all Jews who wish to hear, that Hashem is the Creator and the sole Ruler of the world. If in any way, you don't listen to His commands or don't accept the fact that He is the King (heaven forbid), you will be severely punished. You must understand that Hashem punishes us only in order to teach us and show us the right way. But if you don't understand this, you will have to be taught it, until you reach perfection.

"I ask you: whenever you meet an unfortunate person like me, pity him. Have *rachmonus* on him. Treat him with respect, because he was once just like you. If Hashem caused you to meet him, then know that He wants you to learn from it.

* * *

Yisroel Dovid, a nine-year old autistic child speaks very poignantly: "Ima, I want tell you how much I love you and appreciate your love for me. I know how much pain I cause you. I remember the time you first learned that I wasn't a regular child. You still continued to hope that I would get over my problems. But Hashem planned things differently and you learned that I was autistic. It was a terrible blow for you. You felt guilty. You thought you had faults and that they had caused my situation.

"You and Abba aren't to blame for my situation. I'm to blame. I am a sinner, who must undergo a *tikun*. Ima, all of your love is precious to me, all of the sleepless nights you spent because of me. I *daven* for you and Abba, and for the entire family, and hope that we will merit to greet the Mashiach soon."

* * *

Shlomo, a six-year-old brain damaged child sees his situation quite maturely. He says: "Ima, I know how much you love me. You don't have to feel guilty for my situation. I feel that I have to go through life in this form because of the sins I committed. My life is a decree from Hashem. I am happy that I have two very righteous parents. Tell that to Abba. He suffers very much because of the way I am. He should study more. He should attend a *shiur* every day and *daven* with love and joy. Ima suffers a lot too, but not only because of me. She has to learn to accept her difficulties with love.

"My parents blame the baby-sitter. They say that she dropped me and caused my brain damage. But that's not true. She's not to blame. Don't blame anyone. Hashem decreed that I be this way. I brought about my own situation because I committed many sins in my previous life."

* * *

Shulamis, an eleven-year-old Down syndrome child says: "I need love. Children are entrusted to their parents by Hashem. Are pure souls like mine any less in the mind of the Creator? No one tries to understand me. I don't have a teacher who understands me. Don't you believe that Hashem loves pure souls like mine?

"I want people to love me. When people look at me, I walk very slowly. My soul recognizes the *chessed* Hashem shows me. The good in this world is unlimited. The whole day I ask Hashem never ever to leave me. I know which *mitzvos* I didn't fulfill in my past life. I didn't fulfill my obligations."

* * *

Shaul, a fourteen-year-old brain damaged child tells us about his suffering: "I returned to this world because I sinned with my speech. My mother holds me when I am sad. I suffer here [in my residential facility] because there aren't any Torah activities. I think that this form of communication [FC] will help many of the kindergarten children. In time they will be able to master the method. Every child who is ready should be taught it.

"Tell the teachers and counselors that they have no idea how much Gemora study will help all of the children here.

* * *

A mentally disabled child in a Christian institution has a very stirring message: "Take me out of here. The people here aren't Jewish. I am Jewish. Don't leave me here.

"I want to tell people about my inner being. My soul isn't damaged. I live on *mesiras nefesh*. I am suffering because of my sins. People don't see the blessing in my situation. They regard it as a curse. But I prefer to live a bitter life and not to suffer in the World of Truth. Because I have spoken to you so openly, I plead with you: ask Hashem to take me back to the World of Truth.

* * *

Noam, an autistic child of four-and-a half has an interesting view of life and himself: "Music is a cure, especially for children like me, who yearn to study Torah but can't . Music nourishes our longings, and is food for our hungry souls. All autistic children love music, and if I were to hear a song sung by a *tzaddik*, who really and truly yearns for Hashem, and isn't just trying to make an impression on people, I could complete my *tikun* faster. But its very hard to find someone like that."

* * *

Galia

Galia's mother went to a store to buy her a dress. Of course, Galia wasn't with her, because Galia, a thirteen year old CP child, is in a residential facility, and can't sit or stand. At the store, thoughts of Galia's pathetic situation flood her mother's mind, and she broke out into uncontrollable tears. On a visit to Galia, the following conversation took place.

G: Ima, please don't feel sorry for me.

M: What do you mean by that?

G: When you went to buy me a dress, you felt sorry for me, and burst into tears in the store.

M: How can I not pity you when your situation is so dreadful. You can't even stand.

G: I'm not pitiful, Ima, because my *tikun* is nearly over. I may look unfortunate, but you are probably more unfortunate than I. I am closer to the truth. I am not confused and sense Hashem's love for me every moment. You suffer from confusion, which is worse than my form of suffering. No. Ima, I'm not so unfortunate.

M: Do you feel that your soul is being held captive by your body?

G: Yes. But my body is less of a prison than that of a regular person.

M: Why is that so?

G: A normal body can inflict harm. A body like mine can't.

M: Galia, you suffer so much and are so dependent on others. From where d you derive the strength to accept all this so calmly? Poor thing. It must be so hard for you.

G: Ima, I accept everything with love because I know that my suffering will perfect my soul. So that it won't remain in an incomplete state in *Shamayim*. One can only perfect his soul here, in this world. Ima, suffering atones for sin. I accept all my pain with love, because I know what awaits me in the end. After withstanding the terrible afflictions of this world, I'll know infinite tranquillity and infinite pleasure. This suffering is insignificant when compared to the unlimited good in store for me in the World to Come. I'm not sand or despondent because this suffering is so transient and passes so quickly — like life itself. You have to learn to relate t the essentials rather than the trivialities. All that counts is *Olam Ha-ba*. People must make every effort to be worthy of *Olam Ha-ba* even if this involves suffering and affliction, which are negligible when compared to the eternal good.

While Galia dozed, she and her mother had the following conversation

M: Does it bother you if I communicate with you while you are asleep?

G: No.

M: Is it possible to facilitate with all disabled children?

G: Yes.

M: Do some parents of special children fail to take advantage of the opportunity to communicate with them?

G: Yes.

Amazing. Amazing. You must have a special *zechus*, that you've been given the ability to communicate.

G: I have a *tikun*.

M: Does your *tikun* include conveying messages?

G: Yes. But I don't understand why you are so amazed. Although our bodies are restricted, our souls are just like yours. But the truth is that healthy minds are even more restricting than impaired ones.

M: Your soul expresses itself far better than mine. How is that possible?

G: Hashem decided that, at this point it is important for special children to convey messages to the world at large.

M; Are you obligated to transmit these messages or can you decline to do so?

G: I must. I have no free choice on this point.

M: So I was also chosen to be the one to ask you these questions.

You were chosen to do *teshuva*. I have already explained that to you.

*   *   *

My Life without Communication

Jenn Seybert is currently a college freshman, who communicates by means of FC. This transcript is presented precisely as she wrote it . at an OMR Statewide Convention, in Hershey, PA on February 24, 2000. It has not been edited:

"My life without communication was 24 years of a living hell. Imagine yourselves sitting in your seats and having your thoughts constantly interrupted by thoughts of terror, your own voice sounding like a seemly thunder of garbled words being thrown back at you, and other folks screaming at you to pay attention and finish your task. You find your body and voice do unusual things, totally realizing you aren't in control. Now add to this that you cannot talk maybe a few words but nothing consistent with language.

"With all this in mind, welcome to the world of a non-verbal Autistic individual. My life was always upside down. Nothing made sense. I kept trying to please but was not able to let anyone know what I was trying to say. We are a confusing lot. We are able to have intelligent brains, but our outward appearance is looked at as severely retarded. You are able to sit in your seats and have total control of your mind, voice and body. That isn't how we work. We are not in control all the time, and some of us folks, never. We want to comply, we want to please, but we can't make it work all the time.

"Some of you out there have the understanding, the education, and the ability to help folks like us. Then why is it so difficult? You don't listen to us. You don't take time to watch our body movements, our cries of frustration, and our want to be free of the hell of autism.

"We are so much like each of you in our wants and needs it is almost scary. Believe it or not, we have a lot of similarities. Individuals like myself don't like to be touched.

Some of you don't like to be touched. We shy away from loud noises; some of you don't like loud noises. We are realizing that we are not so different, aren't we? However, we experience life very differently. You have a voice, but the reason I am able to talk is only through the support I get from a facilitator. As you can see, we are different, but not aliens from another planet. Without a way to express our voices, we use behavior to try to get your attention. I want you to understand the frustration we feel and the inability to have our frustrations understood without the means of communication.

"You see, for the first 24 years of my life, my behavior was appalling, and I was aggressive, very unhappy, and always frustrated. Four and a half years ago, I was introduced to facilitated communication and my world became unlocked in an instant. That is when my whole life opened up and the hell of being locked inside of myself disappeared. It wasn't easy to allow myself freedom from autism that holds you together like a cult.

"Opening my mind to healthy thoughts of life was very hard. We managed to work through issues as they came up. I struggled with how to tell good strategies from bad ones. In the beginning I needed a lot of support, both emotional and physical. Like you, I will always want and need support from family and friends. My need for physical support, however, has been reduced to practically nothing at times. My thoughts are normal like yours, but my motor planning issue causes me to stall on each thought without the help of my facilitator to give me a gentle lift so I am able to get my next thought out. The whole thrust, from my first evaluation/assessment, was getting me to type my words independently as soon as I was ready.

"A few friends in my Lonesome Doves group are well on their way to being independent, and so am I. The group I have just referred to is a group I organized and began two years ago. We are all unique, and our problems are manifested in many ways. But our common thread is the ability to use various sources of communication, and we are all fighting the same battle each day of our lives — the battle of belief and acceptance. You can see from my appearance that I look mentally disabled. The motor planning issue I have to live with makes me not respond immediately. When you are talking with me, I appear to drift off or am not listening. I utter involuntary sounds or words. You must understand that my typing is not accepted everywhere, and we who use it are constantly challenged in every step we take. These battles are never ending and painful to go through.

"It isn't fun to experience being called a liar or having your facilitator accused of controlling your movements. You don't enjoy it when these words are thrown in your face time after time. You are squirming in your seats. I hope you are listening to my thoughts.

"I think you are ready to hear how this process has put me where I am today. I am blessed to be living in a county that really wants to reach out to their people. I am part of the Luzerne/Wyoming MH/MR family. They believed in me from the beginning, and I didn't let them down. I was fortunate to have them help me with technology and dollars and the trust to have me implement my own program so I don't have to attend a day program. It is called self-determination, and I have done it through person-centered planning.

"I was helped in this process by Rosa McAllister. She, along with my circle of support and my family, encourages me to wish, dream, and set my own life in order. Then they plan with me to make the necessary changes. It is because of these planning sessions that I am now a degree student at Penn State University, Hazleton Campus. But here again I had to prove who I was, and I did it one course at a time until I fulfilled my status as a provisional student.

"You are looking at an incoming freshman, and I have the grades to prove it. I have worked hard for them, doing double duty trying to pick up where the lack of a high school education hampered me, and at times the going is rough for me and for my parents.

"You are looking at a person who has a family that loves her, but love is not enough. Love started the journey. Because of love, came a means to communicate, followed by a circle of support and backing from my county. To those of you who sit in silence, there is hope for you in my words because you can have these things too.

"To those who are caregivers, teachers, case managers, parents, and staff, I urge you to think hard of at least five people without communication that you support, who are in a day program, in a group home, or one of your family and friends. I want you to think of my thoughts you have just heard and of these people who sit in silence before you. They need your help to find a means to communicate because there *is* a way out of silence.

"Your views about our outward facade must change. It is of great urgency that you begin to look beyond our disability and really get to know us. Remember, love is not enough. Giving us a direction and helping us with our choices is what self-determination is all about. This is where *our* lives begin with you hearing *our* thoughts and working with us to realize them. To those of you who sit in silence, there is hope for you, and it is my prayer that folks who are your teachers, case managers, directors of your agency, your parents, and your staff, will help you find a way out of silence. I want you to leave encouraged and empowered to reach out to us who are sitting in silence. I want to send an encouraging thought of hope for people like me to find the way out of the hell in which autism holds us. It's not a simple process, but with trust and perseverance you can make it work."

Section III

Our Heroes

- Ima, I Love You
- Beila Holds Her Own
- Rivkie Triumphs
- "My Soul Thirsts" — A Visit to Pisgat Yehuda

Introduction to Section III

Our Heroes

Galia, Beila, Rivkie, Ben, Shaya, Aryeh, Meir and indeed all of the very special people whom we have presented in this book are truly heroes. Defying adversity, they make a quantum leap towards achieving perfection. As they march ahead, they draw others along with them, leading them toward an understanding of life's true aim. Fasten your seat belts, or better yet, unfasten them, and soar to the heights with our beloved heroes and heroines.

9

Ima, I Love You

We have already met Galia, who is totally incapacitated and lives in a special residential facility for CP children. Galia's mother received a BA in education and criminology from Bar Ilan University, and continued her studies at the Hebrew University. She did *teshuva* as a result of her exchanges with Galia, and has written a book about Galia in Hebrew. When these FC sessions took place, Galia was ten years old.

Galia's mother relates: "Prior to my first session with Galia I had prepared a series of questions to ask her. I had wanted to open with "I love you," but Galia preceded me, and opened the session on her own initiative with "Ima, I love you."

In these touching exchanges, the deep spiritual bond between mother and daughter comes to the fore. But they are far more than personal exchanges. They are songs of hope, songs which highlight the eternity of the soul. They also stress that these children have returned to earth to complete their *tikun*, which is to draw as many Jews as possible back to their roots. Especially striking are Galia's efforts to advise her mother and to gently rebuke her when necessary, something which confirms beyond a doubt, that Galia's comments originate with herself.

Session 1: Ima I Love You

> G: Ima, I love you, but I have something to tell you. I am the soul of your grandmother Simcha, who passed away. Ima, I was sent from Heaven to rectify a sin. Yes, it was because I didn't give my children a proper upbringing. You have *zechus avos* (merit of the forefathers) and I was sent here to influence you to do *teshuva*[1].
>
> Ima, you have to understand that the end is coming, and that I am very worried about you. You are angry, but Hashem isn't angry at you. He wants you. He loves you. But you are far from him. Your life is difficult, Ima. You must reach the truth. This world is false, and you must serve Hasem with all your heart. You constantly search for love, but don't find it. You love me so much because I need you and your love. I love you very much.
>
> But Ima, in this world you won't find the love you seek. Only Hashem's love can satisfy you.
>
> M: What can I do to help you? How can I ease your *tikun*?

---

1 The workings of Heaven are amazing. Savta Simcha failed to give her children a Torah-true upbringing. As a result her granddaughter grew up in a secular environment. Savta Simcha returns to earth in the form of Galia, in order to influence her very own granddaughter (Galia's mother) to do *teshuva*!

G: You can't do anything physical to help me. But you can do much from a spiritual standpoint that will help me complete my *tikun*. I failed to give my children a Torah education, and if you do *teshuva*, that will help me. Don't be angry at Abba. I'm not angry at him. We are all messengers of Hashem, Abba too.

M: Do you want me to tell Abba anything special?

G: Tell him that I forgive him, and that he is in great spiritual danger. He hasn't found his place in this world, because he thinks that falsehood is truth. He has to search for the truth. Now he is unfortunate. I feel very sorry for him. I am very happy that I am finally able to tell you this.

M: Are you angry at Abba?

G: One who knows the truth can't be angry. Abba simply forgot about me.[2]

M: Do you want to say anything to your brothers?[3]

G: They won't understand me. They are too involved in this world. I don't have anything to tell them now, because we have no common language.

M: I am afraid of Hashem. I feel that fear in my heart.

G: Ima, you fear death, not Hashem, because if you really feared Hashem your life would be different, and I wouldn't have had to return to earth in order to

---

2 Galia's father hadn't visited her for a long time.

3 She has two older brothers, one of sixteen and one of nearly twenty.

influence you to do *teshuva*.

M: Is that why you returned to earth?

G: Yes. You are in general afraid of everything. One who truly feels Hashem's presence isn't afraid, because he knows how much Hashem loves him.

Session 2: Ima, You're Not Alone

I am so happy being able to communicate with you.

I love talking with you too. I know everything you did this week, and am so happy.[4]

How can I influence your brothers to do *teshuva*?

First strengthen yourself. Then set an example for them. Ima, you feel lonely. But you are not alone. Hashem is with us. I don't feel lonely because I see the truth more clearly than you do. Ima, you are not alone.

Session 3: The End Which is the Beginning

M: What is the key to happiness?

G: *Chessed.* Abba is good, but he doesn't understand the true meaning of *chessed*.

M: What is genuine *chessed*?

G: *Chessed* for the sake of Heaven.

M: You said that the end is nearing. To what end are you referring?

---

4 Galya's mother had spent four days at a seminar for *baalei teshuva*, along with her sixteen-year-old son.

G: To the end which is the beginning of a new world — a world of truth and not of falsehood.

M: Will I be able to bear that difficult period? Will your brothers?

G: With Hashem's help.

M: Will you be healthy in the new world?

G: Yes.

M: Do you mean to say that a miracle will occur, and you'll suddenly be able to talk and do everything?

G: Yes.

M: Galia, if I ever offend you, I beg your forgiveness.

G: You're a *tzaddekes*, Ima. I have nothing against you.

M: Can I ask you everything?

G: Everything.

M: Tell me when you want to stop the session.

G: O.K.

M: Do you want to communicate with anyone else?

G: No. I feel closer to you than to anyone else on earth.

Session 4: Ima, You're Changing

M: Can you read thoughts?

G: Yes.

M: Do you know what goes on at home when I'm not here?

G: Sometimes. I know that this week you experienced a great change. The world seems much clearer to you, and you have more direction and hope.

M: I did *teshuva* before I began to communicate with you and kept Shabbos before that. But my bond with you and our talks have been very helpful to me, and have enabled me to become much stronger. What merit do I have? *Zechus avos* [the merit of one's forefathers]?

G: Yes.

M: If you also have *zechus avos*, why have you returned to earth as a reincarnated soul?

G: I've already told you. I returned in order to influence you to do *teshuva*. The fact that I was born this way drew your attention and caused you to feel an emptiness and to long for your parents' home. I'm very pleased that you're on the true path now.

M: Why did I descend to this world?

G: In order to achieve true faith and trust in Hashem.

M: How can I strengthen my love of Hashem?

G: Do *chessed*.

M: What must we do in order to survive the war of Gog and Magog and greet Mashiach?

G: Ima. Stop worrying. Draw closer to Hashem and everything will be fine.

M: How can I allay my fears?

G: You're afraid, because you don't feel close to Hashem. Your fear stems from of a lack of faith. It is a symptom of the Golden Calf.

M: You're a reincarnation of my grandmother Simcha, who passed away forty years ago. Yet you were born ten years ago. Where was your soul during the interim?

G: Souls wait in a special place in Heaven, until they return to earth.

M: Is it good there?

G: Yes. But it's still a waiting place.

Session 5: Abba Loves You, Too

M: Were you sent back to earth of your own free will?

G: Yes. But everyone's situation is different.

M: Abba says that you were selfish. You should have come back to earth in a healthier form, one which wouldn't make those who love you, like he does, so unhappy.

G: Abba has complaints against Hashem. As long as he thinks he can decide how to run the world, he won't be able to understand the truth.

M: I told him to come and visit you. I believe he loves you.

G: He loves me because he has feelings. But he is far from the truth.

M: Can I use our conversations in my outreach work?

G: First you must cover your hair, and learn how a religious woman should behave on a daily basis. After doing that you can publicize these conversations.

M: Can I give the transcripts of these conversations to Rabbi S., who is very active in outreach work?

G: Yes.

M: How can I help you?

G: Go to the Kosel.

M: Should I read to you?

G: Yes. Read me the *parsha* of the week when you come.

M: Do you want me to come more often?

G: Once a week is enough. But please read me the *parsha*.

Session 6: The Truth

M: Is death frightening?

G: It depends for whom.

M: Is it frightening for a good person who keeps the *halochos*?

G: It depends how deeply one is attached to this world.

M: I don't understand.

G: Those who love the pleasures of this false world will

find it very hard to leave it.

M: Is truth ascertained only after death?

G: A *tzaddik* can see the truth even in this false world. A true servant of Hashem who nullifies his ego and performs *mitzvos* purely for Heaven's sake can see the truth.

M: Why do I feel ill at times?

G: Because you're uneasy, and still haven't found *beis Hashem*.

Session 7: I'm Never Alone

M: Do you communicate with other souls?

G: Yes. I'm never lonely.

M: Do you communicate with the other children in the dormitory?

G: They're souls too.

M: Do the souls of living people ever go up to Heaven?

G: They are here, but every soul reaches Heaven.

M: Even while they are alive? When they are sleeping?

G: In general!

Session 8: Why Did You Cry?

M: Why did you cry last night when I visited you? The evening counselors say that you cry every night.

G: I cry, because Jews are supposed to cry and *daven* all night.

M: Precisely at night?

G: Yes. During the day they should study, do *chessed*, and draw Jews closer to *teshuva*.

M: Do souls sleep at night?

G: No.

M: Never?

G: No. No. No.

M: Why did you point to the word "no" a number of times?

G: To stress that the answer is obvious.

M: Why is the failure to give one's children a proper education so serious a shortcoming?

G: By failing to give children a Torah upbringing one kills entire generations.

M: What was wrong with the way you raised your children in your past life?

G: I didn't stress the most important goals in life: Torah and good deeds. As a result, my children grew up with a spiritual flaw and strayed from the true path.

M: Your younger brother has begun to put on *tefillin* and to believe. But your older brother still doesn't believe in anything. What can I do to influence him to do *teshuva*?

G: Hashem will bring him back. But you must pray for him from the depths of your heart. You must cry when you pray for him.

M: Have I also failed in the *chinuch* of my children?

G: No. As we were growing up, you weren't aware of the truth. Your *teshuva* will also help your children.

Session 9: My Soul Knows

M: Do you know how to read?

G: Yes and no. I can't read like regular people, because I am brain damaged. But my soul is complete and knows everything.

M: How can I comfort you when you cry at night?

G: Say *Tehillim* next to me.

M: Which chapter?

G: It doesn't matter.

Session 10: Pray for Me

M: I also cry when people are killed in terrorists attacks.

G: You only cry over the people who were killed. I cry over the Jewish Nation from Adam and until eternity.

M: My neighbor, Channa doesn't feel well. Can you help her or pray for her?

G: No. She should ask a *tzaddik* to pray for her.

M: Can we pray for your benefit? Can we pray that

your *tikun* be easier?

G: Of course. It's important to pray for me.

M: Who should pray for you? What should they pray?

G: Whoever wants to pray for me should do so, whenever they please. What helps me most is your *teshuva*.

M: Should we visit the graves of *tzaddikim*?

G: Yes.

M: Should I go alone, or do you want to come with me?

G: Let's go together.

M: You said that Hashem loves me. How do you know?

G: I simply know.

M: My sister has high blood pressure. What should she do?

G: I'm not a doctor.

M: Do people know how long they'll live?

G: No

M: Do you know?

G: No one knows, except for a few outstanding *tzaddikim*.

M: Are souls reincarnated in animals, plants and objects?

G: Don't ask such questions.

M: What kinds of questions?

G: On Kabbalah.

Session 11: Take Me Home for Pesach

G: Ima, please take me home for Pesach. It will be an important Pesach and I want to spend it with you.

M: Are you saying this because other children have said the same thing?

G: No. I want to go home because I feel that a great danger is hovering over our heads.

M: For the whole Jewish Nation?

G: Yes.

M: Specifically on Pesach?

G: It hovers over our heads all of the time. But Pesach is a special time for the Jews. Great miracles can happen then if we are deserving. Ima, don't tell anyone what I said. Hashem can change things, but this is what I feel.

M: After Pesach, can I tell people what you said?

G: Yes.

M: Galia, I love you very much, and I planned to take you home for Pesach even before you asked. I bought you a new dress for the Seder, and cried in the store.

G: I know. Don't pity me. Ima, I love you so much too. We are from the same soul.

Session 12: Hashem Teaches Through Love

M: Why do I deserve such suffering, such pain?

G: Ima, Hashem loves you, and wants you to reach a high level. Without suffering, you won't reach that level. You have to be as trusting as your family in Heaven.

M: What family? Who?

G: Your forebears from generations past.

M: From which side — my father's or my mother's?

G: Both sides. Those generations were closer to Hashem than we are. But your suffering and the efforts you are making to reach Hashem will propel you to great heights.

M: I read in the *Zohar* that women have special chambers Above — the chambers of Miriam and of Batya.

G: It is forbidden to study what you can't understand. The *Zohar* isn't only words. Even *talmidei chachomim* don't study it, unless they have reached a certain level.

M: I study what I understand and enjoy it very much.

G: You just think that you understand.

M: Why am I so afraid of Hashem and of the unknown?

G: In general you're afraid of many things. You're afraid of punishment. But your life isn't a punishment. It is *chinuch* through love. In this way you will learn to be more G-d-fearing.

M: Whose love?

G: Hashem's love for you. He teaches you through love.

M: Did you choose to return to this world?

G: Some people are given the opportunity to choose whether to return. I wasn't.

M: In our last conversation you told me that you came here of your own free will.

G: True. But I wasn't given the opportunity to select my *tikun*. I came back to earth to correct my sins. I am happy that I was given such an opportunity.

M: Is everyone given the chance to rectify his sins?

G: No. Some are purged in *Gehennom*.

M: Even the righteous person who only committed a small sin?

G: It depends on the sin.

M: Will Heaven be angry at me for asking you so many questions like these?

G: No. But only *avodas Hashem* can accumulate merits for you and protect you.

M: Is my interest in Heavenly workings included in *avodas Hashem*?

G: It has no value other than to bring you to *avodas Hashem*.

M: When a person dies, do the deceased members of his family come out to greet him in Heaven? When we die, after 120 years, will we meet? Will I meet my mother and my other relatives?

G: They will come out to greet you. Meeting one's relatives is one of the stages the soul experiences after death. It is a *chessed* from Hashem meant to prevent the soul from being frightened.

M: Does the soul have feelings? Can it sense anger, fear and sorrow?

G: The fear a person feels after he dies is a result of his sudden detachment from the body he occupied until that point, and to which he was so closely connected.

Session 13: I Still Want to Ask

M: When the soul of living person goes up to Heaven during sleep, does the body remain without a soul?

G: No. At such times the soul remains linked to the body.

M: One of my teachers said that time was created only for this world, and that in the World to Come there is no time. Is that correct?

G: Yes.

M: Can I ask you more questions?

G: Yes.

M: Does the soul ever get sick?

G: The soul suffers from various ailments. But they are

spiritual ones which must be rectified.

M: Do the souls of the righteous in Gan Eden ever get sick?

G: No.

M: Does the soul have a human form? Does it have any sort of form?

G: No.

M: I thought that souls look like people, even though they are not corporeal.

G: Ima, you can't understand. These questions are beyond you. I told you what you have to do now. Such questions won't help.

M: Does it bother you when I ask such questions?

G: No.

M: Were you happy to see Abba?

G: Ima, I'm so unhappy. You're progressing so beautifully, and he's backsliding.

M: Would it help you if he did *teshuva*?

G: Of course. But first of all it will help him and my brothers.

M: How can I influence your father and brother to do *teshuva*?

G: Set an example.

M: Yossi doesn't want to come to the Seder. How can I set an example?

G: You invited him. That's all you can do.

M: Do you have a message for Z.? He said that if the communication with you is valid, he'll do *teshuva*.

G: Yes! Tell him that he won't do *teshuva* even if I reveal the numbers on his identity. card, because this is not the way to do *teshuva*. One has to search for the truth and to love Hashem. But he's not searching for it. He doesn't know what true love means.

M: Whose love?

G: Divine love, real love. Tell him exactly what I said.

M: Yossi wants you to reveal the winning Lottery numbers. What should I tell him?

G: Tell him that it's preposterous to think that Hashem sent us to earth to help others draw away from Him, and into the world of falsehood.

M: I told him that you don't have permission to interfere in such affairs, and therefore won't give him the Lottery numbers. Is that correct?

G: No! Tell him that winning the Lottery won't make him happy.

M: Does your name, Galia, hint to the fact that Hashem reveals (*megalah*) spiritual secrets through you?

G: Ima. First worry about the evident, and only afterwards the esoteric.

M: What's a woman's role in life?

G: To be a helpmate to her husband, to help him study Torah, to create holiness, to raise her children with the love of G-d, and to build a small sanctuary in her home.

Session 14: They're Crying over Abba in Gan Eden

G: Ima, tell Abba that I know Saba is crying over him.

M: What's his name?

G: Menachem.

M: Why is Saba crying over him?

G: Because the Redemption is near and our family still hasn't done *teshuva*. Saba is suffering because there will be no continuation for the family. If Abba would observe the *mitzvos*, if he would be a servant of Hashem, Saba's distress would end. But Abba's stubborn and is causing Saba untold suffering.

M: Is Saba in Gan Eden?

G: No.

M: Do you know where he is?

G: No. I only know that he is suffering, and in Gan Eden people don't suffer.

M: What must Abba do in order to help Saba enter Gan Eden?

G: He must keep Shabbos properly.

M: Galia. Do you like communicating?

G: Yes. I enjoy communicating and *must*

communicate. Communicating releases me from my prison and links me to you and to this world.

M: Sometimes you have a message and sometimes you don't. Why?

G: I don't know. I simply feel that I have something to say, and that I need the services of a facilitator in order to express myself clearly to this world of falsehood.

M: Who tells you what to say? An angel?

G: I hear a Heavenly echo.

M: Do you hear a voice and words?

G: I can't explain that to you.

M: Do you have the patience to continue?

G: Yes.

M: Last time I was here, you didn't seem happy about communicating with me. The week before, though, you were happy when we "spoke." Why?

G: I'm always happy to communicate with you.

M: When I read to you, does your soul hear me?

G: I feel your words in my heart.

M: How do souls remember?

G: Not like regular people. We are dependent on Divine knowledge.

M: Are you told in advance what to say?

G: No, only at the moment you ask me a question.

M: Even when you are asleep?

G: Yes. Our inner essence is not asleep, while our external substance is linked to the facilitator.

M: In what manner is it linked to the facilitator?

G: The energy of the facilitator and the knowledge activates our bodies.

M: What characteristics must a facilitator possess?

G: He have at least some potential for belief. But not every believing person succeeds at facilitation. Hashem selects facilitators according to the situation.

M: Are you referring to religious belief?

G: Yes.

M: Will those who are wise here also be wise in the World of Truth?

G: If they served Hashem in this world, their souls will be healthy and complete.

M: By "healthy and complete" do you mean wise and more knowledgeable?

G: No. I mean that their souls will be capable of delighting in the sacred light.

M: Can a person who is not wise, be wise in the World of Truth?

G: If he was righteous and served Hashem in this world, he will occupy a good place in the World to Come.

M: What do you mean by "the sacred light?"

G: The *Shechina*.

M: I asked you this before. But it is very important for me to discuss this problem with the women who come to my lectures. If a woman undergoes an artificial abortion, is she a murderess?

G: It depends. In each case one must ask a *rav*.

M: If a *rav* forbids a woman to abort her baby, yet she does so anyway, is she a murderess?

G: She's worse than that. She's rebelling against Hashem!

M: Will Z. do *teshuva*?

G: I don't know.

M: I took you to the grave of Shmuel Hanavi yesterday. How did you feel there?

G: People seek succor there. They seek relief from their ailments. Your *teshuva* is my cure.

M: How did you feel when we visited King David's grave?

G: I felt that Mashiach is here.

M: Did you feel that King David *is* the Mashiach, or that the true Mashiach is amidst us?

G: I feel that he is amidst us.

M: What did you ask for at the graves?

G: That Hashem pity the entire Jewish Nation.

M: I felt very calm at the Kosel. How did you feel?

G: I yearned for the spiritual world.

Session 15: Ima I'm Terribly Worried About You

G: Ima, the Redemption is approaching and there's no time. You must complete your *teshuva* now. Ima, I am so worried about you. A terrible decree is hovering over our heads, and we must *daven* and do *teshuva*. I sense that Torah observant Jews are in danger. They must do *teshuva*. Ima, I am so worried about you. I love you so much. Hashem is sending many warnings. Those who don't understand, lose eternal life. Ima, I'm worried about Abba. But I'm even more worried about you, because we are one soul.

M: Why do you cry every night?

G: I told you, because there is a decree against the Jewish people.

M: When you cry at night, the counselors think that you are hungry and feed you cereal. Does that make you feel better?

G: The cereal only pacifies my body. They don't understand.

M: What did you mean when you said I must complete my *teshuva*?

G: Move to a Torah observant neighborhood.

M: Z. refuses.

G: Persuade him. Ask Rabbi Z. how to better strengthen yourself.

M: Are only religious Jews in danger?

G: The entire world is in danger. But the religious will suffer a heavy blow.

M: How can we revoke so harsh a decree?

G: *Teshuva, tefilla* and *tzedakah*. Love every Jew.

M: Why are you worried about Abba?

G: He's so far removed from the truth.

M: Don't you feel well today, Galia?

G: Not that well.

M: What can I do to help you?

G: Hug me.

M: When you come home, I'll hug you all the time.

G: I want to go home.

M: Did you notice that I arranged your room so nicely, with pictures and curtains?

G: Ima, I want pictures of my grandparents and of *tzaddikim* — pictures of the Babba Sali, placards with *Bircas Habayis* and *Eishes Chayil*.

M: I'm a bit busy now, Galia. As soon as I have time, I'll go to town and buy you the pictures you like. But there are pictures there already—pictures of birds and animals. It's not forbidden to hang such pictures in children's rooms.

G: Maybe not. But they don't suit a Jewish soul.

M: It's a room for little girls, and those pictures suit girls your age.

G: That's not so. They're nice for *non-Jewish* girls my age.

M: Will you eat when you come home? When you don't eat and drink at home I become very upset.

G: I'll try. Just take me home.

M: Don't you like it here?

G: It's OK. But I like being with you, and right now, it's especially enjoyable to be with you.

M: Why now?

G: Because when we're together we're closer to the truth.

M: You've been close to the truth for a long time.

G: But we are connected and I can't be complete without you.

M: I'll take you home for Shabbos. I want to facilitate with you. Will you cooperate with me?

G: I'll try. Please don't lose your patience.

M: Write short sentences and try to point to the right letters.

G: I'll try, Ima.

M: You won't be angry at me if I hold your hands or feet tightly?

G: Ima, I can't be angry at you.

M: Why not?

G: Because I love you.

M: You love me, like I love you. I can't be angry at you either. Last week you said that you were sad. Do you feel better now?

G: I still feel sad.

M: Are you worried about the decree?

G: Yes. But I also don't feel well.

M: How do you know that a decree has been issued?

G: I have a strong feeling on that point.

M: Can decrees be canceled?

G: With Hashem's help.

M: What will happen to those who won't rise up in the *T'chiyas Hameisim* [the Resurrection of the Dead]? Will their souls exist forever?

G: I don't want to tell you.

M: Can you tell me what is meant by *kaf ha'keleh* [a form of Heavenly punishment]?

G: No. But understand that Hashem is a just judge, and those who do not accept the yoke of Heaven before the Redemption will be denied eternal life.

M: Will their souls remain in Heaven?

G: Their souls will vanish into thin air.

M: How does my doing *teshuva* help you?

G: Our souls are linked. Thus I am incomplete if you are incomplete.

M: What do souls do in Heaven, while they await

T'chiyas Hameisim?

G: Ima, worry about the Day of Judgment.

M: Does the soul after death retain the same personality that it had while alive?

G: Certainly.

M: Do the souls of people with senses of humor retain that characteristic in Heaven?

G: I don't want to answer that question. It's too complicated.

M: How can I improve our facilitation sessions?

G: Be patient. I love facilitating with you. I'm so happy that you're coming closer to the truth. Bravo!

M: Do you have anything else to tell me?

G: Serve Hashem day and night.

M: I *daven*. I keep kosher. I recite *Tehillim*. I observe the Shabbos. What else should I do?

G: *Chessed.*

M: What kind of *chessed?*

G: Help other Jews.

Session 16: Your Tears Don't Vanish into Your Pillow

G: I know that you cry a lot at night. But your tears don't vanish into your pillow. They go up to Heaven.

M: I don't cry a lot. I cry when there are terrorist attacks. I cry over the soldiers who are killed. I cried about the couple murdered by the Arabs near Beit Shemesh.

G: The heart cries.

M: Do you know what goes on at home?

G: Sometimes.

M: Can FC harm you? After all, your soul is far more vulnerable than that of a regular person, because it is not covered by an external sheath.

G: It can't harm me.

M: Is that so because *mitzvah* emissaries are not harmed?

G: Hashem who created us, also protects our souls.

M: Is Hashem pleased when we appeal to Him for help?

G: Very pleased.

M: Does Hashem answer only the righteous, or does he also answer people on my level?

G: He decides. There are people who reach the level of *tzaddik* in a very brief period of time.

M: Does He answer such people without fail?

G: It depends. You won't understand.

M: When I pray, I am besieged by external thoughts. I rebuff them, but they return.

G: Don't give up.

Session 17: A *Tzaddik* Passed Away

M: Something seems to be bothering you. Is everything all right?

G: No.

M: What's wrong?

G: A *tzaddik* passed away today.

M: Is that good or bad?

G: Bad. But when a *tzaddik* dies his merits benefit the community. The *tzaddik* who died today had many merits.

M: Who was he?

G: Rabbi Kessler, the rav of Kiryat Sefer.

Session 18: Do You Have a Mind of Your Own?

M: What do you think about the meeting at which FC was demonstrated?

G: I don't know.

M: Do you have ideas of your own, or do you only repeat things you hear emanating from Heaven?

G: It depends on Heaven.

M: Does communicating with me cause you emotional problems?

G: No.

M: Your counselors say that you are spoiled, and that I spoil you too much.

G: You can listen to what they say. But don't accept it.

M: How can I make you happy?

G: Study Torah with me.

M: Should I read to you from the *parsha*, or from *T'nach*?

G: Whatever you want.

M: The angel taught you the entire Torah before you were born. Why study?

G: Ima, I'm also a human being.

M: But your soul remembers everything it was taught before your birth, and I don't remember anything on a conscious level.

G: My body must also be treated kindly.

M: How can I help you?

G: Found a yeshiva for girls.

M: Will the girls study by means of FC?

G: Yes.

M: I haven't heard about a yeshiva for girls.

G: Call it whatever you want, as long as we can study there.

M: Why are you crying?

G: A sudden sadness has overcome me.

M: Why?

G: I don't know.

M: Have I done anything wrong?

G: No Ima, I just hope that Am Yisrael is faring well.

M: Should I pick you up, or do you want to remain in bed?

G: I want you to hug me.

M: When you smile does that mean that you're happy, or do you smile even when you are sad?

G: Ima, you must understand. The Jewish Nation is undergoing a very difficult and dangerous period. We function on many levels. I am always happy when I see you, especially when you hug me. But that doesn't eliminate the danger.

M: Why did you say last time that the danger hovers precisely over the heads of religious Jews?

G: Believing Jews are the spiritual center of the Jewish Nation and Hashem's servants are scrutinized first.

M: Rabbi S. asks if a modest woman adds to the merits of the Jewish Nation.

G: Of course. One of the current problems is the lack of modesty. Vulgarity prevails instead of refinement. Only those with noble character traits can draw near to the Creator.

M: I was invited to speak at a program featuring Rebbetzin Kook. Will I succeed?

G: Yes.

M: Should I accept invitations to speak at private homes?

G: Yes.

M: Rabbi S. heard that a few days before the elections two snakes crawled out of the Kosel. One was killed, the other was snared. What does that indicate?

G: It indicates that during the forthcoming elections, the heretics will lose power. But the victors are also dangerous, because they don't serve Hashem either. Hashem will bring the Redemption, but not through them.

M: Through whom will He bring it?

G: The *tzaddikim*.

M: Rabbi S. asks if souls have memories?

G: The further a soul is from this world, the weaker its recollection of it.

M: I am referring to a soul like yours, which resides in the body of a living person.

G: I don't recall everything. I say what Hashem permits me to say.

M: Hashem is so great and powerful. Does he relate to people like me and you?

G: He relates to every single detail of His creation.

M: Hashem Himself?

G: Yes.

M: I conceive of Hashem as remote and as having little connection with us.

G: Hashem is within every person.

Session 19: You Are Also Speaking With Me

M: Why doesn't Heaven let us communicate much as I want?

G: Because I say a lot of things which have no consequence.

M: What do you mean by that? Do you say things which aren't worth saying?

G: No! You ask too many questions, which at this point have no answers.

M: Do you mean that Heaven doesn't let you answer them now?

G: No! There's no purpose to such discussions.

M: To whom, then, am I really speaking, to you or to your soul? Is your soul merely a vessel which passes messages to me?

G: It's a vessel. But you are also speaking with me. There are a number of levels to this form of communication.

M: With whom else am I speaking?

G: Only with me. But that part of the soul which is close to Hashem, can only act for Heaven's sake. It has no free choice. The part of the soul which interacts with the body, has more choice.

M: Do you mean that the soul has a part which is close to Hashem, and a part which is close to the body?

G: Not exactly. More or less!

M: How does one explain Hashem's existence to a skeptic?

G: Ask him how so intelligent and educated a person can ignore the obvious fact that the world is too complicated to have come about randomly. A person like Abba understands that idea, but also contests, because he doesn't want to be Hashem's servant. He wants freedom, even if the freedom he imagines he has is really a prison for desire. Y. is just like Abba.

M: Why is Y. like Abba, and Z. like me?

G: That's life.

M: Can I read to you when you are asleep? Do you hear me then?

G: Of course.

M: I don't understand.

G: You don't have to understand. The soul doesn't sleep.

M: If I don't read out loud, but in my heart, without words, will your soul hear me?

G: Yes.

M: Deep down?

G: Deep down.

M: When you come home, and the TV is on, do you understand the programs?

G: I understand that there is impurity in the room.

M: Should I turn off the TV when you come home?

G: Yes.

M: This month, I'll take you home only on weekdays. I'm afraid that you won't feel well, and that it will be hard for me to take care of you by myself on Shabbos.

G: If it's hard for you, Ima, you don't have to take me home.

M: I love taking you home, and I am certain that you like coming. But during the week it's easier to take care of you.

G: Don't worry, Ima. Take me home whenever it's best for you.

Session 20: The 17th of Tammuz.

M: Why are you crying?

G: I feel that you don't understand the true meaning of this day. If you understood, you would also cry and be sad. All you care about is when the fast will end.

M: To whom are you referring?

G: To everyone.

M: Are you crying because of the fast?

G: Of course. I'm very worried. I worry every fast day, but today I feel that the danger is especially imminent. I feel that something is liable to happen soon. Ima, this Tisha B'Av in particular, we have to feel what we have lost. If we want to merit to build the third *Beis Hamikdash* we must cry over the Destruction of the Temple *as* if it occurred yesterday.

M: How can I influence Y. to do *teshuva*?

G: You can't. Just set a good example.

G: How can I set a good example if he doesn't visit me?

G: Be patient and daven. Ima, I want to tell you once more, that I think very highly of you and admire you for having done *teshuva*. Don't be afraid of being alone. Our Father in Heaven watches over us all the time. His vigil is constant. He is always with us, and we are never alone. Dearest Ima, don't cry. Go out and do Hashem's work. Bring Jews back to Hashem. Be confident. Be enterprising. Hurry up, Ima. There's no time. Work quickly. Be dynamic.

M: I feel drained.

G: That's because you're too involved in this world. Improve your relationship with Hashem, and don't worry. Don't be afraid.

M: How can I do that?

G; By engaging in outreach work.

On *erev* Shabbos, angels accompany men home from *shul* Do they accompany women too?

G: Ask a rav. But I think they accompany only the men. Women are repositories for good. They make certain that the good angel remains in their homes. They prepare the home and set the table for *Shabbos kodesh*.

M: Does the angel remain in the Jewish home all Shabbos?

G: Yes, it depends on the woman.

M: What else can I tell the women at the lectures? Should I publish a pamphlet with transcripts of our sessions?

G: It's best to talk to them face to face.

M: An article about your dormitory appeared in *Maariv*. One part is especially moving. Should I read it to you?

G: Yes.

M: After describing all of the difficult cases in the dormitory, it says: "At the end of my visit, in the nicest room of all I saw a sign which read: 'To my sweet Galia, from Ima, with love.' It had been hung over a series of pictures which lined the wall near the bed. Tears welled up in my eyes. That note made me realize that all of the children I had seen that day were really someone's children. Loving them and living with them don't necessarily go hand in hand." Moving, isn't it?

G: Yes, but the author of the article doesn't understand the essence of parental love, nor the meaning of the love of our Father in Heaven. The entire article hurts me. It's sad that these silly pictures represent love to the author. She doesn't understand that when you hung them, you loved me less than you do now. At this moment your heart belongs to me and you don't need pictures when you have me, your daughter, Galia. She doesn't understand that with or without pictures, all parents suffer. All parents love their children, and want them to be healthy. Enough. I'm through.

M: I'm happy that I finally have a real girl.

G: Everyone makes that mistake.

M: What do you mean?

G: We, the mentally disabled have always been real children. But only a few parents realized this.

M: Did they realize this even without communicating with their children by means of FC?

G: Yes. There are parents who feel this even without FC.

M: It's a great privilege to communicate with you. Most parents don't facilitate with their children.

G: You have many merits, Ima.

M: Last time your answers were very short. I wanted to receive long answers. Today, I am pleased. Your answers are long. Tell me the meaning of love.

G: Love can be defined as one's need for social contact, the need to feel that others are concerned for him. Love is a haven in our grim world. But this explanation pertains only to non-believers. For believers, there is a different explanation. Love, for the believing Jew, must be for Heaven's sake. It must be based upon the Torah's laws. Hashem's love is the paragon of genuine love. He loves us unconditionally.

M: When you say "us," are you referring to mentally disabled children?

G: No, to believing Jews. Even if His children rebel against Him and draw away from Him, He continues to love them.

M: You brighten my day. Tell me more.

G: True love is unconditional, it is for the sake of Heaven. The love between husband and wife must be sacred and not based on physical factors. Husbands and wives build, together with Hashem, a mini-sanctuary and fulfill the verse, "Be fruitful and multiply." All of their deeds must be for Heaven's sake and they must rejoice at having been given the opportunity to do His will.

It is also the same regarding parents' love of their children. Parents who do Hashem's will and train their children to be *ovdei Hashem*, this is the greatest love and joy possible for them. All love comes directly from Hashem Who is entirely love.

M: But when we love, we don't realize that we are fulfilling Hashem's will. The capacity to love our children is inherent.

G: The love to which you refer is not genuine love. It is an offshoot of man's need not to be alone.

M: Why does Hashem love us so much? Why is His love for us like that of a mother for her children?

G: He created us, and we accepted His Torah when we said, "We shall do and listen."

M: When we die, does Hashem embrace us like a mother embraces her children?

G: Ima, you worry too much about death. Know that everything is the way it should be. Don't worry.

M: I am starting to feel closer to Hashem.

G: I'm very happy for you. That's a high level.

M: How do you manage to write on the language board without looking at the letters? You even write when you are asleep.

G: Through you I feel the letters.

M: But you don't look at the letters.

G: Not with my eyes. I feel them.

M: Do you feel them with your imagination?

G: You don't understand, Ima.

M: You said that Hashem might use the motorcycle to teach Z. that his true place is in the *beis medrash*. How can a motorcycle convey such a lesson?

G: Tell Z. what I said.

M: I've already told him.

G: One day, he'll understand. But its would be better if he understood this on his own — before! It would be better for him to enroll in a yeshiva — before! Tell him that.

M: Should he continue to ride his motorcycle?

G: He must do *teshuva* now. There's no time. He can't live

it up, and then settle down. He must do *teshuva* now. Z., listen to your sister. Her words come from Above.

M: I'm flabbergasted. That's exactly what Z. said. He told me that he would do *teshuva* after having enjoyed life. What should I tell him?

G: Tell him that he's not the one who makes the timetable.

M: How can I explain to him that time is of the essence?

G: Hashem won't let him ruin his soul. At the age of 20, a person is held accountable for his deeds. He is part of your family and your righteous ancestors demand that he also be righteous. I've had enough today Ima. I only want to tell you that it's getting late. Difficult times are around the corner for *klal Yisroel*.

M: How can I overcome my pain?

G: Direct all your energies to prayers, *mitzvos* and good deeds. Direct your love to Hashem.

M: Are you happy that your *tikun* is nearly over?

G: Yes. I'm tired of this place and of my situation. I yearn for the *yeshua*.

M: Do you yearn for the era of Mashiach when you will be healthy and like the other children, or do you yearn to be in the World of Truth?

G: *Oy*, Ima, may we merit to greet Mashiach soon, because when he comes, there will be Gan Eden in this world.

M: What do you love best in this world?

G: You!

M: What do you dislike most of all?

G: The sins of the Jews. I suffer terribly when Jews sin.

M: I'm still uneasy about what you said regarding the end of your *tikun*.

G: Ima, we are all in danger. *Daven! Daven! Daven!* Hashem sent you to earth to arouse people to do *teshuva*. Rise. Go out to war.

M: Do you feel well?

G: I told you, today, the 17th of Tammuz is a terrible day for the Jews. Great dangers loom above our heads. Enough, Ima. Now I want to be alone with my sorrow. I need time to *daven* for the Jewish Nation. Enough for today. Enough, Ima.

M: Pray for me.

G: Ima, I always pray for you, and always will.

10

Beila Holds Her Own

Drama at the Meeting Hall

A few years ago, a well known facilitator held FC sessions with various mentally incompetent children at an auditorium in Jerusalem. The purpose of the meeting was to explain the technique to the public at large, and also to motivate people to do *teshuva*.

The meeting was very dramatic and emotion filled. Ben Golden appeared, as did Beila T., an eight-year-old CP child, and a number of other mentally disabled children.

Beila's mother, a very devoted and understanding woman, didn't want her to attend. By means of a facilitator, Beila's mother expressed her reservations. Beila, though, held her own, and in the end, her will prevailed.

Following is a transcript of the exchange which took place between Beila and her mother. Although it was moderated by the facilitator, Beila addressed her mother directly.

> F: Beila, your mother doesn't want you to speak at the meeting.

B: Ima, you're wrong. You can overcome your unfounded shame. Speaking at the meeting is part of my earthly mission, part of the task assigned to me by Hashem. You don't want me to go, because you are afraid that people will pity you for having a handicapped child. That's what's really bothering you.

F: Beila, your mother has reasons for not wanting you to go.

B: Ima, you're making up excuses. The real problem is that you're ashamed to have a child like me. I know that you love me. But you're also bewildered by the fact that Hashem gave you such a child. You're afraid of what others will say. You think that you'll feel uncomfortable when people learn about your situation.

Ima, it's very important for me to go to the meeting on Tuesday night. I want to convey a message to the audience, and to help people do *teshuva*. When they see me, they'll be frightened. The pure soul within me will be evident to everyone, and they'll be so shocked that they will be aroused to do *teshuva*.

F: What will you say at the meeting?

B: I can't tell you now. Ima, you have to let me go. What I have to say can save many people. I know it's hard for you, but if you let me go, you'll benefit too.

F: Your mother is concerned only about your welfare. She wants to help *you*.

> B: Every heart I influence and penetrate absolves me of part of my punishment, Ima. In my past life I didn't think that I had to help other people. Now, I must rectify that serious sin. I had many opportunities to help others, but didn't utilize them. I knew that I was supposed to help, but I just didn't .
>
> F: Beila, your mother still wants to know how she can make you happy.
>
> B: The only thing that can make me happy is knowing that my sins have been forgiven.

After these heartrending conversations, Beila's mother finally agreed to let her appear at the meeting. The night of the meeting arrived. In full view of the audience, Beila, with the help of her facilitator, wrote:

> I want to warn everyone that there is little time, but much work. I am an example of an unfortunate soul who must undergo a *tikun*. Look at me. Are you frightened? Are you shocked and alarmed? If you don't want to have to return to earth in the form of a hapless child like me, listen to what I have to say: *loshon hara* and behavior towards other people are the biggest problems. Time is very short.

At the meeting a man said that he doubted the validity of FC and claimed that the facilitator was moving Beila's hand. On her own initiative, Beila turned to him and said, by means of the facilitator:

> I want that man to understand that if the validity of FC were clear, people would lose their

freedom of choice, and the Divine attribute of justice would prevail even more strictly [if they would persist in their ways].

She also turned, to a soldier in the audience. He was in the early stages of *teshuva*. The following exchange took place between them:

> B: Soldier! Do *teshuva* now. Don't wait until its too late. Take a Gemara and study. Don't wait.
>
> S: But I've done *teshuva*. I also study Gemara. Do you think that I should study more hours a day?
>
> B: Yes. Study more, and with all your heart. You're still a bit uncertain about your new course in life.

Beila's Mettle

Mrs. H., an activist and fund-raiser visited Beila at her home. The following conversation took place between them:

> Q: Are you aware of someone here who experienced a tragedy?
>
> B: You came here today because you are suffering, and not in order to help children like me. Your *chessed* is really a front for your sorrow. I want to tell you that every soul has a mission in life. My earthly mission is no less important than yours. I was once a healthy person. I am no less important than you. It's difficult to recall our Divine roots when the world blurs us with its lies. I am only a part of your search for the truth. You must search for the truth within your soul. That's

where it is located. I feel sorry for you, and commiserate with your bewildered state of mind. All of the mentally disabled see the clear truth. We are not beset by lies which, under ordinary conditions, would confuse us too. That's what I have to tell you.

Q: Can you tell me what type of tragedy I suffered?

B: I think you're testing me. I know that you suffered a loss. I know that you are still suffering. Now you have proven that what I wrote beforehand is true. You came here for yourself and not for our sake. You are immersed in your own problems. We aren't really uppermost in your mind. There are enough proofs to confirm the fact that we deserve *chessed*, and are special souls, and are entitled to study and express ourselves. How many other people know what it means to be ignored, to be scorned and ridiculed? With Hashem's help, when the Mashiach comes, we will be healthy. But all that I hear from you is talk, without any genuine progress. I don't even think you like me.

A person must constantly examine his intentions. The ego is a clever fellow. He lures us into thinking that we are absolutely righteous. This doesn't mean that you don't do *chessed*. But you must know that you have to improve the quality of your *chessed*, and that your *chessed* should be for Heaven's sake. Rid yourself of your ego. Do *chessed* without expecting anything in return, and without feeling that you have done your share. Feel the plight of those people for whom you collect money. Empathize with them.

Place yourself in their shoes. Feed them; clean them. Only after you have felt their pain, will you be able to nullify your ego.

Q: Why do you think that I don't like you?

B: Because you aren't sharing your heart with me, only your thoughts.

Beila Inspires a Rebbetzin

Q: Should a woman's *chessed* be limited to her family and her home, as they say, "Charity begins at home"?

B: True and not true. People say that charity begins at home, but that is a non-Jewish idea, and many people apply it mistakenly. It is true that one has to care for his family and they are naturally the first recipients of our *chessed*. However, part of *chessed* to one's family is to show them what *chessed* is. Our children must be taught that our lives are empty shells unless they are filled with *chessed*. We must open our homes to the needy. There's no such thing as a private life. That's a ridiculous notion, formulated by the indolent. Abraham set an example for us. Did he and Sarah have private lives? Did Yitzchak feel neglected because of their lifestyle? Why are we any different than Sarah and Abraham? Why do we need private lives? What are private lives? Does Hashem go on vacation and leave us alone? Do whatever you can every moment of the day. You are a rebbetzin. You and your husband must teach others that we will have to give an accounting for every wasted moment of our lives. Scary, isn't it?

A person who doesn't live Hashem's truth during his life cannot see that Divine truth when faced with tragedy. The truth is that we are all here in order to fulfill a mission. A child who dies before the age of twenty has completed his earthly mission, and is free of sin when he leaves this world. Such a child's situation is much better than that of his parents, who must still cope with the difficulties of life and with their *nisyonos*. Everything that Hashem does is for man's benefit. It's easy to say this when one is not faced by tragedy and devastation. It is preferable for people who have undergone the loss of a child to devote themselves to their other children, and to become involved in *chessed*. Their personal pain will help them to feel the pain of others.

You asked me if I could tell you the names of the other children in your family. That's hard for me, but if you insist I'll do so. But that doesn't prove a thing about the validity of my messages. I have messages for certain people, and that's all. If the disabled could divulge such information accurately 100% of the time, we would become show pieces, and the seriousness of our messages would turn into a joke.

Beila Encourages an Activist

B: I want to tell you that Hashem is with you in your prolonged suffering. I'm so happy that you have finally come to see me. I've been waiting for you. You must continue with your important work. Time is ending for the world as we know it, and we have to save as many Jewish souls as possible. Your home life has nothing to do with your mission in life and you must refrain from confrontations.

Q: I have many health problems.

B: You must do *teshuva*. Look into yourself and, in all honesty, search for your weak points. One of your main problems is that you are too pre-occupied with your emotional problems and don't concentrate enough on your relationship with Hashem. You have a great influence on many people, and must devote more time to prayer and to the study of *mussar*. You should study *Messilas Yesharim*.

Q: I study it all the time.

B: But you still haven't nullified your ego. It is too strong. You won't be able to maintain a genuine link with Hashem, as long as your ego is so strong. It is your real religion. In order to nullify your ego, you have to engage in the most difficult kinds of *chessed*. You should volunteer to work in a Chevra Kadisha once a week. Facing the deceased will cause you to contemplate life and its meaning, and help you realize that life endures only one hundred and twenty years. Practice what you preach. Examine the motives behind every one of your deeds. Think more of others. You can rise to a higher dimension. Be more selfless. That's what life is about.

Q: How does my ego manifest itself?

B: You are very concerned about your emotional

needs. However, because you are so important to your Creator, He wants you to draw closer to Him. He feels that the very talent He has given you to help people has become an ego trip separating you from Him. He wants you to return to Him.

Q: What will working in the Chevra Kadisha teach me?

B: That the body dies, but not the soul.

Q: I help people with their emotional problems. I guess you could call me a "soul worker." Should I continue with my work?

B: Yes. But make sure that the people you help don't connect more to their souls than to Hashem. Tell them that if they pray, they will feel His presence.

Q: How can I feel His presence?

B: Pray with a broken heart.

Q: But I'm so broken already. I feel crushed all of the time.

B: Your sense of physical security has been undermined. If you truly felt close to Hashem, you wouldn't feel so broken.

Q: Should I seek the help of a spiritual therapist?

B: Turn directly to Hashem. He is with you. He is your father, your husband — everything. You must know that Heaven feels that you are very capable. Moshe Rabbenu was the greatest of all men, yet the most humble. Try and help others without thinking about your emotional needs. Find yourself a Rav. Turn to Hashem for encouragement. The purpose of your suffering is to bring you back to Him. Visit me again.

An Inspiring Talk with Rabbi A.

Q: Can you tell me details about my previous incarnation?

B: I don't have permission to divulge such information to you. I want to tell you, though, that it's preferable to worry about your current incarnation. Your present life determines your future. Improve your *mitzvah* observance. Do *chessed*. We are here for so brief a stay. You are wasting your precious time searching for the hidden, and fail to see the obvious.

Q: But the Arizal told R' Chaim Vital who he was in a previous life.

B: You aren't R' Chaim Vital, and I haven't been given permission to tell you the hidden.

Q: What is my root?

B: I guess I'm not expressing myself clearly. I can't answer such questions. If you think that if you ask the same question in another form,. I'll answer you, then you're in for a surprise. I'm not interested in such questions. I'm here to help people who need help, and am not a research specimen. I, and all of the other mentally disabled children and adults, have been sent here to help Jews overcome their evil inclinations. Some believe, some don't . But that doesn't matter. The message gets to the right person at the right time. I want to tell you that you are a serious person who is seeking the truth.

Q: But what is the source of my soul?

B: Forget about the world of souls; forget about incarnations. Roll up your sleeves and join the battle of saving Jewish souls before it's too late. That is your *tikun*. Feel the suffering of your fellow Jews. Help them out of their confused worlds. Help them find life. Draw them closer to Torah and *mitzvos*. Draw them closer to Hashem. I have nothing more to tell you. That's the message I was sent to convey to you. I hope you understand.

Q: But I have to work on myself first. I don't feel ready to give to others. I haven't perfected myself yet.

B: One can't wait until he's achieved perfection, because by then the person dies and is of no help to anyone.

Q: Does *ruach hakodesh* rest on me?

B: Yes. But it is only good if you do *chessed* to suffering Jews. Not just a little in order to discharge your obligation but enough to save souls, like Avraham Avinu.

Q: I have a *kollel* for which I provide support.

B: Yes, the *kollel* is good, but it is part of your ego. It is a *mitzvah* with "strings attached." *Kiruv rechokim*, to save souls, is today's war.

Q: I consider myself a private person, and not a public activist. I lack the means to go out and save souls.

B: You may not say "What can I do?" The Heavenly Court will use these words against you.

Q: Do you see the Divine Presence?

B: No, though at times I feel it very strongly.

Q: If so, how do you know that it rests on me?

B: Because that's what Hashem tells me. I know nothing by myself, He tells me what to say.

Q: Are my prayers accepted?

B: They are accepted, but they lack compassion, and are not uttered in a broken hearted manner, nor have you shed bitter tears over the lowly state of the Jewish People.

Q: Is there anyone in this generation who merits to see *Eliyahu Hanavi?*

B: I do not know.

Q: What about the 36 hidden *tzadikkim?* Do they exist?

B: Yes. Of course. There are some in *Eretz Yisroel* and some abroad.

Beila Describes the Heavenly Court

Q: What can you tell me about the Heavenly Court?

B: All I can say is that it is awesome. The judges scrutinize every single detail of man's acts. They are

Hashem's emissaries. Even the righteous tremble in fear of them on the Day of Judgment.

Q: In which Heavenly Court did you appear?

B: *Netzach, Hod* and *Yesod* (kabbalistic terms).

Q: Who were the judges?

B: Either the *Shechina* or the *Ze' er Anpin* (a kabbalistic term).

Q: When will the Mashiach come?

B: I don't know , but surely soon.

Q: "Soon" in material terms, or "soon" according to spiritual calculations?

B: According to material calculations.

Beila Speaks with a Rabbi L., a Prominent Outreach Worker

B: You are doing an outstanding job. You are helping to save many Jewish souls. You must work day and night. But don't stop studying Torah. You are in the midst of a raging battle. Your are waging Hashem's wars. Many will die spiritual deaths. Your Torah study will give you the power to persist and succeed in this battle.

Q: What guidelines can you give our organization?

B: It's the end. Very soon the world will have to grapple with the final test. Half of the Jews in the world are wallowing in illusions. You already know what I mean. Everyone requires *chizuk.* Our generation is lowly, and it is sad that it is so engulfed in darkness that one must come to the mentally disabled to find sparks of light. But this is the darkness before the great light. We, the mentally disabled of this world, have been sent to disclose the truth. This is part of our *tikun*. Genuine Torah Jews will recognize the truth. The Jews with whom it is most difficult to contend are religious ones who regard themselves as *tzaddikim*, and who think they have no need to repent. They are certain that their place in the World to Come is ready and waiting for them. No one tries to work with them, or to help them improve their ways. No one dares.

Now, I want to tell you about the State of Israel and the current government. They also have the function of carrying out Hashem's will. They built a lie which includes all of the lies. But Hashem will destroy the edifice they built. Hashem is all-powerful, and will wipe out the corrupt. But beforehand they will see how the monster they created dies before their very eyes. The current government is wicked. Its members can't save themselves because they deny their Jewish roots. They deny their G-d.

Beila Encourages a Ben Torah

Q: Who am I?

B: You don't have to ask such a question. What's the difference? Be a Jew who studies Torah, *davens*, and does *chessed*. That's the type of Jew you should be.

Q: What do you think about my *chiddushim*?

B: I'm not a *talmid chacham*. Ask a prominent *rav*, and not a child like me.

Q: Why have I come to this world?

B: To study Torah and do *chessed*, and to teach others the truth. *Chessed* is the key. You must give of your life to others. You are too wrapped up in yourself. Give to others, freely, generously. Do *chessed* which is hard for you to do. Of course you must study Torah and pray, but if you do *chessed*, your understanding of the Torah will be more profound, and your prayers more sincere.

11

Rivkie Triumphs

Rivkie is currently eight-years old. She suffers from a serious case of CP and her entire body and brain systems are paralyzed. Her sixteen-year-old sister, Miriam, learned how to use FC and communicates with her. Rivkie refuses to live in the residential facility in which she is registered. She claims that she has nothing to do there and feels out of place. She says that she is treated like a baby, while she is interested in studying Torah. At home she asks her family to help her skim through *sifrei kodesh*, telling them which one she wants to study. She even advises them in which store to purchase the *sefer*! She also insists on being taken to the lectures of great rabbis. When her parents demanded that she return to the residential facility like all of the other CP children, she staged a hunger strike. Of course the facility wasn't willing to assume responsibility for a child who doesn't eat, and her parents were forced to keep her at home. Whenever the members of her family are lax in a particular area in Yiddishkeit, she rebukes them and makes certain that a high ethical level prevails in her home.

Once, as her mother was speaking on the telephone, she

heard screaming. The mother asked Miriam to find out what was wrong. It soon became clear that the mother had spoken *lashon hara* and that Rivkie was trying to prevent her from continuing the conversation. She wrote: "Ima stop talking right now. You're speaking *lashon hara*."

On another occasion, when the mother was arguing with her husband about something, Rivkie wrote "Ima, be calm." Her mother replied: "I'll try." Later on Rivkie wrote to her mother: "You were tested today, and passed the test with flying colors."

On another occasion, Rivkie wrote to her sister: "Please call your teacher, Mrs. Shapiro. I have an important message for her. I want to tell it to her in person, in her house." At first Miriam refused to comply with her sister's request. How could she tell Mrs. Shapiro that Rivkie wanted to convey an important message to her? That would appear very strange. But Rivkie didn't relent. She continued to pressure her sister who finally agreed to discuss the matter with Mrs. Shapiro. The teacher invited Miriam and Rivkie to her home, where Rivkie wrote: "I, Rivkah M., ask you to light a candle in memory of C. (the name of the teacher's father who had died a short while beforehand). Light it near his grave. An electric candle will do. He will be very grateful to you for this." The teacher was stunned at the child's words, because this matter was very much on her mind during the past few days. After her father had died, she had lit a seven-day candle at his grave every week. Due to certain circumstance she had stopped these visits, and was very uneasy about it. Rivkie's sister surely knew nothing about this matter, because Mrs. Shapiro did not share personal problems with her students. How did Rivkie know all this?

An Interview with Rivkie

F: Have you anything special to tell us?

R: Very soon, great miracles will occur. But beforehand, you must return to Hashem. We are being tested now with terrorist attacks because Israelis are making so-called peace. People are mistaken. When you do *teshuva*, there will be real peace.

F: On what should we focus?

R: On Shabbos and the laws of family purity.

F: There was a terrible attack in Beit Lid. Was it related to the Shabbos desecration in the Prime Minister's residence?

R: Yes.

F: What about the Foreign Minister's disparaging remarks about King David?

R: Yes, it was because of that too.

F: Were the occurrences in the Holocaust linked to the birth pangs which are supposed to precede the arrival of the Mashiach?

R: It's best not to ask such questions.

F: Your parents say that you don't want to communicate with them, because it causes you to neglect Torah study. But aren't women exempt from Torah study?

R: They are exempt from Torah study, but I want to study Torah because it is so vital.

F: Do you have anything special to say?

R: We need the prayers of the entire Jewish Nation, because the Redemption which will be of benefit to the Jews in the Diaspora must come.

F: Why has the Redemption been delayed?

R: We must want it to come.

F: Will the Redemption come because we want it, even without *teshuva*?

R: If people want the Redemption to come, they will also behave in a manner which will make it come!

F: But the irreligious are happy in their situation. They don't know that there is more to want.

R: We must show them that their situation is not good.

F: You don't look at the language board. How can you see the letters?

R: I see without looking.

F: Why must we look, while you see without looking?

R: Your mind prevents you from seeing.

F: Do you sense that you have a body and a soul?

R: Yes.

F: Do you feel that there will be terrorist attacks?

R: We have to trust in Hashem.

F: Do you have anything else to say?

R: I want to remind everyone do *teshuva*, before its too late.

F: *Teshuva* for what?

R: For *lashon hara*.

F: Why has this type of communication been discovered only recently?

R: It is a means to draw the Redemption closer.

12

"My Soul Thirsts" — A Visit to Pisgat Yehuda

Following are verbatim messages and essays composed by the children of the Pisgat Yehuda yeshiva. It was originally located in the northern city of Zichron Yaakov, and has now moved to its new quarters in the center of the Har Nof section of Jerusalem. In this unique yeshiva, autistic children study Torah by means of FC. It was founded by Ben Golden's father, at Ben's urging. The students interviewed here are above the age of twenty.

Aryeh

Yes, I am very affected by the situation that is now developing in the Middle East. The fact is, it is not only here in the Middle East that is affected. The whole world is at stake. The talk is about nuclear weapons, biological weapons, gas, deathly gas again. This is a problem for the whole world. What will be the end to this terrible threat that is hanging over our heads?

I cannot answer my own question, but I can tell you

what can make a difference. We as *Yidden* are brighter than most. We see further than most. We have the means to analyze a situation better than most. But of course this is only when our heads are clear, not filled with nonsense that has seeped in as a result of the distorted media. Stop reading the news. Stop hearing the news. It is nonsense anyway. We are not getting truth through those means. Listen only to the voice of *Gedolim*. They are on top of the true situation. They see things clearly. They don't let themselves be swayed by the broadcaster's charm. *Yidden*, turn to your *Gedolim* for direction. Any major decision should be made with their help and no one else's. Listen to me. It is a good piece of advice.

Shaya

Our point is to help you all through the danger, to give you all good advice that no one else will give you. Listen my friends. Aryeh is right. Only listen to *daas Torah*, even on matters of the world. There is no one better informed than the *Gadol Hador* how we as *Yidden* should behave in a time of crisis.

No gas mask will help if the inside of the sealed room is filled with outside garbage to sully our homes. Make your home a home of *kedusha*. Take out all that can be held against you according to *halacha*, according to better judgment for a Jewish home. If it is not appropriate for the *Beis Hamikdash*, it's not appropriate in our homes. We know what we have that doesn't belong in a place of *kedusha*. Get rid of it now, when that threat is over our heads and when we beg for mercy that our homes should be protected.

Meir

I want to tell you all what I think you should now be busy with. We all want mercy from Heaven. We want Hashem to look upon us with love and compassion. We must make that situation happen. Picture this: can Hashem send destruction to a nation that is busy with Torah and *Chessed* every extra minute of the day? Can He destroy those that are in His army of soldiers bringing those less informed Jews closer to Him? Can He hurt His children who are busy taking care of their brothers who are less fortunate than them? Now is time to show Hashem how much *chessed* we can really pile into our lives. This is the time to push ourselves to the limit to make ourselves indispensable in the world of *chessed*. There is no time to waste. No time for vacations. No time for messing around. No time for good times for the sake of fun. Only *tachlis*, every minute of the day. *Tachlis le'shem Shamayim.* No time for anything else. I will add a little secret over here. The joy you will feel in doing what I say will bring you more satisfaction and joy than you attained from any party, from any vacation or from any time of relaxation. This is what gives us strength. Not rest, not sleep. Only work *le'shem Shamayim.*

Dovid

I will take another aspect of preparation in times of crisis for a frum Jew. This is the time to check our prayers. Are we davening with the right intentions? Are we thinking of our day's plans instead of concentrating on what the *Anshei Knesses Gedola* intended for us to think about during our prayers? Stop now. No more lip-service. It's time to put meaning into our prayers. A time to feel the flicker in our hearts of fear and reverence for the One we are standing in front of. We must realize that we are begging for mercy from the One who has our lives in His hand. Do you realize that? Imagine standing in front of the Judge in court that is condemning you to death for a crime you did not commit. You would scream, 'til the windows of the courtroom would shake, to beg for mercy to see your point. Use that same desperate feeling to approach Hashem and beg Him for your life, for your children's lives and for your friend's lives, for the lives of all of *Klal Yisrael*. "Help us. Listen to us. Listen to your children begging for forgiveness. They are sincere. They mean what they say." These words must be true. Not just words. *Am Yisrael* wake up! The situation is desperate. Don't stick your heads in the ground and leave the davening to the next person. Everyone must make his effort to change things, to move things in *Shamayim* in our favor.

Ben

I want to start with *teshuva amiti*. I already wrote the 10 steps to *teshuva*. I would like you to attach that to this essay.[1]

We are all in a very desperate situation. Don't let anyone belittle the danger that is hanging in the air over our heads. We are now in a time of judgment. Desperate judgment. It is not a court that has a lot of time. It is a desperate court. The kind that is set up when people are in a desperate

---

1 Ben's ten steps to *teshuva* can be found in the appendix.

situation and big decisions must be made. Listen, I will tell you the only way to get out of this court with positive results. *Teshuva*. Massive *teshuva*. Only that can save. You are all asking how can we be held responsible for all those that are so stubborn and don't want to change their ways. Remember that *posuk* that says "Open a small opening and I will open the opening to the opening of a great hall." That still applies to us today. We must all make the greatest effort to change what we personally can. We must ask Hashem to open the hearts of those that are so stubborn to see the truth. Miracles do happen and can happen. It is in the hands of those who understand. It is in the hands of those who already know the truth. The ignorant will be awakened if the knowing truly beg Hashem for that. But it must start with us, with all *frum Yidden*. We are the nucleus of this special nation. We must do something because we will be held responsible for neglecting this very important mission.

The next preparation for ourselves in time of crisis is cleaning out our mouths. What comes out of our mouths cannot ever be retrieved. You all heard this already. This is the time to apply all that you've learned about *shemiras halashon*. This time is a time of crisis. We must all do what we can to perfect ourselves. We need our mouths to be pure for the saying of *Tehillim*, for the *davening* for the begging Hashem for *rachmunus*. It can't be the same mouth that is dirtying his friend's reputation. One cannot use the same *kli* for both good and bad at the same time. If we want our prayers to make a difference, we must clean out our mouths and use it only for *kedusha*.

The next step is to clean out our homes. Our homes are

our *Beis Hamikdash*. We live in our homes in *kedusha*. That is the way a Jewish home should be, a *Beis Hamikdash* of *kedusha*. Sometimes we allow foreign matter to seep in and affect the *kedusha* in our homes. We don't pay much attention to this for we are busy and it doesn't seem to be important at the time. But now when our homes are vulnerable to the outside destruction, we must check very carefully and remove anything that doesn't belong in a house of *kedusha*. Not just T.V., not just video, not just dirty books. All outside things that have no purpose in a Jewish home like secular books, secular magazines, secular advertisements, statues and art work that are not appropriate for a *Beis Hamikdash*. Anything that is questionable for a growing child to see must be removed now.

Number two is to check all *Mezuzos*. Make sure all the *Mezuzos* on the doors of your home are kosher without a doubt. Every *Mezuza*, not just the main one. Check them all twice in seven years. Also the *tefilin* you use, make sure it is checked twice in seven years. This is a must now, you can't imagine how many people are living in homes with *Mezuzos* that are *posul*.

Now I want to talk about your children. You are mothers that are in charge of precious lives, children of Hashem that must be protected. Without a doubt they are not responsible for today's *matzav*. They are innocent and put in our hands for protection. We must not fail them. We must stay on top of the situation and make sure that we know where they are at all times. To make sure that they play with appropriate toys, that they play with appropriate children, appropriate friends and most important make sure that they continue to be *mekayem* the *mitzvos* that they can do in order to sway *Beis Din shel Maaloh* in our favor. Children should *daven*, should say *Tehillim*, should eat only what is absolutely kosher. These are the protective devices we have for our charges. They are relying on us, we must not fail them. The children learning together in *cheder*, davening together so innocently wrapped up in their concentration in the *sefarim*. This is the picture that moves hearts in *shamayim*. This is how one should see our children. This is where they belong, not on the street roaming about without purpose.

Now I will write about our husbands and big sons. This country has an obligation to protect our nation from foreign invasion. Now I am talking physically about our army. The army of Israel is supposed to be a holy one. *Am Yisrael* always had an army, always had an obligation to protect its borders. The heads of the historical armies of *Klal Yisrael* were Avraham Avinu, Moshe Rabenu, Yehoshua, the Chashmona'im, all great *gedolim*, well versed in *halacha* and devoted to Hashem. Now we are in the hands of an army of *kofrim* of anti-frum, of non-believers relying on their own strength for victory. Yidden, we must compensate. We must create our own army. How, you may ask. Who will allow us to take over? I will tell you. Our husbands and sons must create an army, a *ruchnius* army. They must sit down every opportune moment to learn Torah without a stop, without a wasted moment. This is time of war. All is not regular time. The army is in readiness. So our army must also be ready. All Yeshiva *bochurim* must realize that our *gedolim* fought for their exemption to physically fight in order to ensure that they can continue to learn and protect us with their learning. Today we have no other protection. The army of *Talmidei Chachamim* is all we have. Men make haste. No time to waste. You are what we have. You are the army that counts. Take it seriously. It is a big responsibility. It cannot be ignored. All capable men between the age of 20 and 60 are *mechuyav* to serve in the holy army. No exemptions. Each one makes a difference. Not one to spare.

I would like to close with a *bracha* and a *tefila* that Hashem should protect us with great *rachamim*. So that there can be a tremendous *kiddush Hashem* in the coming of Mashiach very soon.

Appendix

- Inspiring Interviews
- Golden Strands
- A Religious Viewpoint
- Startling Implications of FC

I

Inspiring Interviews

The Glory and the Struggle

Nechama and Mrs. Levi

Q.: Good morning Nechama. Do you have anything special to say?

N: Judaism involves hard work. It's not like being secular. The secular do what's easy for them. Jews have come to this world to serve Hashem day and night. Yet many people still don't understand this.

Q: I miscarried a number of times.

N: The soul of an infant who dies in its mother's womb has achieved its final *tikun*, and ascends directly to Heaven. You were the means by which these yet unborn infants achieved their *tikun*. Everyone has his own special *tikun*, his own special problem.

Q: There were times when I felt terrible during those pregnancies.

N: You felt the souls of those infants who were undergoing special stress. It was a *tikun* for both of you. Therein lies the glory and the struggle. You must perfect the trait of self-control, and resist negative feelings. They stem from the *yetzer hara*, who is trying to topple you. Your childhood was difficult, and you still bear emotional scars from those days. But now you are mature enough to overcome your loneliness and the feeling that you are unloved. In your mind, you know the truth, which is that every person is alone in this world. Most people don't love others more than themselves. But our Father in Heaven loves us, with all our deficiencies, even more than He loves Himself. We are alone in this world. In the World to Come, we are inseparable parts of the *Shechina*, although we are human. In this world we long for the good which awaits us in the World to Come. We are constantly searching for it here, and seek to receive it from other human beings, only to be disappointed. What we must do, is to draw closer to the Creator.

Q: What must I correct?

N: That's an interesting question! I understand that you feel you have already achieved perfection and are searching for whatever else there still is to do. I assure you, that the first thing you lack is genuine love for Hashem. If you felt Hashem's presence in your heart when you prayed, you would be on a level in which you could correct all of your shortcomings. The fact that you have come to an autistic child for guidance indicates that you lack such love. If you truly felt Hashem's presence in your heart, you wouldn't have come to me.

Q: How can I reach such a level?

N: You have to try and see in your life the extent of Hashem's love for you. Observe how all of your suffering is really for your benefit. Study the fact that Hashem is a loving Father Who personally attends to the needs of each and every Jew, every moment of the day. A child who perceives how much love his father lavishes on him, has no choice but to reciprocate that love. Doing *chessed* for the sake of Heaven also helps one appreciate Hashem's love for him. Learn to love every Jew because his basis is holy. One who loves every Jew will have no problem feeling Hashem in his heart.

Q: Who was I in my previous life?

N: Silly people ask me that all the time. Why don't they ask: what must I do in order to save the generation?

Q: Should I change my name?

N: You must ask a *gadol*. Don't wait. That's a very important question, because the name of a person is indicative of his future.

On the Essence of FC
an interview with Chana, a nine-year-old autistic child

Q: Why don't I facilitate well with children like you?

A: You have difficulty communicating because you're not strong enough inside.

Q: What do you mean?

A: The entire connection is hazy to you. You have to feel it from inside. You're working with your hand and the board, but don't form inner bonds.

Q: What do you mean by inner bonds?

A: I can't explain. You have to feel the hand from inside. There are people who understand, because they are very sensitive to it.

Q: Which of the facilitator's traits do autistic children use?

A: I'll try and explain. We use the facilitator's lingual and verbal ability and the knowledge that his mind and experience have gathered. It's easier for us to express our ideas by means of a flexible and open person. It is important, too, that he or she be G-d fearing, because *yiras Shamayim* is the basis.

Q: Why does the facilitator become tired from these sessions?

A: Because we are working together, and making use of his abilities. It's very hard for the facilitator. It doesn't tire me at all. My body can sleep. But my soul doesn't sleep.

Q: Does it matter at which time these sessions take place?

A: No.

Q: Do all disabled children communicate in the same manner?

A: No. Children who were born regular, and became brain damaged due to various situations or mishaps, are more limited than those who were born disabled.

Q: Does age count?

A: The older the child, the better it is. But after the age of three, age doesn't matter.

Q: Did the angel strike you?

A: This is not a question. I am mentally disabled and that is the biggest blow of all. My soul knows everything, but on a personal level, I am mentally disabled. I answer only those questions Hashem permits me to answer.

Q: Can you convey messages to other autistic children?

A: Yes. When necessary.

Q: When is it necessary?

A: When Hashem wants us to communicate with them.

Q: Do you know our thoughts?

A: Yes.

Q: Do you have free will? Can you sin?

A: No.

Q: You said that when you *daven*, your prayers pierce the Heavens. What do you mean?

A: The soul prays about the Jewish Nation, because the soul knows the truth, which is that there is no individual, only "together".

Q: Is it conceivable for the soul of a wicked person to speak against the Torah?

A: I don't think so. But a facilitator can influence the answers he receives, or he can lie. The ability of the facilitator to nullify his ego is very important in FC. His ego can influence the answers.

Q: Do the answers you give vary, in accordance with the number of people present at the session?

A: It depends on the situation.

Q: Some autistic children know hidden facts such as the identity card numbers of others.

A: I don't know such things. Perhaps others do.

Q: Can you decide what to say?

A: I can't convey ideas which I am not allowed to express. I have special information to bear to select people. Except for that, I can say whatever I please.

Q: Sometimes the levels of the answers differ. Why?

A: It depends on the intellectual levels of the people asking the questions. If I give a very profound answer to people who aren't on a high level, they won't understand me. I accommodate my answer to their levels.

Q: What have you to say to FC's opponents?

A: The *yetzer hara* tries to extinguish all light. Don't worry. Hashem will reveal Himself in the near future.

They won't succeed in stopping us or in extinguishing the truth. They don't feel Hashem in their hearts. They are tied to this world, and are afraid of the World of Truth, because they are so far from it.

More About FC
Interview with a 9 year-old autistic child

Q: Should FC be publicized?

A: Yes. No one wants to suffer bodily and spiritually. Hearing a soul speak about Hashem's glory and grandeur has a profound influence on people.

Another child gave a totally different answer. She said: "There is no purpose to revealing the worlds of the soul, because a person who sees miracles in the hidden world does not need the messages conveyed by the souls, while a person who does not see these miracles won't see them even if souls speak to him."

The Successful Facilitator
an interview with Chaim, an eleven-year-old CP child

Q: What traits must a person possess in order to succeed in facilitating with you?

C: He should believe strongly that I want to relate to others like a normal person.

Q: Why have you stopped answering the volunteers who come to communicate with you?

C: The teachers don't communicate with me by means of FC the way they used to. They forgot that my thirst to write only actually reaches the letter board by means of a strong-minded attempt to force the soul to be revealed.

Q: Does this mean that they should be more forceful with you?

C: Yes.

Q: What else do you want to tell them?

C: To expect that I have answers to all their questions.

Q: Why don't you cooperate in communicating with Abba?

C: He's too emotional. He must learn be how to suppress his feeling of love for me while he facilitates.

Q: How can we teach him?

C: Explain that FC works only when the facilitator is firm. That's all Abba lacks.

Q: If he is firm, will you communicate with him?

C: Yes.

Q: Do you have anything else to say?

C: I love Abba, and didn't intend in any way to speak disrespectfully.

You are My Printer
an interview with: Shmulik, a 9 year-old autistic child

Q: Do you derive your ability to write from my power?

S: Yes.

Q: If so, then perhaps you are merely reading my thoughts?

S: No. That's not correct.

Q: Explain, then what's happening?

S: You are my printer, the means by which I express my thoughts. I arrange my words in a specific order.

Messengers
an interview with Amos, a twelve-year-old CP child

Q: Can you explain the nature of your messages?

A: They are warnings in which Hashem exhorts the Jewish Nation to do *teshuva*.

Q: Are your messages prophecy?

A: We aren't prophets. We are reincarnations of people who sinned in past lives and returned to this world in order to help Jews see the truth. Doing so is part of our *tikun*.

Q: Tell me more.

A: I receive messages directly from Heaven.

Q: How do you receive and impart these messages?

A: They issue from Hashem to the deepest recesses of my soul. From there, they pass to its upper parts, and then, with the help of the facilitator, to the material world. However the messages don't always reach this world in their original form, because as they pass from the spiritual world to our earthly one, changes can occur.

Peeking Through the Veils

Shaul, a Down syndrome child and Yossi, an autistic young man describe other aspects of the process of receiving and internalizing these messages.

> Shaul: "We are mentally incompetent. We have been sent to bring a message to the Jewish Nation, to peek beyond the veil which separates this world from the World of Truth and to receive a spark of the Sacred Light — only a small amount, amidst the dense darkness. We are only messengers.
>
> Yossi: "I am not the one who conceives these messages. They come from under the Throne of Glory. Hashem *wants* His people to repent. He *wants* to bring *Mashiach*. Only prayer and *Tehillim* can save the world. I once more repeat: I am only delivering a message."

We Have Work to Do
An Interview with Yerachmiel a 20 year-old with CP

> F: What have you to tell us?
>
> Y: I'm very happy that you finally arrived. I've been waiting for you for a long time. We have important work to do, and can't postpone it any longer.
>
> F: What work?
>
> Y: We have to warn the Jews who don't believe that Hashem is all-powerful: Return before the end.

F: Is it possible to heal you by [kabbalistic] means?

Y: No. We have a mission to do in this world and until we complete it we will not be at peace.

F: Can you tell us what sins you committed in your previous life?

Y: I won't tell you because that's not important.

F: It will help other people do *teshuva*.

Y: Just seeing someone like me writing is enough to cause people to do *teshuva*.

F: What must we do in order to bring Mashiach soon?

Y: *Teshuva*. Complete *teshuva*.

F: You're deaf. How can you hear my questions?

Y: I hear them with my soul.

F: How can you point to the letters without looking?

Y: I've already told you, through the eyes of my soul.

F: For which sins should our generation do *teshuva*?

Y: For *lashon hara*.

F: What about the other sins between Man and Hashem?

Y: Our generation belittles everything, whether it be the honor of their fellow man or the honor of Hashem.

F: Why did you preface the honor of man to the honor of Hashem?

Y: Because one learns to respect his fellow first.

An Interview with a Shomronite

F: Do you have anything special to say?

S: I don't want to talk, because I don't want to discuss Torah[1]. All I want to say is that Hashem is the King of the entire universe.

F: Why did you come down to earth in this form?

S: In order to praise Hashem. Very shortly all will recognize the true greatness of Hashem, even the members of my sect.

F: What is the difference between a Jew and a non-Jew?

S: I didn't come here to answer such questions. I came here only to praise Hashem.

F: In what manner do you praise Hashem?

S: I testify to the fact that Hashem is the King of the Universe, and the Prime Mover.

F: Since you can't speak or write, how can you testify to this?

S: Now you are giving me the opportunity to fulfill my mission in this world.

---

1 It is startling that he knows that a non-Jew is forbidden to study Torah as it is written "A non-Jew who [studies] Torah is subject to the death penalty, as it is written Moshe commanded us the Torah a legacy [for the community of Jacob] — a legacy for us and not for them" (*Sandhedrin* 59a).

F: Do all non-Jews know this fact?

S: Those who are alive and healthy, don't know. But every soul knows.

F: Do non-Jews have a share in the World to Come?

S: Not a full share.

F: Have you anything else to say about yourself?

S: Hashem is treating me very kindly.

F: What is the difference between a Shomronite and a non-Jew?

S: We are closer to the Jews. However our sin is greater, because we had the opportunity to know the truth, and squandered it.

II

Golden Strands: Essays by Ben Golden (verbatim)

Mashiach

Mashiach our King is here. He is right in our midst, standing next to us in a crowd. He *davens* with us in shul. We take no notice of him because we see only ourselves and our own needs. When will he be able to reveal himself? When will the time come? It must be very soon, because time as we know it is ending. Either we will reveal him or Hashem will.

Hashem created a King to lead a nation of *tzadikim*. When we become that nation Mashiach will be able to be crowned.

The work to make *baalei teshuva* is the most important effort to save Jewish souls and bring Mashiach without much suffering. When we can through our efforts bring all of *Am Yisrael* back to Torah, then maybe we will be able to crown Mashiach in peace.

Understand well what I am about to say. Mashiach is a person who is part of *Am Yisrael*. He is the greatest *tzadik*. He is G-d's representative and he is the human bridge between G-d and His people. But in order for *Am Yisrael* to recognize their King, they must be like him in holiness. When this happens it will become clear to holy eyes our holy Mashiach.

I must add here that if we will not work day and night to save Jewish souls, many many will be lost and Mashiach will arrive with great suffering. Those religious Jews who ignore their unenlightened brethren and make no effort to save them, it will be held against you.

I plead with my brothers and sisters, save us all.

Divine Love: One

All the people in the *midbar* were reliant on Hashem for all their sustenance. Where did *Bnei Yisrael* find the perseverance to wait each day for their food without having rebellious thoughts and fears of abandonment by Hashem? They would go out each morning and know that the *mon* would be laying on the ground waiting for them. There was no doubt in their minds. There was only strong *bitachon* and steadfastness in *emunah* that Hashem loves them beyond a doubt and that he would not betray them. The food would be there no matter what. Of that they were sure. What gave them such assurance? What signs did they get that Hashem wouldn't abandon them? They all knew that Hashem loves beyond a doubt and nothing would stop that love, that devotion to them, that deep-felt emotion. All of *Bnei Yisrael* knew that Hashem will provide their sustenance as long as they needed it. He wouldn't abandon his loved ones. He wouldn't let his people go hungry when they all relied on him for every morsel of the day. Hashem provided their needs whenever they needed. He provided their emotional support also whenever they needed it. Moshe was the *manhig* that Hashem sent to *Bnei Yisrael* in order for them to be able to withstand the *nisyonos* that Hashem put in their way.

He was the greatest teacher in the history of *Klal Yisrael*. He was the only one who could encourage the people to go on against all logic and rely entirely on Hashem. He was able to do this for he loved the people he governed. He loved them no matter what they said to him. He encouraged them even though they sometimes misbehaved. He was a true leader, a pillar of strength and an *anav* at the same time. He was able to govern an entire nation by himself without helpers only as long as the people believed in his love. They believed in it without doubts. Once doubts set in the influence weakened and helpers were necessary. Only with love, unconditional love, can a person trust completely his lover. Love is an emotional feeling that surpasses any other emotion.

When one is loved by Hashem he can rely on Hashem to take care of every physical and emotional need. He can rely without a doubt on Hashem to be there for him wherever and whenever he needs Him. Only Hashem can love so completely without jealousies, without envy without any outside interference. Love of this kind is unconditional and comes full force under any condition whether wanted or not, expected or not, or anticipated or not. Such love is unavailable among humans. Human emotions interfere in such love and distort it. Anyone who receives such love knows what it's like. It brings joy beyond comprehension. It brings ecstasy and excitement into one's life that was not felt ever before. It brings the ultimate happiness to a person.

Divine Love: Two

All of *Am Yisrael* were standing by *Har Sinai* when they received the *Torah* from Hashem. Moshe was in *Shamayim* and the *Yidden* trusted he would return to them. They were afraid — they were petrified, but they didn't run away. All *Am Yisrael* stood and didn't turn their backs and run away. They stayed and bore the fear because they knew Hashem loved them beyond a doubt. This love kept them standing in place even though they were overwhelmed with fear. They thought they will die with fear. All the *Yidden* stood and waited for the *nissim* that Hashem would bestow on them. They stood at attention in complete subservience to the G-d that they loved in return. They loved beyond a doubt. They loved with all their hearts. All the *Yidden* were glued to their places in love and service to their Creator. All the Yiddin were glued. All the *Yidden* were stuck to their creator. They were one with him at that moment and unable to move. They were glued to their Father in Heaven. They were one being, one *klal* one colony of people only serving one G-d. They had nothing else on their minds but Him. He was the focus of all their attention at the time. All their devotion and all their love. No one could distract them.

When *Am Yisrael* left the *Har Sinai* after the open revelation of the *Shechina* and Hashem's presence, they got shaky and fearful. They felt insecure and worried. They felt abandoned by their Lover. They needed the closeness of their Lover continuously after that to keep them intact. They could not be without it anymore. They felt what being one means and couldn't leave their Lover behind. They needed that show of love constantly and regularly in small doses in order to continue their existence. All the *Yidden* felt it and all of them needed it. All of them together missed it and as a unit were rebellious before Hashem and created the *egel hazahav*. All of them as a unit became insecure and made a mistake. They didn't know that Hashem is still there. They didn't know that Hashem would never leave them. They didn't know that it's temporary and He will return to them in forty days with the *Torah*. All the *Yidden* together sinned in their oneness. Oneness can trip also. Togetherness can also make mistakes. Oneness doubles the feeling of rightness. One must be careful that the decisions made in unity should be the right ones, should always be the will of Hashem and not the will of self. Yes. One must be careful to do what is expected of him and not his *ratzon*. He must do what is cut out for him to do and not his decision.

Divine Love: Three

All the *Yidden* in the *midbar* were devoted to Hashem's *Torah* and *mitzvos*. Yes. All the *Yidden* followed the letter the law. They all did everything exactly as they were supposed to. No deviations, no exceptions, no alterations. All the *mitzvos* were done exactly how Hashem decreed them on *Har Sinai*. There were no questions which yes and which no. All the *mitzvos* were of equal importance to the people. Everything was new and fresh in their mind. They couldn't make a mistake. Their teacher was beside them guiding them every step of the way. There was no room for deviations with Moshe around. You did as you were told. It was clear, absolutely clear, no errors. Only clarity, brightness, light. At the time of *Har Sinai* Hashem gave the Torah and made it very clear who was their Hashem, yes. Who was their G-d. Who was their light to follow. There were no doubts, no questions, only doing what was expected of them. Why, you may ask did *Bnei Yisrael* listen without doubts, without questions? Why didn't they argue a little here and a little there? They knew that the Torah was given with love and when love is involved in giving there is no doubt as to the intention of the giver that the motives are just for the benefit of the receiver. There can be no ulterior motives. Only good can come from love bestowed on a friend. Only good can be transmitted from one friend to another when love is involved. Giving from love is beautiful, it's wholesome, it's reassuring. It reassures the receiver that the giver is there for him and no one else. He is reassured he is not alone and is cared for. Giving from love is the *middah* of Hashem that we try to emulate the most. It is the hardest to achieve but the most gratifying. Giving enables a person to receive the love that Hashem has in store for us. By giving to others, Hashem's love can come upon us without interference and without interruptions. It flows freely like a river without stones, like a river without rocks. Only smooth flowing waters rushing in one direction to spill over onto the receiving pond to fill and become a lake of vastness and magnitude beyond the view of the naked eye.

Divine Love: Four

All the *Yidden* in the *midbar* were subservient to Hashem for everything. As we've said before there was no problem with who is boss. All the *Yidden* without exception knew that Hashem is One, the Creator of all and that He is Ruler of all. They knew that whatever Hashem did was for their good.

When Hashem said *Bnei Yisrael* should prepare themselves for receiving the Torah they were excited in their anticipation. They were thrilled that Hashem is bestowing on them a present with love. They knew if Hashem is giving them something of His *mi'Shamayim* it would be special and beyond human comprehension. They knew no human could create a divine Torah. No human could create a gift that was as perfect as the one Hashem created Himself.

All the *Yidden* trusted Hashem and waited for His presence to appear. They were frightened and trusted that nothing would happen to them to hurt them. Hashem wouldn't trick them. Hashem wouldn't trip them. They are His loved ones, his precious children, how could he hurt them?

Divine Love: Five

All the *Yidden* in the *midbar* relied on Hashem for all their sustenance. As we've said before, they were totally dependent on their Father in Heaven. Yes, yes, they all knew beyond a doubt that Hashem loved them and would never do anything to hurt them. Yes, when Moshe was told to fight the nations of the world for the benefit of *Bnei Yisrael* he didn't question. He just did what Hashem asked him to do. War came about as a *kiddush Hashem*. To be *mekadesh Shem Shamayim* is the highest *madreiga* a person could reach as a human being, living and breathing on this world. It is the closest one can get to the *kisei hakovod* from *olam hazeh*. *Kiddush Hashem* is the *mitzva* that comes from extreme love and utter devotion to *Melech Malchei Hamelachim Hakodosh Boruch Hu*. What is *Kiddush Hashem* you may ask? I'll explain. *Kiddush Hashem* is when you would give up everything of this world in order to sanctify Hashem's name, even if it is embarrassing, even if it is out of character, even if you are the only person doing it and everyone else laughs at you. Yes, *Kiddush Hashem* is a devotion to *Hakadosh Boruch Hu* that no one can uproot. It comes from love and giving that humans usually are incapable of. It comes from selflessness and servitude. A true *eved Hashem* is one who knows who his master is and serves no other. All his being is in service to the Master. Every limb and every organ. All for Hashem. A servant like this has no chains on his body, no chain on his soul — it's all for Hashem.

When one is serving Hashem like this there are no ulterior motives, no ego involved, no caring about impressing your fellow man. Yes, just doing what is expected without questions and without self-consciousness. It's a total giving up of one's physical needs and luxuries. Whatever one takes part of in this world it's so that he could better serve his Master in Heaven. It's not easy to be an *oved Hashem*. To remain on this *madreiga* one must be stubborn and steadfast in *emunah* and *bitachon*.

Davening with all his heart that Hashem should help him maintain this level of servitude without faltering, without falling off the top rung of the ladder to *Shamayim*

With conviction it's possible to reach these heights but the ego must disappear. There is no place for ego in a Jew coming closer to his Maker. Ego is selfishness, ego is self-centeredness, ego is anger. It distorts true servitude. It destroys true loyalty. Ego is a curse that clings to the person like a leech and won't let go unless the person wrenches it off and throws it away for good. How, you may ask, does one do this? By *davening* with a broken heart to Hashem that the ego should disappear. By practicing suppressing one's anger in every situation that would normally erupt into anger. By controlling one's *ta'avos* in everything such as food, dress, relations and household needs. By needing less — only what is absolutely necessary to continue functioning in this world, and to always know that what is given to you is given by Hashem for that purpose only — to better serve Him.

The *Matzav* Today

When all the *Yidden* are living according to the Torah the atmosphere in the world is one of harmony, peace, and tranquillity. When they live their lives in *sheker*, there is turmoil, distress, pain, conflict and disunity among brothers. This is our choice. It is black and white; either, or. We make the decision. Yes, yes.

All Jews no matter where they are must return to their Father in Heaven. They must show Him who is their G-d, who is their Creator. Yes. Must show Him that they believe it deep in their hearts and nothing will shake it. No fears, no threats. It has to be a steadfast *bitachon* in Hashem that is immovable under any condition.

Jews, wake up. It's your last chance. Now or never. No time to waste. War or peace, turmoil or tranquillity, upheaval or harmony. It's your choice. Do something together. Make a demonstration of devotion and maybe Hashem will change the *gezeira*. No time to waste. Now. In history, there were many *tekufot* of persecution and *tzarot* for *Yidden*. There were many times of uneasiness and terror. They were times when Hashem concealed his attention to us. They were times when *Yidden* felt that Hashem had deserted them. But really he was with them all the time. His presence couldn't be felt because no one was attuned to it. They were far-removed from him.

Now in our times in this *tekufa* of Purim he is hidden from us. That is because we are in need of true *teshuva*. Not the kind people are doing today. It is a *teshuva* that we today have not yet accomplished.

- Step one is *teshuva amitit* which is accomplished when one is totally immersed in his *avodah*, in Hashem's *derech*. It is total devotion to Hashem in *shamayim* and *bitachon* that whatever He does is for our good. *Teshuva* accomplished with these things in mind has to be *teshuva amitit*. The problem today is that the preconceived ideas that people use as a prerequisite to their *teshuva* destroys that *teshuva*. Then it is no longer *teshuva amitit* and therefore doesn't bring the *geula* that we wait for with such longing.

When one is about to begin his journey to true *teshuva*

one has to rid himself of all old baggage, all the old ideas that one has carried with him through one's lifetime, and start accumulating new valuable acquisitions that one can get from our former *talmidei chachamim* in their holy writings. There are all kinds of very important works written by *tzadikim* that help us realize who really is running this world. One does not have to be a *talmid chacham* to read these works. There is much written today in English on the issue.

- Step two is to learn *halacha*. We must know the correct way to do the mitzvot that we do anyway, but don't do right. All of us do *averot beshogeg* because we don't know halacha. We must all learn the fundamental basics of our Torah. One cannot be a good Jew without this. It doesn't come naturally to us like it did to Avraham Avinu. We must learn the halachot in order to do the mitzvot.

- Step three is that all good *Yidden* must get rid of all negative feelings against his fellow Jew. One cannot do true *teshuva* with negative feelings in one's heart against another *Yid*. *Yidden* must love one another. No choice. It is a commandment in our holy Torah. Just like eating kosher or putting on Tefillin. No difference. If one has difficulty with this, our *chachamim* have also set down guidelines how to accomplish this. One must work on this with the same diligence one works on his concentration in *davening* or any other *mitzva* that comes with difficulty. The feeling of accomplishment when one has conquered this is enormous.

- Step four is *Chessed*. That is a *yesod* in our behavior with our fellow Jew; the way we behave with our friend is the way Hashem will behave with us. *Mida kneged mida*. We set the tone. Practice the love of your fellow Jew when doing *Chessed*. It is easier to do *chessed* with one you love than one that disgusts you. When one has acquired love for all Jews then *Chessed* comes easier.

- Step five is that *teshuva amitit* needs *tefilla*. *Tefilla* with a broken heart for Hashem to accept our *tefilot*. Hashem waits for His children to daven. He wants to hear our cries of anguish so that he can answer them with his kindness. Even Moshe Rabeinu had to ask Hashem to forgive His children in the *midbar* after the *chet ha'egel*. It wasn't enough to just think those things. He had to plead with a broken heart for forty days before Hashem forgave His children.

- Step six is *emunah* in Hashem that all comes from Him. This comes as a result of true Torah observance. It comes as a result of true mitzva doing. It is the vehicle to bring us to true *emunah* in Hashem. When one is on a path of teshuva, *emunah* is a must. If not, then there will be many setbacks to trip him. But with *emunah* he will push forward no matter what obstacles come in his way.

- Step seven is that: *Yidden* must be aware of their surroundings at all times. No *traifos* in the air. No *devarim asurim* influencing their delicate make up. Outside influences have a definite negative effect on a holy Jew. We must always protect our surroundings and guard that no *tumah* seeps in.

- Step eight is that no Jew can accomplish true *teshuva* without learning *Hilchot Teshuva*. Again there are many *sefarim* written on this subject. It is very important to know the *halachot* of *teshuva*. Whole *sefarim* were written for this purpose. Use the direction of our holy *tzadikim* to guide us through the steps of *teshuva*.

- Step nine is love of Hashem. Love of Hashem comes through his mitzvos as well. But the difference here, between this and acquiring *emunah*, is that in loving Hashem one must acknowledge that he is our Father, and loves us as a father loves a son, with no hesitation, no question, no interference, only true love of a parent to a child. Then we can return His love in the same way we get it. Without it being attached to the things we get. One can love Hashem out of poverty. One can love Hashem out of sickness. One can love Hashem even when one doesn't see the end of his *tzarot*. One must love Hashem no matter what one gets from Him. It is not dependent in anything. Only in his own conviction to be devoted to the One who has created us and given us life.

- Step ten is *Simcha*. Without *Simcha* there is no life worth living. It is void of all the things that Hashem has created us for. *Simcha* in one's heart comes from the awareness that Hashem is our Creator, our Lover our Benefactor and He is devoted to no one else but His children here. The whole world was created for us. The Torah was created for us. This awareness should bring us to such joy that we should be able to dance from morning to night. With *Simcha* one can conquer anything, even one's own heart. With *Simcha* we can accomplish true *teshuva* and bring Mashiach in the fastest way possible.

Salvation

Our people for generations have been living lives of uncertainty. We have been persecuted and ridiculed and killed just because we are G-d's chosen. Our suffering has a few reasons. One is to be *mechaper* on the *chet* of *Adam Harishon*. Second is to be *mechaper* on *chet ha'egel*, which we still suffer from today. Third is the *tikun* that every Jew must do until the time of Mashiach.

The sin of the first man is cured by death. The person's individual *tikun* is in his hands to remedy. If he fails to do his mission, he is helped by Heaven through suffering in this world and *Gehennom* in the next world until his soul is pure. If an individual is a complete *rasha* and no merit can be found for his eternal existence, then he and his memory are wiped out.

Chet ha'egel is the sin that all generations have suffered from since the time it occurred in the desert so many years ago. Our generation is carrying the most intense effect of this abominable sin. We are the generation closest to Mashiach. We can reveal him if we can truly repent for the sin of the golden calf. This is not a simple task. No generation has been able to achieve this goal. Why should we succeed when greater generations of *tzaddikim* have failed?

Now let us define what the sin of the golden calf is. It is tied in with the sin of *Adam Harishon*. It is the lack of complete trust in Hashem, to be absolutely sure that He is in total control of the world and our individual lives. It is a lack of real faith in G-d. This is the only sin that includes all of *Am Yisrael* and every generation since it happened.

This lowly generation is steeped in the gold that the calf is made of. Most people, even "believers" put their real trust in man-made institutions such as the medical establishment, the weather man or the almighty army. Man is sure that he is in control. If he saves money in a pension fund he will be able to retire with security. If he has a very equipped army he will win the war. If he takes vitamins he will live to 120. Money, comfort and false security are more easily attained than ever before. Have no doubt, this trust in material toys has seeped into the *frum* community as well. We too are guilty. We are also keeping Mashiach away. Let the righteous know we carry this sin as well and we too will be held accountable.

This generation is lacking the sparks of *kodesh* that were so strong in previous *dorot*. We are so engulfed by *olam hazeh* that simple truths are no longer evident. Our generation is buried under the lies of this false world and we keep digging ourselves a deeper hole to completely hide G-d's Truth.

However, precisely because we have almost lost all visions of *emes*, we also have the greatest ability to effect complete repentance. Because the darkness is so deep, one thin ray of light can dismiss the night and bring the day in its full light.

This generation wallows in selfishness. The worst of all evils is selfishness and the greatest of all good is selflessness. Only this self-centered sin is total and open rebellion against Hashem. Hashem created us in his image. He is more than a Father. We are actually part of Him, really inseparable. But you silly normals think you can go about life doing things that your Father absolutely forbids without paying the price of separation. Voluntarily separating yourself from your source will ultimately bring you to physical and spiritual death. Make no mistake, there are many righteous people in this world. However they are hidden away by the "Sodom Syndrome", that prevails in all of the world including the Jewish people.

The *frum* Jewish community is also suffering from this malady. The situation lately is worse because, sadly, the greatest lights of Torah are slowly disappearing and like the Jewish people at the foot of Har Sinai, they make a Golden Calf because they feel alone. We, the Jewish people, are at fault. We are without desire to accept truth fully. We demand but are not ready to give. We quickly make a golden calf to take our Father's place (Heaven forbid) and so we voluntarily separate ourselves from Him. We tie ourselves to this temporary world and its self-centered lusts.

There is only one way out of this black, terrible situation. Collectively each and every Jew must find the Truth and accept it whole-heartedly. We can achieve this highest of all spiritual levels in one of two ways. Either Hashem will bring a terrible tragedy (Heaven forbid) that only He can save us from by doing open miracles, or the Jewish people as a whole must seek that Truth and accept it voluntarily.

Adam Harishon was the greatest human ever to exist. All souls find their source in his. He was the perfect creation. However Hashem created him with free will and this point only *Adam Harishon* himself could perfect. He failed and we, the sparks of his soul have been trying ever since to be *mitaken* this obstacle to perfection. This is precisely *Chet Ha'egel*. If we manage to achieve pure *teshuva* and total *bitachon* in Hashem's Kingship then this lowest of all generations can achieve perfection.

I am an autistic young man without speech. I can do only basic things for myself. I depend on the *Chessed* of kind people. I am an out-cast of life. Yet, in this lowly world, if I write: "Do *teshuva* now or else" people get scared. I guess it's as if a mule would suddenly start to speak words of *mussar*. Our beautiful holy Rabbis are ignored and strike up no fear. Only the words of a grotesque creature like myself may ignite the sparks of terror in the hearts of the sleeping.

G-d is Holding Back His Divine Anger

G-d is holding back his Divine anger. He is waiting and hoping that His children will return to Him. He is causing all kinds of tragedies in order to wake us up to reality. Will the lazy never realize, will the frolickers never leave their illusions, will the righteous never come back? Will the Creator have to destroy them all?

Mashiach is waiting for the signal to enter but we are keeping him from coming. Every day that we waste will make his arrival harder.

Wake up, wake up, Jews, come out of your stupor. Your time is almost at an end. Pick yourselves up. Crush your false idols, empty your cinemas of lies, discard all your materialistic junk, trample your intellectual pursuits. Strip yourself of ego and approach your Maker with nothing but love.

You Jews who arrogantly defy your Maker and obstinately oppose Him, beware. If you do not do *teshuva* now, you will be wiped out of existence. Your counter force cannot exist together with the all powerful Force of creation.

To the lazy, you too are in mortal danger. You slipped into the comforts of life, ignoring your soul's needs and the Mitzvos of your Maker. If you don't run after Truth with all your might, you too will have a sorry end.

To the religious, check your deeds with careful scrutiny. Then do *teshuva* with all your heart. You also have an obligation to bring back lost Jewish souls.

To the non-observant Jews, ignorance will not be an accepted excuse on the day of judgment. You must also seek truth.

G-d is Creator and Ruler of the world. His way is all good and love to His creations. His creations cannot decide what is best. Only His *derech* will prevail.

Go to your synagogues and pray that your stubbornness will not prevent you from reaching the delights of His Divine Truth.

Let me describe in a way that most humans can understand, the great reward given to *tzaddikim*.

Each soul will be given his own place in the Heavenly dwelling. Each soul will bask in the Divine Light which is the utmost pleasure in existence. The greater the soul, the closer it will be to the Divine Light. The G-dly Light is Torah, and those souls that searched out G-d's truth in Torah and Mitzvos during their lifetimes or supported such a search will be able to reap the greatest pleasure, men and women alike.

One last plea before I close. Jews, beloved of your Maker, His chosen people, His bride in the desert, His cherished children — come back to your Father and live.

The Arab Israeli Conflict

Reasoning people will agree that in a military conflict the force with the most seasoned soldiers, the most advanced military machinery, and the most advanced technical knowledge has the best chance to win the war. Sometimes the weaker force wins, but that is always easily explained logically. For example in World War II, Hitler with his stronger army was stopped at the Russian front by the snow, cold and huge amount of Russians.

Here in the Middle East, Israel has won several wars against her Arab neighbors. Israel is a very small country with a very small population and still she has managed to defeat her enemies who are great in size, population and financial wealth. But such victories are easily explained by logical Jews and gentiles alike. The reasoning goes something like this; really the Israelis had the upper hand because America helped her with money, equipment and technical knowledge. The Israelis, the people of the book, are well educated with the most advanced technical knowledge. Her enemies are largely uneducated and primitive. In light of this argument it is easily understood why the Israelis won and continue to win.

How are Jewish wars really won? Who are the real enemies of the Jews? Were the Romans or Germans our enemies? In present times are the Arabs our enemies? The terrible truth that logic hides is that we Jews have always been our own worst enemies. All the other so-called enemies of the Jews have grown out of distancing ourselves from our Creator. This is the way it works. When the Jews individually and as a group have *Bitochon b'Hashem*, complete faith in G-d, when they know that G-d makes everything happen, that we are only His servants here to do His will, to learn Torah and do *mitzvot* then we the Jewish people are completely protected by our Maker.

We may think that once the Arabs are defeated or when we are at peace with them, then we are safe, Israel is safe. Ridiculous reasoning by blind people. The truth is if we are doing Hashem's will fully and put our complete trust in Hashem then we are totally safe. We then have no fear or worry.

Jews listen to my words. I have nothing to gain from what I am writing to you. Take the truth into your minds. Understand what I am saying and accept it with all your senses. Close your minds to the lies of the nationalists, the deniers of G-d's greatness. Stop the advocates of democracy — freedom to reject Eternal Truth by popular vote. Put on your *teffilin*, wrap yourselves up in your *talleisim*, cry out to your Maker for help and accept wholeheartedly G-d's Kingship. Strip away all your false gods and direct all your desires into doing His Will. Know without doubt that He is All. Do not make the mistake of *Adom Harishon*, that can destroy us all. We are not G-d, even though He created us in His image. There is only one Creator and we are His servants.

When all Jews accept this truth and not the lies of the war mongers and peace makers alike, then salvation will come and the *Beis Hamikdash* will be reestablished and we all will be safe in our Father's loving arms. When every Jew can say *Shema Yisroel* with full trust and belief then we will have finally won the eternal war and will have defeated the true enemy, the only enemy that ever posed any danger to the Jewish people — the *yetzer harah*.

B'yemei Shefot Hashoftim

Shefot Hashoftim — this well describes the period before the crowning of *Am Yisrael's* King — Dovid *Melech Yisroel*. It was a time of chaos, a time when respect for the leaders of the *Am* was at a terrible low. But from this sad situation G-d's Kingship was established through a Moabite princess and a judge of Israel.

Today this much lower generation that we live in finds itself in a similar situation. *Shefot Hashoftim* is a common deficiency among observant Jews. The non-observant population to a much greater extent suffers from this malady and they have reached very low levels of disrespect for true justice, human feelings and life itself.

But we will not deal now with the terrible situation that prevails among the non-observant Jewish population in Israel. Instead we will focus on the so-called religious segment of the population. There are many types of Jews today that call themselves *frum*. Each one of these groups is sure that they have found the true way. But we are not going to investigate the pros and cons of each group's claim to eternity. No, we will go straight to the center of all of these outer circles and zero in on the ultra-Orthodox Jewish population.

Respect for our Torah scholars is the most basic concept in Judaism. Those who (Heaven forbid) lack respect for our *chachomim* will (Heaven forbid) soon not respect the words of their Father in Heaven. Sadly we are witnessing just such a time. *Shefot Hashoftim*, we judge our holy scholars and accept their judgments only when it coincides with our own desires. Yes, I am talking to the so-called *tzaddikim*. Our *bitachon* is sadly lacking and one of the major reasons for this is our lack of trust in G-d's representatives. Even the words of Torah have become ideas to say amen to, but not to become our reality in life. Troubled people declare in their misery, "There is no Rav to speak to. I have been to so many and have not gotten an answer. No one can help me." The answer they most certainly got, but just didn't want to accept it because it went against the tendency of their hearts.

The heart is the key. If the heart desires the truth then man can achieve total *bitachon*. But the heart of even the *frum* man is lusting after the delights of this world. Mild as his desires may seem in comparison to his non-religious counterpart, still they separate him from his Torah.

We must educate the heart as well as the mind to G-d's truth. We are failing in our efforts to educate our children's hearts. We live in a generation that considers a boy who learns Torah with diligence and wants to continue learning Torah after his marriage, the only kind of boy that most girls and their families want for a *choson*. A generation with so many *kollels, yeshivos,* and *cheders,* why then is the respect for our *Rabbonim*, our *Gedolim*, so low? Because we are educating the minds of our children to Torah but the heart we ignore. We have a *dor* that speaks holy words of Torah with a heart that desires the opposite.

Fathers and mothers, look into your hearts. Try to discern if the true desire of your heart is to serve your Father in Heaven. If not, then go to your Rav and tell him that you want to make your heart's desire Truth. Beg him to give you a program to achieve this goal. Then accept what he says and do it even if it goes against your opinion or desire. The Rav, the *Gadol Hador* is G-d's representative on earth and if you ask him for help then your puny opinion of what he tells you means nothing. Stop criticizing the Rabbonim of other groups of Jews. Woe to the *dor* whose children openly tell jokes about Rabbonim, Rebbes and other *Gedolei Hador*, all with parental approval. How can you hope to educate your children in such an atmosphere of disrespect?

Pitiful generation, raise yourself up, unite yourselves with your *Gedolim* and lust after Divine Truth. Humble yourself before the world of men so that eventually you will be able to reach the ultimate humility when you stand in front of the Divine Court on the day of judgment. If (Heaven forbid) you fail to achieve this great humility, even the fearful knowledge of Divine retribution will not help you to repent. The heart will be hardened by years of neglect and even the threat of oblivion will not soften it.

B'nei Torah, humble yourselves. Bring Torah into your hearts. If you fail (Heaven forbid) the Torah that you have learned will only work against you in *Shamayim*. Because Torah without heart is not Torah.

Only a generation that accepts G-d's chosen representatives will one day witness the crowning of Mashiach.

To Be a Jew

To be a Jew is an awesome responsibility. Every Jew must keep the entire Torah from his Bar Mitzvah to his death, 613 laws which dictate everything that a Jew does from when he wakes in the morning until he lays his head to rest at night. Every movement, every thought, every ripple in a Jewish heart is covered by G-d's holy Torah.

The Jew has no rest in this world. First he must spend his entire life learning Torah so that he will not fail in his obligations because of ignorance. He is also obligated to educate his heart to the Torah approach to life. No time to waste, since every Jew has a mission in this world that he must fulfill. Now you may think that, from what I wrote above, it is much too difficult for a poor Jew to bear. How can a weak human being be expected to live such a difficult life? A Jew is not expected to live such a life, he is obligated to dedicate his whole life to Torah. What gives the Jew the strength to live such a dedicated life? What gives him the fortitude and determination to keep G-d's mitzvos even in the face of mortal danger? The answer is the Divine Love that Hashem has directed to his beloved children and the love that *Am Yisrael* feels for their Father in Heaven.

What is Divine Love? It is G-d's all, His everything, His very essence. His relationship with the Jewish People is Truth and Divine Truth is Love. The Torah is truth and love. Therefore, the Jew that lives a life of Torah lives a life of

Eternal Truth and Divine Love.

G-d's love for his Jewish people has no limits. His only reason for the creation of the world with man at the center, was to create an extension of Himself. A man that could live a physical life in a G-dly way. But man let foreign matter enter his purity. The *yetzer hara* entered which brought pure man into an impure conflict with himself. Man fell from his greatest heights to his lowest depths. The Jewish people were created to bring man back to his former glory. They were given the Holy Torah to guide them every minute of their lives so that they would not fail. What great G-dly love! What great Divine *Chessed*! Hashem gave his people exact guidelines of how to attain immortality and the delights of the world-to-come. What extreme kindness! Now all a Jew has to do is live his short life in this world according to the Torah. So beautifully simple.

The *yetzer hara* knows that when a Jew leaves his Torah for even one split second, he can enter the Jew's heart and destroy him forever. However, G-d's great affection for his Jewish people allows a truly repentant Jew to return to his Father's loving home. Throughout history, there have been Jews who gave up their lives rather than give up their Torah. To die on *kiddush Hashem* is the greatest act of love a Jew can show his Creator. Still, many Jews have given up their Torah for the false idols of this world.

History is coming to an end, and the day of reckoning is drawing near. The rejecters of G-d's love will perish forever and peace will descend on the world. Mashiach will be King and Torah will be life. Then the light of Divine Love will fill every corner of the universe and beyond. The Heavens and the earth, men and angels will sing G-d's praises. Then He will be One and His Name One. And the earth and the universe and the Heavens will be filled with His Love.

Ben and Rabbi M. Discuss High-priority Issues

Q: What would you like to tell us today, Ben?

B: *Kevod HaRav* is surely aware of our nation's woes. Many yeshivos but little Torah, much kind deeds but little love of Hashem, illnesses – many and strange, many young people dying, many youths who have abandoned the right way of living, children born disabled every day, especially among the Orthodox. But no one asks why. No one asks what must be done.

There are organizations which direct the sick to appropriate doctors. Jews run hot-lines for yeshiva drop-outs. But no one is attempting to tackle the problem at its core. No one is attempting to deal with the root of the problem. Drought, pestilence, natural calamities. What does all this mean? Why are we silent? Why?

The root of the problem is our lack of unity with Hashem. We must be one entity: *Am Yisrael* and Hashem. But how can we achieve this when we are so deeply immersed in this world?

It is true that many people study Torah, true that Jews seek more and more to draw closer to Hashem. But they disregard the simple and direct means for acquiring *ahavas Hashem* and *bitachon*. Our society is disjoined, divided — rent asunder by groups, sects and religious parties. There are many *baalei teshuva*.

But dissension and confusion run amok. Everyone feels lost. The Nation is confused and is suffering. But no one understands why. People search for answers. They turn to fortune tellers, kabbalists and even autistic children.

The situation is tragic and menacing. Someone has to stand up and say "No." No! Stop relying on this world. Rid yourselves of the *kelipos* (a kabbalistic term meaning "covering" or entities which obstruct man's spiritual progress).

Weeping is heard. Tears are shed. Heaven is crying because the Nation has failed. Warnings are issued every day. But people don't heed them. People hold rallies. But afterward their enthusiasm wanes and the world continues.

HaRav, I know that what I am saying is not new to you. But something must be done. There isn't much time. We, the mentally incapacitated aren't *talmidei chachomim*; we aren't rabbis; we aren't kabbalists; we aren't prophets. We have come, at least some of us, to tell the truth — the simple truth that if we don't take steps to correct the situation, Hashem will take measures and then our suffering will be very great. Hashem loves his His people and wants them to unite with Him. Mashiach is waiting to arrive, bringing perfection with him. Why should we suffer for no reason? Something must be done. We are merely conveying a message.

Q: What must be done?

B: It is not I who says this. Binyomin Golden is

nothing, only a body which Heaven has assigned the task of conveying the truth. The people must be gathered, and shown the situation in a clear manner. They must be brought to *emunah*, to love of Hashem. But before that, they must be shown harsh reality and brought to tears. Most of the people suffer but doesn't feel that someone understands. The people must be brought to tears. Then they must recite *Vidui* together, place ashes on their heads and pray in unison. After that they must maintain the new level they have reached, a level on which they heed the *rabbonim* and realize that their concern is the welfare of the whole people, rather than their own. Once we have reached that level, great miracles will occur, and Hashem will save us.

Q: What can I do?

B: You, and others like you, can do a great deal. Jump into the water. All that is needed is one "Nachshon." Don't be afraid. Tell the world the truth. Speak to the Nation. Speak the truth. Show people that you understand their situation, that they are confused. Make order fearlessly.

Q: What do you mean by order?

B: Order means living with trust in Hashem, not placing one's trust in doctors or in the army, not depending on the government's National Security (Bituach Leumi), etc. It means being dependent only on Hashem. Only in this way will the evil be eradicated.

Q: Which sin is the worst?

B: The sin of the Golden calf.

Q: What do you mean by the Golden Calf?

B: *Olam hazeh*. What I have said is true and you know it. That is why you have received this message. What you do with it is not my affair but you have heard the truth. What is the law when one Jew sees another Jew in mortal danger and he is able to save him? What does the law require him to do?

Q: Are there so many afflictions for everyone?

B: This is an epidemic.

Q: Who are the *gedolim* that one must obey?

B: I mustn't say but the people do not recognize them. If the *gedolim* will stand firm they will receive the whole people together. Together they will repent. Then everything will change and there will no longer be so many illnesses and tragedies.

Q: How much more time until Mashiach?

B: Little, but hurry up. Now is a most dangerous time, all of the natural calamities, all of the difficult suffering and the *tzoros*, are warnings meant to hint to us that a terrible calamity will bring about the *yeshua*. But if we change, we can prevent the tremendous difficulties of this great change.

Q: How should we reach the people?

B: Directly. Assemble them and speak.

Q: What should we tell them?

B: I've already told you. Describe the situation. That will bring them to tears. Then tell that that Hashem wants to help. But first of all break their stiff necks, and cause them to humble themselves. Then tell them to place ashes on their heads, and recite *Vidui* — Ashkenazim Sephardim, Chassidim, Litvaks, jointly. It doesn't matter if at the beginning only a few convene. Keep up your efforts. Many more will come, and the impact of such a rally will be colossal. It will also bring those who are not religious and non-Jews because this will be true and be recognized as truth. Therefore there is all the suffering, in order to bring the people to the truth.

Q: Regarding which sin should we exhort the most?

B: The most severe sin, which brings to all other sins, is the *egel hazahav*.

Q: How should we influence people to do *teshuva* and increase their *yiras Shamayim*?

B: As I have said. It will start slowly, and the trend will gain impetus. Hashem wants to save the Nation. He will help, but together with others. Speak the truth exactly as I have put it.

Q: Why are cancer and Alzheimer's disease so prevalent?

B: Hashem wants to warn us, in order to bring us closer to Him. The people are distant. The source of all these illnesses is spiritual.

Q: What should one do in order to live long?

B: One must cleave to Hashem. May Hashem give you the strength to fight his battles. Shalom.

Ben at a Women's Rally (5759)

Shalom to all of you. Shalom to all of the women who are searching for the truth. The truth is very harsh. Every week terrible calamities occur not only in Eretz Yisroel, but all over the world — every day a new tragedy. There are more sick people among the chareidim than among non-Jews, more mentally disabled children, while non-Jews undergo more natural calamities. The amount of young people who have left the Torah path is very disconcerting. Some have dropped out of yeshiva and out of seminary, and we know who they are. Others are in the Beis Yaakov seminaries and yeshivas, and we don't know who they are. But they are tottering. The word is topsy turvy and nothing is clear. We don't know who is good and who is bad, who is a friend and who is a foe. Up is down, backwards is forwards. No one knows. Everything is confused. But people are afraid to ask "Why?" They are even afraid to think about this situation. As a result, they don't speak out and they bury the dead in the earth, continuing with their daily lives as if nothing had happened. Hashem addresses us, yet we are silent. We shut our ears in order not to hear, our eyes in order not to see. Only sometimes we sigh but we continue on. Never have there been so many problems in *shalom bayis*. There are problems of peace between Jews, between non-Jews, between countries. While such problems have always existed, never were there so many. And the trend is escalating. There are many *baalei teshuva*, many yeshivos, many synagogues filled with people who have come to pray. Nonetheless we lack unity with Hashem. That which is written *"Hashem echod u'Shemo echod"* means that we need to be one with Hashem. That's unity. Unity means accepting the dominion of Heaven on oneself and together. "Togetherness," rectifies the world. "Together" — *be'yachad*. Our generation seems to be the furthest removed from this state, but it is precisely this generation which must reach this state. Every fool can see that there would be no place to run if there will be anti-Jewish violence. Actually there will be, in the whole world. There will be no place of refuge. The harsh weather wreaks havoc the world over and not only in our own region. Slowly, the world is becoming smaller. More and more we are all in danger. Our *tikun* is *achdus*, meaning accepting the dominion of Heaven in full together, under Hashem's banner.

Why have you come here today? Because action must be taken. Just like in generations past, women can save the situation. Many of you have already begun to organize groups for the reciting of *Tehillim*. It is particularly important that they be recited in groups. For some reason, men do not concentrate on the recitation of *Tehillim*. As a result, the women must recite *Tehillim* as a means for saving the men. If every day, as many groups as possible meet to say *Tehillim*, even the non-religious will be positively influenced. We must recite *Tehillim* together in groups.

There are so many who have begun practicing Judaism but the quality of the observance of many of them is shallow. They notice the many shortcomings among the religious, such as the failure to be careful with one's fellow's money etc. But the recitation of *Tehillim* in unison, will have a positive effect on everyone. The recitation of *Tehillim* can propel one directly to the Throne of Glory. Love of Hashem and *Tehillim* are interlaced because *Tehillim* is a song of love for Hashem. It emerges from one's mouth, and streams into the soul, from where it from the goes directly to the Throne of Glory. Organizing groups to recite *Tehillim* is women's work. There isn't much time. All want to hear prophecies. *What will be?* they ask. This is silly because everyone can see the dangers. Great rabbis and kabbalists and even scientists sense danger. There isn't much time. Work swiftly. Hurry up. In order to save the Nation, we must approach the Throne of Glory with tears. *Im yirtzeh Hashem*, there will be a rally at the Kosel, and then we will come together to *daven*, to cry, to recite *Vidui*, and to beg for pity. There is a drought. There are calamities. Many people die. There are sufficient reasons to take out the ark with the Torah, place ashes on our heads, to recite *Vidui*, and to cry and beg for mercy and deliverance.

Ben Speaks at a Public Meeting

Q: Why did you come to Israel?

B: I have to be here, because that is what Hashem wants. I must study Torah in a yeshiva in the Holy Land with Hashem's assistance.

Q: How many languages do you know?

B: I only know one language, the language of the

soul. *Lashon Hakodesh* — the Holy Tongue — is the basis of all languages. The languages you know are good only in this world. There is only one language in the World of Truth.

Q: How has the new method of communication helped you?

B: It has helped me to communicate with my surroundings, to study Torah and to clearly convey that the *yeshua* can come only through Hashem.

Q: What message do you wish to convey before the High Holy Days?

A: Prepare for the fact that the end is nearing. We're not ready. *Teshuva! Teshuva! Teshuva!* Influence every Jew to save himself from spiritual death. Time is against us. Now! We must do *teshuva* right now. There is no time.

Q: What particular sins must we rectify?

B: We must concentrate on our interpersonal relations. They are the key to Gan Eden.

Ben Speaks at a Rally, Prior to Rosh Hashana

At the meeting, a man who doubted the validity of FC hurled derogatory remarks at the facilitator. The audience demanded that he leave the auditorium. Ben pleaded on his behalf, and said : "Shortly before Rosh Hashanah, I ask of you not to be angry with this young man. I know that it is difficult to believe that the mentally disabled have souls like other people. Our souls are like yours, except for the fact that our vessels — in other words our bodies — are broken. A *rachmanus* on you. I have nearly finished my *tikun*. You have a long way to go. In Heaven my situation is far better than yours, even though you believe that you are the ones who must pity me."

At that meeting the following exchange took place:

Q: Do you have a special message to convey?

B: I came here to say: We need a yeshiva just like other children.

Q: What must we do in order to be judged favorably on Rosh Hashanah?

B: Don't skip words when you pray, so that your prayers will penetrate your heart.

Q: Does this answer apply only to me, or to the entire audience?

B: To everyone.

Q: Should a woman with children try and recite the entire prayer service?

B: She should try.

Q: What is our *tikun*?

B: Don't speak *lashon hara*. Improve your interpersonal relationships. Torah study must be accompanied by *chessed* toward your families and toward every Jew. There are many Jews who study Torah, but don't do *chessed*. Guarding one's tongue is also a form of *chessed*.

Q: Do you have anything else to say?

B: Every Jew contains the Divine good. Even this generation has the merit to greet the Mashiach. Hashem loves His people and wants them to return to Him. I'm tired. I once again want to say that I don't like to make requests. We are in the hands of others. You, *boruch Hashem* don't know what it means to be dependent on others. Today, so many chidlren are born with difficulties and handicaps. I don't understand how a healthy person doesn't cry when he sees me, or others like me. Pray that there won't be any more cases like ours. There are enough.

III

The Religious Viewpoint

Although the amazing phenomenon described in this book has caused thousands of people to strengthen their level of religious observance, there are those who oppose FC on the grounds of various halachic prohibitions. We wish to address these issues and respond to them.

Some Torah Jews compare FC to the practice of communicating with the dead, which the Torah in *Devarim* 18:11 forbids. However it is important to note that even though there is a superficial similarity between the two, FC involves communicating with *living* people. This cannot be compared, for example, to a seance, where the participants purportedly communicate with the soul of a *non-living* person.

One rav has claimed that FC involves communication with *trafim*, because some of the children have presentiments about the future. Whether or not there exists a connection to the *issur* of *trafim*, however, is irrelevant. The reason is that the prohibition of communicating with *trafim* applies only to asking questions about future events. This is something which we are particularly careful to avoid, in accordance with the guidelines we have received from *Gedolei Yisrael*. What is more, those who do ask special children about future events invariably receive the response: "We are not permitted to answer such questions."

Others feel that FC might violate the injunction, "You shall be completely committed to Hashem, your G-d," (*Devarim* 18:13), which is also regarded as a prohibition against seeking foreknowledge of future events. However once again, as long as one does not ask the mentally disabled for information about future events, he need not fear violating this command.

HaRav Nissim Karelitz, *shlita*, has stated that one must not base his faith on the messages conveyed by children by means of FC. We asked him if it could not be used, however to arouse people to increase their fear of Heaven by showing them living, vivid examples of people who have felt the full force of Divine judgment, and yet justify Hashem's decree and accept it with love, knowing that the punishment is actually a form of kindness.

HaRav Karelitz agreed with this approach and has no objections to using the messages conveyed by the mentally disabled for this purpose. One must realize, of course, that the phenomenon presented in this book is a totally new discovery, something which was unknown in past generations. We must also bear in mind that the validity of this method might one day be definitively refuted. As a result we must not rely solely on them as supports for our faith, and remember that the genuine and unshakable foundations of our faith are the miraculous events of the Exodus from Egypt and the Giving of the Torah which we witnessed as a Nation.

However, in our somber times, we are justified in grasping at any straws which can strengthen our commitment to Torah, and especially at those which will motivate us to reach out to those of our yet non-observant brothers. We should be infinitely grateful to Hashem for revealing this new means of communication in our generation. The striking stories which have been revealed by means of FC have already borne fruit in the form of the many, many *baalei teshuva* who have been inspired to return to the Torah, not to mention the many Torah observant Jews who have found strength and been brought closer to Hashem as a result of these communications

IV

The Startling Implications of Facilitated Communication

by Rabbi Yechiel Sitzman

> *Rabbi Sitzman, an expert in the field of Facilitated Communication, has published a number of articles on the subject, and is currently preparing a website which will explain the subject in much greater detail than is possible here. He is presently teaching at Yeshivat Dvar Yerushalayim (The Jerusalem Academy of Jewish Studies).*

Rabbi Eliyahu of Vilna, better known as the Gaon of Vilna, explained the thirteenth blessing of the Amidah, which ends lauding G-d, "Who is a support and a trust for the righteous", as follows: When G-d wishes to save the righteous they must first trust in Him to deserve His intervention. He therefore supplies them with evidence of His activity on their behalf, to "support" them in developing the degree of trust that they need to deserve His full deliverance.

Example 1: To enable the Jewish nation to have sufficient trust in Him, to be willing to leave Egypt for the desert, a location without food or water, he first showed them His supernatural direction of events when He brought the ten plagues upon the Egyptians.

Example 2: After the decree of Haman to destroy the Jews, they needed to repent for their sin, motivated by their *love* for G-d. During their three-day fast, they only succeeded in repentance motivated by *fear* of G-d, which would not have sufficed to overcome the decree. G-d therefore showed them Haman leading Mordechai in royal garb and on the King's horse proclaiming, "This is what is done to the one whom the King desires to honour." When the Jews saw this, they realized that G-d is about to save them. This inspired them to trust in Him and to feel the emotion of love for Him. With this love they increased their repentance to the required level.

Example 3: Before the arrival of *Mashiach* (the messiah), G-d will display miracles similar to those which He showed at the time of our leaving Egypt. He will do this to enable us to develop the degree of trust in Him which we will require to weather successfully the process of redemption.

The phenomenon of facilitated communication (FC) could be a part of this preparation. During the past few years, a good number of disabled people, most of them Jewish (but also some non-Jewish), have transmitted messages with spiritual content via FC. These messages include descriptions of past lives, judgments for their deeds in past lives to which they were subject in the celestial court of justice, and warnings to individuals and to groups to prepare themselves for the imminent coming of the Mashiach and the troubles which may accompany his arrival.

There have been many people who have disputed the validity of FC. Even among those who accept the validity of FC, there have been those who have questioned the value of the spiritual messages which have been received via FC.

In 1998 and 1999, three books, *Venafshi Yodaat Meod, Galiah,* and *Galiah-Praidah,* were published in Hebrew, discussing this topic and reporting many of the spiritual messages which were written using this method. Tens of thousands of these books have been sold, and the messages have also been discussed on the religious radio here.

Venafshi Yodaat Meod includes an article written by myself, dealing at length with the various controversies regarding the FC phenomenon. My article is also available in English on the website of Yeshivat Dvar Yerushalayim: *www.Dvar.org* and on the website *www.goldenfc.com.*

In this present article I describe the dual role that FC can play in the process of the impending redemption. The redemption is described as transforming both the world at large, and also specifically the location, orientation, and political structure of the Jewish nation. These two transformations are interrelated, however, two different aspects of FC can be instrumental in affecting these two different groups.

Almost all cultures until the time of the French Revolution believed in spiritual entities and interactions. At that time, influential sectors of society adopted unproven materialistic axioms that have played a major role in the formation of the contemporary culture.

The philosophy of Amalek has been described as the denial of, and the opposition to, the concept of anything spiritual in the world (*Michtav M'Eliyahu* Vol 3 p. 217, Vol 5 p.333). The redemption is dependent upon the destruction of this philosophy, and the phenomena of FC can be used to help to defeat Amalek.

FC can only be explained adequately as an interaction of the spiritual components of the personalities of the disabled, whom we refer to in this article as the communicators, and the personality of the one who holds his hand, known as the facilitator. The controversy in the academic world as to whether they are really expressing their *own* thought is a result of academic unwillingness to admit to the existence of the above-mentioned spiritual interaction.

The undeniable fact is that, using FC, many people who are autistic and/or were previously thought to be severely retarded and illiterate, are able to communicate and exhibit a level of intelligence far above that which they had previously been thought to possess. Many of these people have never spoken and many others who do speak have very limited verbal vocabularies. Many of them were never taught to read or spell. How can one explain their suddenly discovered literary abilities?

Most of those who consider FC to be valid maintain that these people are not really retarded and that their inability to communicate normally is caused by motor problems. They suggest that the technique of FC enables the communicators to overcome these motor problems. As they are credited with possessing normal intelligence, it is claimed that they taught themselves to read and spell by observing television and other written material.

Those who deny the validity of FC cite the conclusions of many studies that prove that these people are actually retarded. These opponents of FC explain that the facilitators *unconsciously* and *unwittingly* cue or guide the communicators to point to the letters. Even though this explanation is very strange, the proponents of FC think that they are forced to admit that this process sometimes operates in this manner because there are instances when it is clear that the message that is spelled out has been influenced by the attitude and/or knowledge of the facilitator.

The proponents support their own position by bringing evidence of many messages which were written which contain information the facilitator did not know and therefore he could not have hinted to the communicator the appropriate letters.

Each side of this controversy belittles or ignores the solid evidence of its opponent, emphasizing, instead, the strong evidence which supports its own position.

What is the answer to this enigma? Rabbi Eliyahu E. Dessler wrote in *Michtav M'Eliyahu* (Vol. 4, pp.162-3; Vol. 5, pp.163, 199) that through our souls we have the potential ability to know about events and what is in the minds of others in any place in the world. Before we were born, we exercised this ability. After Mashiach comes we will also communicate using this ability. The soul also has an awareness of G-d and the spiritual realm which, were it accessible to our consciousness during our present lifetime, would eliminate our ability to choose to do wrong and thus it would curtail our free will. The main function of the brain is not to be the source of most of our knowledge, as is commonly thought, but rather to filter out that knowledge which is beyond the limitations of the body, time and space, so that we should retain the ability to choose to act properly and reject evil, which is the purpose of our being in this world. Rabbi Dessler explained that in spite of this function of the brain, sometimes such knowledge does reach our consciousness through the cracks (so to speak) in this barrier. Thus he explains telepathy, dreams which include true predictions of the future, diviners who are able to make true forecasts of the future, and instances in which people who are mentally ill sense things beyond the curtain of time and space.

He also suggested that this is the explanation for what the rabbis taught us, that though the classical form of prophecy ceased with the destruction of the temple, a more rudimentary form of it has been given to imbeciles and children, "for their barrier is not so firm." (As their brain is malfunctioning, it doesn't shield them from some spiritual information.) It is likely that this is the explanation for the extensive reports of telepathy that have been reported regarding autistic individuals in general, and also in particular among people using FC.

To mention only some of these published reports, they appeared in these publications: *A Child of Eternity* by Kristi Jorde and Adriana Rocha, *Memoirs of an Autistic Child* by John Chambers, *Qim Tunes* by Tom Smith, *Nobody Nowhere* by Donna Williams, *Paid for the Privilege* by Dan Reed, and,

Je Choisis la Main pour Parler (I Choose Your Hand to Talk) by Anne-Marguerite Vexeau of Paris

That telepathic powers are the solution to the enigma of FC has been explained by many users of FC. The following is a quotation from Ben Golden, who is autistic and non-verbal, which he communicated to his father, Arthur Golden:

> When I FC with you, I hold your index finger tightly around my other three fingers and thumb so your *nefesh* (spirit) which is closely connected to your *neshamah* (soul) allows my *neshamah* to express what is in the truest, deepest part. Since the *neshamah* sees without eyes, such an FC user does not need to look at the [alphabet] board. Also, the *neshamah* hears without the ears, instantly becomes literate in any language known by the facilitator, can access the deepest memories of the facilitator and communicate with other *neshamahs* by thought (which is often described as mental telepathy).

Though the literacy, including the ability to spell, of the communicator is obtained from the memory of the facilitator, the message is usually that of the communicator. This was explained by a 9-year-old girl using FC, who said, "You are my printer, but I arrange the words in a specific order."

According to this explanation, it is the *nefesh*, the spirit, of the communicator, which is actually disabled. The studies which showed that these people are really retarded were studying that part of their personality. In FC, the touch of the facilitator apparently enables another part of their personality, which is usually imprisoned by the *nefesh*, to express itself. This part is what Ben Golden called his *neshamah*. It is the psychic connection between the facilitator and the communicator, and not inadvertent cueing or guiding, which is responsible for facilitator influence.

That the answer to the enigma is that FC often has telepathic elements is an explanation that both sides of the controversy are trying to avoid admitting publicly.

Professor Anne Donnellan, a lecturer at the University of Wisconsin, and a long-time member of the Professional Advisory Board of the Autism Society of America, generally highly respected in the field of autism, was an exception to this attempt to squelch the real answer. She suggested that telepathy might be the solution, but has been severely criticized by her colleagues for such "unscientific" ideas.

In the book, *Emotional Maturity and Well-being: Psychological Lessons of Facilitated Communication*, which she and Paul Haskew authored together in 1992, they reported:

> Shortly after facilitation begins... facilitators often report that their communicators have an uncanny ability to know thoughts in their facilitators' minds, to understand what others think, feel or know, and to transmit their own thoughts to other non-verbal acquaintances, and sometimes to their facilitators. A young man we know told his facilitator what her high

school name was, and that she had a deceased relative who had been a musician. He was correct in every detail, including her feelings about her uncle. A mother told us about the adjustments she has made, knowing that she can have no secrets from her teenage daughter, and another mother told us that her adult son has no need to hear what she and his other two facilitators want him to know: he simply types the responses to their unspoken comments.

In this book, they also advanced a theory regarding telepathy which resembles the above mentioned explanation from Rabbi Dessler, though his explanation goes much deeper:

It may be that a sixth sense is present in all of us at birth, but as speech and locomotion develop, the need for it fades. Still, many people seem to retain vestigial psychic abilities, especially at times of accident or trauma, and there is much anecdotal and scientific literature describing these. For people with impaired communication capacities, the sixth sense may remain active and utilized. The speaking world is simply rediscovering it.

In 1992, in the journal, *Topics in Language Disorders,* Anne Donnellan wrote an article in which she suggested that telepathy might be the explanation for FC. She asked, "Are they learning to 'read' each other in some subliminal way, as some of the present learners have begun to suggest and learners and parents have reported in the past?"

Dr. Howard Spitz, who is a prominent spokesman for the anti-FC group, published his book *Non-conscious*

Movements From Mystical Messages to Facilitated Communications in 1997. In this book he attempts to explain away the phenomenon of FC. He mentions the approach of Donnellan and Haskew, and calls it "bizarre and preposterous". What is "bizarre and preposterous" to him is probably that it assumes the existence of non-physical events, which he rejects. His own attempt to explain what is happening is even more bizarre and preposterous. He claims that through evolutionary processes, organisms have developed "smart, self-organizing processes which can accompany or even displace primary, conscious processes." He suggests that it is these processes (subconscious independent personalities) within the thousands of facilitators who regularly engage in FC, that are the real authors of the many sophisticated and novel communications which have been produced via FC. This occurs without the awareness of the primary personality of the facilitators.

Dr. Spitz apparently doesn't consider it odd that these secondary personalities have no qualms about creating the hoax that it is the mentally disabled clients who are the authors of the communications which are really their own.

This explanation is so far-fetched that it really doesn't require refutation. Nevertheless, the great moral sensitivity demonstrated by the authors of the spiritual messages reported in the 3 above mentioned books and this pamphlet precludes the possibility that they were trying to fool everyone as to the true identity of the authors.

I have discussed the views of Dr. Spitz and others at greater length in an article which is available on the website:*http://members.home.net/qim/notimeforsilence.htm*

FC is able to provide us with overwhelmingly persuasive evidence of telepathy and the existence of a spiritual realm. With the assistance of G-d, we can use this, aided by the conceptual framework provided by Judaism, to overthrow the materialistic philosophy of Amalek. In this endeavor, we can look for allies among the thousands of people who are denied the opportunity to use FC with their loved ones because the establishment has not found an acceptable explanation for the technique.

Many mentally disabled individuals have claimed in their messages via FC that they have been commissioned by G-d to help us ready ourselves for the advent of Mashiach. We know no way of verifying whether this is really so, or of verifying the accuracy of some of the spiritual matters which they convey. In spite of this, many of their messages are so profound and so full of insight that they have had significant effect upon those who have read or heard them. This has occurred among Jews of all levels of commitment, ranging from non-Observant Jews who became observant, to our great Torah leaders who were very moved by their messages.

Hundreds of thousands of Jews have already been exposed to these messages. Some have witnessed FC directly. Many more have read literature, or heard lectures and radio broadcasts quoting them, and we can expect that the dissemination of these messages and of the significance of the technique of FC will increase rapidly in the near future.

According to some opinions (*Yalkut Shimoni*, chap. 227),

the miracles of the ten plagues succeeded in preparing only a minority of the Jews in Egypt for their redemption. The majority who were not sufficiently motivated spiritually did not merit to take part in the Exodus.

Also in reference to the advent of Mashiach, we are told in the Talmud (*Avodah Zora* 4a) that the bright light which will accompany his arrival will be a balm for the righteous, but will cause suffering to those who are not spiritually prepared. FC and the messages authored through it can be a powerful force in enabling many people to ready themselves for the Messianic era.

Glossary

achdus: unity
Adam Harishon: First Man
ahavas Hashem: love of G-d
ahavas Yisrael: love of Israel
amiti: true
anav: humble
averot beshogeg: unintentional sins
avodas Hashem: Divine service
Avraham HaIvri: Abraham the Hebrew
baalei teshuva: those who have repented
bas: the daughter of
Beis Din Shel Maalah: Heavenly court

Beis Hamikdash: the Sanctuary

beis medrash: house of study

bircas habayis: a blessing for harmony in the home

bitachon: trust

bnei Torah: those dedicated to Torah study and a Torah-true way of life

Bnei Yisrael: the Children of Israel

boruch Hashem: Blessed is Hashem (G-d)

bracha: blessing

"b'yemei shefot hashoftim": "during the days when the judges judged." A phrase taken from the Book of Ruth, which alludes to a period when the people judged the judges.

b'yachad: together

chessed: kindness

chet ha'egel: the sin of the Golden Calf

choson: bridegroom

daas Torah: the Torah view

daven: pray

derech: way

devarim asurim: forbidden things

dorot: generations

Egel Hazahav: the Golden Calf

emunah: belief

erev Shabbos: the eve of Sabbath

eved Hashem: a servant of G-d

frum: Torah observant

Gan Eden: Paradise

gedolei Yisroel: Israel's greatest Torah leaders

Gehennom: Purgatory

gezeira: decree.

goy: non-Jew

Hakadosh Boruch Hu: the Holy One Blessed be He

halochos: Torah laws

Har Sinai: Mount Sinai

hilchot teshuva: the laws of repentance

im yirtzeh Hashem: G-d willing

issur: prohibition

kashrus: being kosher

kedusha: sanctity

kiddush Hashem: sanctification of G-d's Name

kiruv rechokim: outreach work

Kisei Hakovod: the Throne of Glory

klall Yisroel: the Jewish Nation at large

kodesh: sacred

kollel: a yeshiva for married men

lashon hakodesh: the Holy Tongue

le'shem Shamayim: for the sake of Heaven.

loshon horah: slander

madreiga: level

manhig: leader

Mashiach: the Messiah

matzav: situation

mechaper: atone for

mekadesh: sanctify

mekayem: maintain

Melech Malchei Hamelachim: the King of Kings

Melech Yisroel: king of Israel

mesiras nefesh: self-sacrifice

mida: trait

mida kneged mida: measure for measure.

midbar: desert

mitaken: rectify

mitzvah: a Torah command

mussar: ethics

nissim: miracles

nisyonos: trials

olam ha-ba: the World to Come

olam hazeh: this world

ovdei Hashem: G-d's servants

parsha: weekly Torah reading

posuk: verse

posul: unfit

rabbonim: rabbis

rachmonus: compassion

rasha: a wicked person

rosh chodesh: the first of the month

rosh yeshiva: the head of a yeshiva

ruach hakodesh: Divine inspiration

ruchniyus: spirituality

savta: grandmother

sefer: book

Shabbos: the Sabbath

shalom bayis: family harmony

Shamayim: Heaven

Shechina: the Divine Presence

Shem Shamayim: Heaven's Name

shemiras halashon: the avoidance of forbidden speech

shiur: a Torah class

shlita: an abbreviation for "may he have a long and good life"

Shma Yisroel: the prayer "Hear O' Israel"

sifrei kodesh: sacred books

simcha: joy

T'nach: the Bible

ta'avos: desires

tachlis: purpose

talmidei chachamim: Torah scholars

tefillin: phylacteries

Tehillim: the Book of Psalms

teshuva: penance

tikun: rectification

trafim: idols

treif: non-kosher

tumah: impurity

tzaddekes: a righteous woman

tzaddikim: righteous men

tzarot: woes

tzedakah: charity

Vidui: a confessional prayer

yahrzeit: date marking a demise

yeshua: deliverance

yesod: foundation

Yidden: Jews

yiras Shamayim: fear of Heaven

Yizkor: prayer recited on festivals in memory of a deceased relative

zechus avos: merit of one's fathers

בשע"ת לר"י שער א' (סי' כ"ז בסופו), לכן מצינו בכמה דורות שהיו שם אנשים חשובים שהתחילו באיזה גילוי נכון מן השמים ונכשלו בגאות והתערבבו הדברים, והבן הדברים היטב. ובירושלים נפגשתי עם פגועת מח ושאלתיה אם הטעם שהגילוי בצורה כזאת מחמת גלות השכינה, ואמרה לי: "כן, נכון, אבל ההסבר הוא מפני שהעולם לא שלם על כן גם הגילויים לא שלמים". עכ"ד. וכבר כתבתי מספיק בזה לדורשי אמת.

וטרם אכלה דברי אחלה פני גדולי הדור ומנהיגיו ות"ח ישרים ואמיתיים שיגיעו להם ענין זה שכתבנו שאל יזלזלו במה שמכריזים ומזהירים אותנו וכ"א יטכס עצה בחכמה לתקן סביבתו ובמה שבידו כי הגיע זמן התשובה והתיקון והכל מסור לחכמי התורה, וגופא בתר רישא גריר, ויש להפחיד וגם לתת תקווה ולעורר האהבה וכנ"ל, והשומע ישמע ויציל נפשו ונפש כל ישראל, ולה' הישועה.

החותם בתקוה לתשובה ישועה וגאולה שלימה
חזקיהו אלכסנדר סענדר יצחק ערלנגער – מבני ברק
בן הרב הצדיק המקובל ר' **חיים ארי'ה מלוגאנא** זצ"ל

ע"כ לא דמי לגמרי לדברי הגמרא בברכות שמביא שם).

והנה תמיה בעיני ע"ד הגמרא ב"ב הנ"ל דכלפי מה שאמרו בגמרא שם מקודם, שיש נבואה אצל החכמים, יש ראיה מפסוק "וניבא ראיה בלבב חכמה", והגמרא אומרת תדע, ומביאה ראיה מהא דגברא רבא יכול לכוון הלמ"מ ע"י טעם וסברא, וזה כעין נבואה (וגם ד"ז צ"ב רחב דמוכח דהלמ"מ בעצם אין בו סברא טבעית לומר שכיוון מצד חכמה טבעית אלא הסברא שבה מרוה"ק כעין נבואה) – וכלפי ניתנה נבואה לשוטים מביא הגמרא עובדה דמר בר"א ואין שום ראיה על זה, ומנ"ל למר בר"א לעשות עובדה עפ"י הכרזת השוטה מבלי ראיה קודמת על זה – **ונראה פשוט שזה היה סוד מקובל אצל חז"ל** והביאו הדוגמא של המציאות באיזה אופן הוא ולכלשון הגמרא ע"ש, **ולע"ד הם סודות עמוקים בסוד יחודא תתאה**, וכמו שקשה להעמיק בענין, כי "ה' הוא האלוקים בשמים ממעל" עוד **יותר יקשה להבין "ועל הארץ מתחת אין עוד"**, (ובספר "דעת תבונות" העמיק בזה) – וגם בספר חסידים ידוע מאד הענין, והגר"א ז"ל בבאור ספד"צ פ"ה, כתב שכל פרטי פרטים מכל פרט דצח"מ רמוז הכל בתורה, קרי לכל הבריאה יש בה גילוי התורה וד"ל) – וכל הבריאה כולה יש בה קיום מכוחות הקדושה בסוד מלא כל הארץ כבודו, ולכן הכרוזים מתפשטים עד שם במקום נמוך – ומובא עוד במד"ר פרשת וארא (סי' י' ופ' ויקרא כ"ב) שהקב"ה אומר לנביאים: "אם אין אתם הולכים בשליחותי יש לי צפרדעים ובע"ח **שהולכים בשליחותי** ע"ש. ומובן שהשליחות הכל מסטרא דקדושה כעין נבואה ואכמ"ל.

והנה נוסח ששמעתי ממנו (מבנימין, וכן ילדים אחרים אומרים כן): **"שהם רק כלי להעביר מסרים מלמעלה"**. ולשון זה של ענין "כלי" כלפי נבואה מצאתי בספר יערות דבש (דרש י"ב), שכ': הנביא הוא עושה רק כמעשה כלי בעלמא ורוח ה' בקרבו ומוציא מפיו את אשר ישים ה' בפיו, ובזה מפרש מה שכתוב: "הרם כשופר קולך" שעושה רק מעשה כלי כשופר שמוציא מה שנופחין וממילא אין עונש אם מזכיר עוונות ישראל, אפילו אומר עם טמא שפתים רק אם אומר מעצמו ע"ש ביע"ד – ומה שהילדים יכולים להוציא רק במעשה כתיבה הוא משום שיש להם מעשה, ואין להם מחשבה, כמו ששנינו לענין טומאת כלים שנעשו ע"י תינוקות בסוגיא דחולין י"ב, והמושג שמתגלה דבר ע"י פעולה, מצינו אצל ריב"ז שהיה מכיר שיחת דקלים (עי' סוכה כ"ח) ופי' בערוך (ערך ס"ח), שאפשר להבחין בנטיית הדקלים ביום שאין הרוח נושב ואכמ"ל יותר.

ז. ביאור ענין גילוי זה מזמננו והתייחסות הגדולים והמשפיעים

ואם נשאל איפה מצינו הנהגה כזאת בדורות קודמים? – לא קשיא מידי, דכל דור יש לו הנהגה משלו, והדבר מפורש באבן שלמה פי"א אות ט' ע"ש היטב, ובמקום שאין לנו מספיק בעלי רוח"ק ופועלי ישועות כבדורות הקודמים, הקב"ה בעצמו ע"י שכינתו בתחתונים מגלה השגחתו וזה ענין השכינה, גילוי השגחה בתחתונים כמבואר בתשו' נוב"י תניינא או"ח סי' ק"ז ע"ש (ובארתי קצת בזה בהמאמרים לפ' "שובבי"ם ת"ת" ענין שכינה שאינו מסתרי תורה והוא ענין נחוץ לדעת אותו) – ובהכרח שיש דברים מתגלים בפועל, והגילוי דוקא באותן שאינם בעלי חטא ובחירה ואז הגילוי הוא קטן ומוגבל (ועי' אבן שלמה פ"ה סעי' ד' סק"ג מדברי הגר"א דהשכינה שורה רק על פועל צדק), ועוד טעם פשוט מפני שאצל אדם בעל בחירה יש נסיונות של גאוה בכל גילוי שהוא מקלקל ומסוכן יותר מגילוי אצל שוטה שהוא בתכלית הפשטות, וכל הסייעתא דשמיא תלוי בענווה כמבואר

י. שאלתי איזה גדול לשאול שאלה ודעת תורה - ענה: "אסור לי להגיד". וכן על עוד כך וכך דברים אמר שאינו ת"ח וזה מסור לחכמים - ועל איזה ענין נסתר ששאלתי, ענה בתוקף "עצור". ועל דברים אחרים אמר "איני יודע".

והנה עוד הרבה דברים בסגנון כזה, שעכשיו הזמן לתקן ויש **הרבה נשמות בינינו החרדים שירדו מהדרך, ומבחוץ נראים צדיקים, וזה הסכנה הגדולה ביותר** וצריך לתקן מהר טרם יחשיך - וכל הרואה דבריו וסגנון תשובותיו, מתרשם מאד שדבר אמת בפיו וזו **אזהרה מן השמים והכל מבחי' החסד העליון** ע"ד שאומרים בתפילה: "ומביא גואל לבני בניהם למען שמו באהבה", וזה ברכת "מגן אברהם" שהוא מבחי' האהבה, ולכן גם דרישת הענין הוא להתעורר באהבה והוא ע"י גילוי פנימיות הנפש בכח התורה ועובדי ה', ועל זה נאמר: "אם תעירו ואם תעוררו את האהבה עד שתחפץ", ובכל אדם מישראל **טמון נשמה ואהבת ה' והחיצוניות המקולקל מעכבו**, והם דברי הרמב"ם הידועים סוף פ"ב מה' גירושין וזה עבודתנו לגלותו, וכדברי הגמרא ברכות י"ז: "גלוי וידוע לפניך שרצוננו לעשות רצונך ומי מעכב שאור שבעיסה" - תקצר היריעה לבאר אמיתת הדבר **ולהשתתומם ממה שמוסרים לנו מן השמים** - וכל מי שפועל להחזיר את עצמו בתשובה, וגם לעזור לאחרים, הוא המקרב תכלית תיקון השכינה והגאולה ומציל עצמו וכל העולם מצרות גשמיות ורוחניות, והן דברי הזוה"ק שכותב על זה הרמח"ל זי"ע (דרך עץ חיים) **שר"ש צרח ככרוכיא** (תיקון ו') וי לון בני נשא דקוב"ה אסיר עמהון בגלותא ושכינתא עמהון ואתמר בהון אין חבוש מתיר עצמו מבית האסורין, ופורקנא דילה דאיהי תשובה אימא עלאה איהי תליא בידיהון בנ' תרעין דחירו עמה לקבל נ' זמנין דאדכר יצי"מ, **וירא כי אין איש דיתער בתיובתא** לתברא בית האסורין דלהון, אלא איש לדרכו פנו בעסקוי דלהון, בארחיו דלהון, איש לבצעו, בבצעא דהאי עלמא, לירתא האי עלמא וכו' ואינון ערב רב **דכל חסד דעבדין לגרמייהו** עבדין וכו' ע"ש כל הענין.

ו. עוד בענין נבואת שוטים, וכרוזים הבאים מלמעלה לעוה"ז

ועתה אחזור למה שדנתי באות א' בתחילה לסיים הענין מעין הפתיחה, **בענין ניתנה נבואה לשוטים** ואעתיק לשון קב הישר פרק ע"א וז"ל **"והנה אף שעכשיו** אין לנו בדור כמו רשב"י שיוכל לבטל גזרות רעות, מ"מ **חסדי ה' כי לא תמנו על כל דור ודור**, ומיד שנגזרה איזה גזירה למעלה רח"ל, מיד שלוחי מעלה מכריזין ומשמיעים הקול **והכרוז ע"י תינוק ותינוקת והן מתנבאים ואינם יודעים מה מתנבאים**, גם הקב"ה מעורר לב הכשרים ויראים שיתפללו על דורם והתעוררות בא מעצמותן", עכ"ל. וע"י שם פי' וניקי קב שמביא דבר זה כבדוק ומנוסה מספר הברית (ח"ב מאמר י"א סוף פ"ה) - ומציין לדברי הזוה"ק שמות ו', ושם כתוב מפורש **שהגזרות מוכרזין ע"י תינוק או שוטה או אפילו עופות השמים**, **ואי זכאין עלמא נמסר לרישי עמא כדי שיודיעו לדור ויעשו תשובה**, ואם לא, לית מאן דישגיח - ומוכח להדיא שדברי הגמרא כפשוטן שהוא נבואה וכרוז מן השמים, והנה בדבר שחוזר ונשנה הרבה בסגנון אחד ע"י שוטה, יש עוד הוכחה בגמרא גיטין ס"ח, דשוטה לא צריך בחד מילתא, וסנהדרין נהגו למעשה עפ"י סברא זו, ע"ש. - והכי נמי בנידון דידן יש לדון כך, והילדים כולם כבר כמה שנים שמזהירים לעשות תשובה ולדאוג להשפיע אצלנו החרדים על תשובה וכמבואר גם בספר **ונפשי יודעת מאד** (וגם בעיון יעקב לבעל ח"י על עין יעקב מצאתי שמפרש הענין מסט' דקדושה, ולא ע"י כדברי המהרש"א, וכבר פלפלתי לעיל דגם לדברי מהרש"א

המרומם לב האדם לעבודת ה') - ואמנם פשוט שגם ע"י עמל התורה בפשטות ישיג האדם זאת אם זה יהי רצונו, ויתבאר עוד) - ומה שנאמר שאהבת ה' נחוץ מפני שלא יקבלו היראה לבד (דהרי פשוט שגם עם יראה צריך לעבוד והרי כל ענין האוטיסטים אזהרת היראה שמאיימים על סכנת הכלל אם לא ישובו), גם זה **מקורו בחז"ל אם באת לשנוא דע שאתה אוהב ואין אוהב שונא** (ע" פירוש הרע"ב אבות פרק א' משנה ג'), ויש להאריך עוד בזה דכוונת אהבת ה' אצלם במסר זה הוא **למשוך לבבות היראים כלפי מעלה** דוגמת דברי הגמרא בר"ה כ"ט: "בשעה שישראל מסתכלין כלפי מעלה ומשעבדין את ליבם לאביהם שבשמים..." - וכל זה נתברר לי מתוך השיחה. ועיקר הדבר שאהבת ה' מתלוה עם תשובה הוא פסוק מפורש - "ומל ה' את לבבך וגו'". והביאו בשע"ת בסעי' הא' מספרו. גם מה שנאמר **לעבוד מן הפנים אל החיצון יש בו דבר עמוק** לגלות פנימיות הנפש דק.

גם מה שענה **לענין ההסתכלות** שתיקן הלב הקודם, הם **דברי הספרי סו"פ שלח** עה"פ "ולא תתורו אחרי לבבכם וגו'", שהעיניים הולכים אחרי הלב - **ועי' חינוך** באריכות מצוה שפ"ז דמנה שניהם "אחרי לבבכם ואחרי עיניכם" במצוה אחת ולא חילקם לב' מצוות, ובאר היטב כל הענין, והכל **מכוון לכל הדברים האזהרות שהוא קורא "עגל הזהב"** כגון ה"מכונית", ה"פלאפון", "הכובע היפה", "השטריימל היקר", "החתן הגבוה", "הכלה היפה", וכו'. גם אמר: "יש הרבה עם ציציות של צמר, כובע שחור וכו' והם מהס"א, **מעט מאמינים יש היום**, הרבה תורה וגמילות חסדים והרבה שנאת חינם" (הכל הם דברי חז"ל על מקדש שני ביומא ט'). ופשוט שכל התיקון אצלנו, בני תורה וחסידים יחד, הכל הוא רק תיקון הפנימיות במדרגה מסויימת, ומזה יתוקן וייראה הכל בפנים חדשות.

ז. **שאלתיו מה גדר האמונה**, האם צריך לעבוד יותר על מידת מסירות נפש וכו', וענה "ענין האמונה בדורנו שהאדם לא יעזוב את השי"ת בשום מצב שהוא, ועם כל הצרות יחזיק חזק לא משנה מה - ומחדירים אמונה ע"י פנימיות התורה". עכ"ד. ויסוד דבריו הרי פשוט בגמרא-מכות כ"ד: **בא חבקוק והעמידן על אחת, 'וצדיק באמונתו יחיה**, וזה יסוד לכל עליה וקיום כל המצוות, ולכן ענינו **להתחזק בכל מצב בה' וזה המקיים כל התורה**, ובין בעוני ובין בעושר אם האמונה בעומק הלב, זה קיומו של כל עבודת ה'. - גם על מה ששאלתיו בענין שידוכים ענה שיש רק שדכן אחד וצריך להתפלל ולמלא תפקידו - ובאיזה ענין אחר בנוגע לזש"ק עבור מישהו ענה שהעצה רק לעשות חסד, וידע שכן היתה תשובת החח"ז"ל וכתוב על זה בספרו "שם עולם".

ח. שאלתי אותו האם האוטיסטים מתפללים לה', וסיפרתי שכתוב בזוה"ק שגם המתים מתפללים על החיים, והשיב: "כן, נכון, **וכל הבריאה וגם דומם מהלל לה'**, והם האוטיסטים מתפללים תמיד על תקנת הדור והצלתו, וכל צדיק ע"י תפילתו מגיע לתורה וגמילות חסדים וגם לתפילה". שאלתיו אם כוונתו להגיע לשלמות ג' עמודים: תורה-עבודה-גמילות חסדים, ואמר לי: "באמת זה **הכל דבר אחד ה' אחד** ושמו אחד ורק אנו מחלקים הדברים כדי שנוכל להבינם ולהסתדר עם זה", עכ"ד. ודברים אלו הם מאד עמוקים וכל **השומע ומבין, ישתומם מי גילה להם רז זה.**

ט. שאלתיו עבורי עצה לזכות לאריכות ימים, ואמר: "איני נביא, אבל יש הרבה עבודה לקיים התפקיד ולהציל את הכלל ע"י התעוררות, עצות וחיזוק לתשובה ועבודת ה', וממילא מסתבר שיש סיכוי לאריכות ימים, ואם משיח צדקנו יבוא הכל יהיה טוב, וכל החיים קשים בלא"ה ואין לחשוב כ"כ על עצמו, ובאנו לעולם לסבול ולתקן ולהתעלות כידוע גם לך" (כך אמר לי)". גם פגועת המוח בתיה מירושלים אמרה הרבה דברי חכמה וזרוז (וקשה להעתיק כל הדברים שנאמרו בפקחות ובחריפות), ואמרה: "אתה רק עבד ה' ועשה תפקידך לשם שמים וכו'..."

ואמר לי דיש בזה תכלית לזכך האדם שיהיה ראוי למילוי תפקידו לזכות אחרים, **וזו היתה תשובה מבלי שאספר עניני**. וזה נכון שהנני מדבר ומעורר לרבים על עבודת ה', **וגם פשוט שזה זכות וצריך זיכוך לזכות לזה**. כלשון חז"ל משה "זכה" וזיכה את הרבים (אבות פ"ה: י"ח), ואי"צ להאריך.

ב. ענה על שאלה פרטית בעניני שאיני רוצה לפרטו, תשובה מדוייקת ביותר ובבהירות, והכל ע"י כמה מילים כאדם גדול בתורה.

ג. על עוד עניינים אמר כמה חידושים, אבל בכל השאלות ששאלתיו יישב העניינים בדברים מדוייקים, וחילק בדברים כמו למדן מובהק.

ד. בעניני ידיעות אחרות ששאלתיו אמר שאינו ת"ח וכל הדבר מסור לת"ח להכריע ולדעת, **ובעצם אומר שאינו יודע יותר ממני רק הוא "כלי" להעביר מסר** (ר"ל דברים שמוסרים לו מן השמים להעביר) **לצורך תיקון העם כדי להצילו** - וכדברים אלו כתובים גם בספר הנ"ל הרבה - ובתוך כל העניני ראינו שדואג להצלת הכלל מעונש וימים הקשים - שזה באמת מתאים לכל דברי חז"ל בעקבתא דמשיחא כידוע, **ודבריו היו ממש דומים בסגנון של רבנו הח"ח ז"ל שהיה מוכיח** לכלל ישראל, ודברי החח"ח כידוע היו **מאד דומים כעין סגנון הנביאים** שהוכיחו את ישראל **והכל בפשטות וישרות ומתוכם נשקף עמקות** גדול למבין, וזה סימן מובהק על אמיתתם כידוע לכל העוסק בתורת אמת.

ה. אין שום התנשאות והתרברבות בכל דבריהם רק פשוטים וישרים, ואין נוטלים שום עטרה לעצמם (היפוך מכל החוזים השקרנים שהיו בכל הדורות), **ורק דאגה וחרדה להיטיב עם הכלל יש להם**, וזה מוכח לעין - **וכל האזהרות סובבים על תורה וגמילות חסדים, והתרחקות מ"עגל הזהב"** שהם קוראים לתאוות וחמדות הזמן, וגם זה מאד אמיתי שעיקר סכנת היצר אין כ"כ בהתאוה כמות שהיא, רק חלק הע"ז שבה, וכל זה מכח הדור הרע הזה שגם אנו נלכדים בו שעושים בטעניהם אלוהיהם, וכדברי חובת הלבבות שער הפרישות פ"ב ע"ש, והם הצבועים שמבחוץ נראים כעושים מעשה פנחס כמו שהביא שם החובת הלבבות, עושים מעשה זמרי ומבקשים שכר כפנחס, וחז"ל אמרו (נדה י"ג): איזהו אל זר שבגופו של אדם זה יצה"ר - וכל אלי דברים ברורים ונכונים.

ו. **האוטיסט בנימין דבר על אהבת ה'** שצריך להחדיר בקרב העם, ושאלתיו הרי היראה קודמת ועקרית ואהבת ה' דרגה גדולה (כידוע מדברי רמב"ם סוף ה' תשובה), ותירץ דאמנם זה אמת אבל עיקר היראה להכניע ולהרתיע דורנו ודור חצוף שלא יקבל זאת, רק אם ח"ו הסטירה וההמכה מגיעה מרגישים, ולכן **צריך למושכם בדרך אהבה** (כ"ה בערך תוכן התשובה) - חזרתי ושאלתיו ע"כ הכוונה **שצריך לעורר הבני תורה** (כיוון שכל דבריו הם סובבים לתקן המובחרים בעם ועל ידי זה יתוקנו כולם, וגם זה דברים אמיתיים כידוע לנו), ע"י דברים פנימיים שבתוה"ק המעוררים את הנשמה ועל ידי זה יגיעו לאהבת ה', ענה ואמר כן **שהתיקון הוא מן הפנים אל החיצון** - שאלתי עוד האם לדבר על האיסור הסתכלות שזה מעיקרי הקלקול כאז"ל אין יצה"ר שולט אלא במה שעיניו רואות, והשיב אמנם שורש הקלקול בלב בו שיש מעט אמונה ומעט אהבת ה' ובדור הזה מעט מאמינים יש, עכ"ד.

והנה משיחה זו למדתי הרבה בס"ד, וכל דבריו אמת ומקורם בחז"ל דהרי **אהבת ה' נצטוינו בקריאת שמע** ואח"כ כתוב תיכף: "והיו הדברים האלה אשר אנוכי מצוך היום על לבבך", ופרשו בספרי דע"י התורה מגיעים לאהבת ה' (והח"ח ז"ל האריך בספרו שם עולם ח"א פרק י"ב), ופשוט שהם האגדות המרוממים פנימיות הנפש ועי' רמב"ם סהמ"צ מצוה ג' (יהוא כל עיקר פנימיות התורה

נמנע הטוב וההתעוררות, וכח התורה הוא יהיה המכריע תמיד. ולמי שאין התורה מכרעת בלא"ה לא ישאל לחכמים (וכעין שאמרו במס' חגיגה לע' ע"ה כלום משגיח עליך ע"ש כ"ב:) – ועניין **הצורך לעורר בנ"א אל התשובה והאמת הוא גדול מאד** גם בלי אזהרות מיוחדות, ועינינו רואות גם אצל היראים אעפ"י שכלפי חוץ מחזי כאכשור דרי, מ"מ אין תוכו כברו (ואפילו בזמן חז"ל חששו לזה כדאיתא במסכת ברכות כ"ח). וח"ו **ביום מן הימים מי יודע איזה נסיונות באים** ר"ל, ואיזה מנהיגים יהיו אז, ומי השומע ע"ד אמת, ואז ח"ו החיצוניות והצלחת הרשעים וכח הרע יתגבר **ויתגלה התוך המקולקל אם לא נמהר לתקנו** כפי היכולת בעוד מועד – **והכל תלוי ביסוד האמונה בלב שלם** וע"ז היצר עובד בתחבולות לקלקלו, וכבר העיד על כח היצר בכלל ובפרט בזה בספר חובות הלבבות שער יחוד המעשה בכל כוחו לרופף האמונה ולהגביר השקר והצביעיות גם בתוכנו – וכבר ניבא דניאל: "ויצרפו רבים והרשיעו רשעים וגו'" (ע"ש סוף הספר) – וע"י עוד חובת הלבבות שער יחוד המעשה פ"ה עיקר פיתוי היצר לקלקל האמונה רח"ל, ובשעת הנסיון אין מה לעשות, רק מה אפשר לחזק ולקדם לפני זה כידוע...

ה. הוכחות שראיתי מתוך דברי האוטיסטים על אמיתת דבריהם והאזהרות שמכריזים

זאת ועוד אחרת – הרי הילדים האוטיסטים הי"ו מזהירים על התשובה ואומרים שיש להם **"מסר מלמעלה" לעורר הדור על התקופה וטרם יגיעו ימים קשים וזה ממש בגדר נבואה קטנה** כדברי חז"ל הנ"ל שנתנה נבואה לשוטים (ר"ל שעומדים במקום הנביאים שהיו מוכיחים את ישראל ובדורות קודמים שדברי ישראל גדולי היו נשמעים יותר ליראי ה' ורוה"ק גלויה לא היו צריכים לזה כמובן), וכפי מה שנתבאר קצת העניין למעלה, ובאמת הרואה ושומע דבריהם **רואה שאין זה דברי שטות**, שאפילו ע"ז אמרו נבואה ניתנה לשוטים, אלא באמת **דבריהם חכמה מדוייקת להפליא**, אלא שהגברא הוא שוטה ודבריו הם חכמה ואמת, וזה בא ע"י מכח הנשמה שלהם וכמו שמבארים בעצמם היטב הדק כל ענינים, וזה עצמו העדות הנכונה בכל מה שמדברים על עצמם הוא ביושר ובדעת נכון **והדבר מוכיח בהרבה ראיות שרוח שדווה נכון מדבר מקרבם**, ואפילו אם לא היינו מוצאים מקור בחז"ל מדברי הגמרא הנ"ל בב"ב, גם היינו צריכים לשקול בעצמנו ולחפש מקורות בזוה"ק ובחכמי אמת, או אפילו לראות כפי ראות עיני חכמי הדור הקובעים בשודא דדייני, **וכל דברי הגמרא הנ"ל מסייעים שלא יהיה סתירה וקושיא, איך יתכן חכמה מפוארה או דברי תוכחה בכלי מכוער**, ויתכן מאד שקושיא זו לא היתה כלל מכרעת רק עכ"פ בגדר קושיא היא – אבל אחרי דברי הגמרא הנ"ל לא קשיא מידי, אלא אדרבא סיוע יש לאמת הדבר והכל אתי שפיר בפשטות.

והנה בזאת אוכיח ממה שראו עיני אמיתת פלאות הדברים:

א. נפגשתי עם האוטיסט בנימין בזכרון יעקב, ולפני שספרתי עניין, הקדימני בשלום, וביאר עניין מחלתי והסבל העובר ושעבר עלי, ונתן טעם שהתקבל על לבי – (כידוע שנחליתי עד שערי מות רח"ל כ"פ בשנת תשנ"ז תשנ"ח – עד שבניסים גלויים ניצלתי), (למרות שלא הוכיחני על תיקון עוונות והייתי מצפה לשמוע גם כזאת, ויש טעם באמת גם על העלמה זו, וכידוע מתוך הספר "ונפשי יודעת מאד" המבואר באורך עניין האוטיסטים שהם נזהרים בגילוי דברים בכבוד הבריות כשא"צ לגלות, כידוע בהל' תוכחה בלאו דלא תשא עליו חטא, והרי היו איתי אנשים אחרים שם) –

כמה טעמים להתנהג בזהירות:

א. לב ההמונים שהם עמי הארץ (והכוונה גם יודעי ספר וקובעי עתים לתורה, וגם המון בני תורה יכולים להיות נכללים בזה אם אין דעתם רחבה,) מאד נמשכים אחרי כל דבר נעלם, מפני ההתפעלות היתירה אחרי כל דבר מוזר, ואין יודעים כלל גדרי העניינים, **וכאשר מתרבה אמונה יתרה בדבר הדומה לנבואה** או גילוי מלמעלה, כבר יקבעו כל התורה וכל מיני הנהגות על פיהם, **והיצר הרע נתפס תיכף לזה**, ואנו **סובלים מאמונה יתרה שלא כפי גדר הנכון** (לפעמים כמעט כמו מכפירה), כי שניהם אינם גדר האמיתי של אמונה שהיא רק בחי' "אמת ואמונה" כמו שאמרו בתפילה בברכות ק"ש, וכן מובא בזוה"ק עניין זה, והביאור הפשוט **דכל אמונה צריך להיות קבוע עפ"י עניין הלכות התורה** ודברי חז"ל, וע"ז באו דברי התורה להעמיד את האמונה עפ"י הדעת האמיתי, וכל סטיה מזה גורם הפסד גדול, ואין כאן מקום להאריך, מכיוון שקשה לפרט העניין והמשך.

ב. כל גילוי מלמעלה **יכול להיות מעורב מטוב ורע**, ועיין הקדמת הרח"ו ז"ל לספרו "שערי קדושה" בזה, והדבר צריך בירור מפני שהיצר נאחז בכל מקום שיוכל, **ואין דבר טוב שאין לו פגע שיפסיד אותו** כל שכן בחובת הלבבות, והרבה דברים טובים בעולם התחילו בטוב וכאשר נתפשטו חוץ למקומם וזמנם נעשה פיגול, דוגמת קדשים כידוע, וזה כלל גדול בתורה שהיא מידת אמת השומרת גדר וגבול הדברים, (ואפילו בחלומו של יוסף הצדיק שהיה גילוי מן השמים לנביא כשר, היה בו תערובת דברים בטלים, כדמוכח שם בגמרא, וזה לא שייך בנבואה כדאיתא שם בגמרא נ"ז ואכמ"ל).

ג. **בענייני הלכה** והנהגה, הקביעות הוא רק עפ"י חכמי התורה **ומה שעבר דרך נשמת חכם חי**, והרי איתא סוף פרק הזהב (ב"מ נ"ט – וע"י' כסף משנה ה' טומא' צרעת פ"ב, ה"ט), לא בשמים היא, ולב בני אדם קלי דעת ואינם מבחינים בזה, וזה מפני מיעוט הדעת והאמונה האמיתית בתורה וחכמה, ומיעוט אמונת צדיקים אמיתיים שכל עניינם עפ"י אמיתת התורה וזה מעלתם – (ובמקום אמונה זו מחליפים אותה באיזה מנהיג שעולה יפה לפי דמיונו של הרוצה להאמין בו וגם רוצה שאחרים יאמינו בו, וכידוע).

ד. תמיד יש לחוש מאחיזת הס"א, ודוקא בדבר טוב ומיוחד יש חשש יותר, וערמת היצר הרע וסכנותיו גדולים, והדברים ידועים מכל הדורות שהס"א מתערבת ומקלקלת ומנצלת הכל דבר לתועלתה, וקל להפוך דברים מאמת לשקר, ואכמ"ל כי נוכל למצוא עוד הרבה טעמים וחששות.

ד. עם כל החששות אין להעלים מה שאמת ונכון עפ"ד תורה

ומ"מ עדיין אין לשלול העניין מחמת כל החששות במקום שיש בו תועלת רוחני עצום (וכמש"ת בסעיף הבא), והרי אנו עומדים תמיד כל היום (הן בשאלות הכלל והן בשאלות הפרט), באותה שאלה של: "אוי לי אם אעשה כך אוי לי אם לא אעשה", וכזאת מצינו בגמרא (ב"ב פ"ט) לגבי ריב"ז שנסתפק אם לדבר על הכלים שעושים בנ"א רמאים (כלפי מה שנוגע לה' טומאה), או שלא לדבר, ע"י' הספק, ולבסוף **אמרה מקרא "כי ישרים דרכי ה' וצדיקים ילכו בם ופושעים יכשלו בם"**, וזו השאלה י"ל תמיד בכל העניינים, וכהיום הזה עוד יותר, וצריך זהירות תמיד בזאת. וגם מאידך גיסא, לא למנוע התועלת והדברים ידועים.

ואם כן בנוגע לנ"ד הרי אנו בדור שגברה המינות ויצר התאוות ואם נמצא תועלת בזה לא

היה ראוי לאותו מינוי ומזה שפט דיש דברים בגו וסמך כל כך על זאת, לבטל מה שחשבו רבנן למנות את רב אחא מדפתי בראש, ומ"מ פשוט שזה נעשה עפ"י ד"ת מפני שהיו מתייעצין בו וזולתו לא היו ממנין אחד, אבל בכל זאת בלי הנבואה יששמע לא היה עושה כזאת ליטול עטרה לעצמו.

ב. אם יגלה דבר שאינו בתחום הטבעי כגון על איזה עתיד והדבר נתקיים, ומי גילה לו, ומזה מוכח שנתגלה מן השמים, והרי מצינו שהרוחות ידעו דברים מאחורי הפרגוד בר"פ מי שמתו, ויש כרוזים מן השמים לפני שהגזרה יוצאת לפועל, וכמבואר גם בזוה"ק שלפני פטירת האדם מכריזין עליו (וע" להלן אות ז'), ועוד הרבה ענינים מצינו בזוהר שיש כרוזים, ולפי דברי ה"תורת חיים" והמהר"ל **זה חלק טבעי בבריאה כמו שיש גזירות יש ע"ז הקדמה**, והוא קשר הקב"ה עם הבריאה בדיבור ומעשה ע"ד שכל בריאת העולם נאמר בו ויאמר וגם ויעש וי"ל בזה ואכ"מ.

ג. המופלא ביותר אם יגלה **דבר חכמה בטעמא דמילתא ואינו לפי כוחו וערך חכמתו, והת"ח השומע מבין דברי חכמה וחידוש**, הרי פשוט שאין זה מעשה שוטה (וכל החידוש בגמ' הוא בדבר שטות שבתחילת ענינו הוא דבר תמוה כעובדא דמר בר ר"א שלכאורה היה צריך לבוא המינוי בדבר כבוד והסכמת החכמים ולא בדבר הכרזת השוטה). ולכאורה יש בזה דרגא יותר ניכרת ממה שאמרו בגמ' לענין נבואת שוטים, דהרי זה **דומה למה שאמרו שם דנתנה נבואה לחכמים לכוון מסברתם הישרה הלכה למשה מסיני**, דלא שייך לומר בזה שבא מכח שכלו דסברת הלמ"מ הוא גילוי מלמעלה, אלא שהגרעון שיש בנבואת שוטה דאינו בא מכח השראת רוח"ק שזכה בו גוף זה, דהרי לאו בר מצוות הוא אלא גילוי מלמעלה ממקור חכמה ע"י כלי פשוט ביותר, והחכם הזוכה במעשיו ותורתו הוא גילוי קדושת תורה ומצוות ונקרא מנביא עדיף ע"ש בגמ' וברמב"ן.

ד. אם יעורר על יראת שמים, אהבת ה' וקיום התורה בצורה מיוחדת, והדברים ניכרים לעובדי ה' ות"ח שהם ממקור התורה האמיתית המסורה לנו, הרי זה סימן גדול שהדבר ממקור עליון (ואין כוונתי דוקא גילויים אדירים, אלא כל **גילוי אמיתי שניכר בו יד ה' עליונה – הוא גדול מאד** להתייחס אליו, והכרעת דברים אלו עפ"י טביעת עין של ת"ח גדולי תורה ויראה, וזה מן החזק שבהכרעות **ומצטרף לרוח"ק של חכמי הדור והת"ח** שרואים בזה אמיתת הענין, והעיקר, שיש לדון על הענין ולא על מי שאומר (פשוט שר"ל בנ"ד, משא"כ אם רשע אומר אפילו דברים נשגבים, מרשעים יצא רשע כידוע).

ה. אם יעורר אמת, הרי **בלי כל ההוכחות הנ"ל צריך למיחש דהרי בלא"ה אנו מצווים להתחזק תמיד**, ובפרט במצוקות הזמן, וביותר בעיקבתא דמשיחא שכבר ניבאו חז"ל ע"ז והזהירונו, וכן המקרים צריכים לעורר על התשובה כמו שכותב הרמב"ם להדיא בה' תעניות שזה מצוה מה"ת ע"ש דברים ברורים פ"א ה"ב ג' וע"ז נוסדה מסכת תענית והלכותיה, **ונמצא שכל נבואתו של השוטה היא מוחזקת מכח נבואת אמת של חז"ל והכל עפ"י התורה** והדבר ידוע לחכמי ישראל שכולנו זקוקים לתיקון, והדורות יורדים ה"י.

ג. באור החששות והטעמים שלא למהר להאמין בזה

ואמנם חשש המסתייגים למהר להאמין בנבואת שוטים (הכוונה בענין הילדים האוטיסטים בזמננו, שעל זה סובב המאמר הזה), וכן לקבוע ולסמוך יותר מדי על הענין הזה, **מובן בפשטות, דגם** אם יתכן שזה זה אמת ברור בו שיש כדי סמיכה והתעוררות ע"ד אמת, מ"מ החשש הוא נכון **מחמת**

בדרגת נבואה ממש ע"ש, אבל אין זה פי' הפשוט לרש"י ע"ש, וגם דברי מהרש"א צריך בירור להמעיין – וגם באוצר הכבוד שם מוכח דהחלום דרגת קדושה).

ובתורת חיים נקט באמת שהוא איזה **רוח עליון השורה גם על אנשים שאינם מהוגנים** (ר"ל שאינם ראויים לקבלת שפע רוח"ק מצד הכנתם), ופירש על דרך משל, למלך שעשה סעודה לעבדיו וסרחו עליו וציוה להשליכה לכלבים. וכן הקב"ה מצידו לא ימנע ואפי' לאחר החורבן מלהשפיע רוחו על ישראל, אלא לפי שאינם עושים רצונו שורה על שוטים ותינוקות, והוסיף עוד דחז"ל **השתמשו בפסוקיך שאמרו לינוקא** ולא חיישינן ל"ניחוש" מפני שרשאי לעשות כן, והוא בדמות נבואה וראוי לסמוך עליו, עכ"ד ע"ש.

ובמהר"ל ח"א על ב"ב כ' להזיא **דהנבואה מן השמים** ומפני כך השוטה שאין לו דעת אין פועל בשכלו לכך מקבל דבר הנעלם מעליונים, והוא כדוגמת בע"ח, שניתנה רשות לבהמה לראות יותר מן האדם מפני שהם תמימים ומקבלים יותר, וכן התינוק ג"כ שאינו פועל בשכלו מקבל נפש המדמה שלו העתידות. אבל החכם פועל בשכלו ואין נפש המדמה שלו מוכן לקבל עתידות כי אינו פני לזה ומבטל בשכלו קבלתו, ובזמן שביהמ"ק קיים שביהש"י היה קרוב לחכמים והיה קרוב אל העולם ואל הראוי לקבל הנבואה, וכאשר חרב ביהמ"ק **והנבואה באה לעולם מצד שכך גזר ה' על העולם – – לזה קרובים השוטים יותר לקבלה**. עכ"ד המהר"ל. ועוד באר בזה מהר"ל בספר "נצח ישראל" פכ"ו הענין, והביא עובדא דרב עיליש בפרק השולח (מ"ג), שהיה לו שליחות אודות מן העורב שצפצף בקולו, הרי דבע"ח ראו יותר מרב עיליש, וזה מחמת פשיטותם מקבלים ידיעות בעליונים, ע"כ.

ומבואר בפשיטות מדברי מהר"ל ותורת חיים דס"ל דשייך השראה עליונה על שוטים והכל מסיטרא דקדושה, ורשאי לסמוך ע"ז, וגם מש"כ מהרש"א שזה ע"י שד, פשוט שלא כתב איסור בזה, דהרי האמוראים סמכו ופעלו בזה, וגם ענין השד לפי דרכו לא ידענו מהו, ולא הרחיק עצם הדבר רק מיעט שאין זו דרגת רוח"ק רק איזה גילוי גרוע ונמנך (וע' מעילה י"ז ודו"ק). מלשון הגמ' נטלה נבואה מן הנביאים ונתנה לשוטים נשמע שהוא בדומה לנבואה, וע"ע להלן אות ז' בזה.

שו"ר בחתם סופר ב"ב שם שכתב וז"ל (אחרי שבאר ענין הנבואה שהוא למעלה מהשגת הנביא דרך כלי שכלו), ועל דרך זה נתנה נבואה לשוטים, כי לפעמים נשמת אדם רואה דברים ולבו אומר לו, אלא שנראה כדברים רחוקים ואין שכלו מניח לו להוציא דברי שטות כאלה מפיו, ובאמת הם דברים נגדרים למעלה, ובעיינינו (נראים) כדברים רחוקים, והשוטה אשר יראה יגיד. כגון, עובדא דרב טביומא וכיו"ב עכ"ל. (וע"ע בס' דובר צדק לר"צ הכהן זצ"ל, דף מ"ו, ביאר ענין זה קול ונבואה לשוטים וכמה בחי' כאלו שהוא גילוי מלמעלה בדרך אחוריים, לא להדיא פנים בפנים, ולכן דרשו חז"ל, מגילה ל"ב, מנין שמשתמשין בבת קול? שנא': "ואזניך תשמענה דבר מאחריך", ע"ש עוד ואכמ"ל).

ב. איך להבחין אמיתת הדברים

המקום והאופן לראות אם יש דברים בגו בנבואת השוטים, הוא על כמה אופנים:

א. אם השואל רואה לפי דעתו **שהתשובות קולעות אל תוכן הענין** והם מתאימים לנושא, וכעובדא דמגל' ב"ב שרב אשי שמע השוטה מכריז דמי מחסיא חותם טבימומי דזה היה חתימתו, והרי שם היה ענין של מלוכה ומינוי ריש מתיבתא ואין השוטה יודע מזה, וגם מר בר ר"א

בחינת דברי האוטיסטים על פי חז"ל

הרה"ג סענדר ערלנגר שליט"א

ביום כ"ו סיון שנה זו (תשנ"ט), נפגשתי עם האוטיסט בנימין במוסד זכרון יעקב – אחרי ששמעתי אודותיו וגם על אחרים כמובא בספר "ונפשי יודעת מאד" – ועל פי זה כתבתי המאמר הזה להציעו לפני גדולי דורנו ה' ישמרם ויאריך ימיהם בטוב, וגופא דעובדא הוי ששאלתיו כמה וכמה ענינים למעלה ממעשה שלימה והכל היה ע"י המתקשרת שהיא גם אשה חרדית – וכל התשובות היו לענין כהלכה תואמים מאד לפי כל השאלות וגם בדרך חכמה ויושר, והיו בדבריו גם חידושים, והם תואמים לדברי חז"ל ומה שכתוב בספרים הקדושים – וכמו שיראו במאמר הזה.

(**ואח"כ** נפגשתי עם עוד אחרת פגועת מוח בירושלים וגם היה הכל היה מדויק על דרך הנ"ל, תשובות מהירות מאד וכולם לענין, ישר, כחכמים מחוכמים. זה היה בי"ד תמוז כבר אחרי כתיבת המאמר הזה).

הענין הכללי היוצא מתוך דבריהם ומתוך האוטיסטים אחרים הרבה, הוא שיש סכנה קרובה (כמובן שאי אפשר לדעת מה זה קרוב, והרי יש מדת ארך אפים וכו'), וצריך לעורר העם לתשובה, ועיקר תפקידנו לתקן הראשים שהם החרדים והבני תורה שיהיה ליבם לשמים, ועל ידי זה יתוקנו אחרים שהם עוברי עבירה בסתר והם בתוכנו, ועל ידי זה יתוקנו אח"כ דלת העם הנדחים ותינוקות שנשבו – ואם, ח"ו, לא נתקן בעוד מועד, צריך, ח"ו, לעבור צירוף חזק של יסורין הן ברוחניות והן בגשמיות, ומי יודע עד היכן, השם ישמרנו.

כל זה תוכן התראתם, והנני מציע המו"מ מה שנראה עפ"י התורה, ולפי מה שראיתי לפני הגדולים ות"ח שבדורנו ואל יהיה עליהם למשא אריכות המאמר הזה כי דבר גדול הוא הענין ורוב דברי המאמר הם לצורך בהירות הענין (והנני מוכן לבוא לפני הגדולים לדבר פה אל פה, אם ירצו לחקור ואיני חושך שום טירחה בזה בעה"ת), וישפטו הם מה לעשות ואיך להתייחס.

א. בדברי הגמרא שנתנה נבואה לשוטים

איתא במסכת ב"ב (יב): מיום שחרב ביהמ"ק ניטלה נבואה מן הנביאים ונתנה לשוטים **ותינוקות**, ומייתי התם עובדא שמר בר רב אשי פעל עפ"י מה ששמע משוטה, **ובמהרש"א** פי' שאין זו נבואת הנביאים שניטלה מהם ונתנה לשוטים, אלא ענין אחר, שנבואת הנביא ע"י השי"ת או מלאך, ונבואת שוטה ותינוק ע"י שד כמו שחילקו בגמ' ברכות (נ"ה): לענין חלום אי הוי ע"י מלאך נאמר בו בחלום אדבר בו ואי ע"י שד נאמר אליו החלומות שוא ידברו, עכ"ד. ודמיון המהרש"א לגמ' ברכות צריך בירור דהא בגמ' הכא בגמ' עשה מעשה עפ"י נבואת שוטה וכן נתקים נבואת התינוק כמבואר בגמ' וא"כ על כרחך לא דמי לגמ' ברכות.

והנה בכל הסוגיא הארוכה בפרק הרואה חזינן דחלום בסתמא יש בו סימן ופקידה ונקרא אחד מששים בנבואה ולדינא יש תענית חלום בשבת והרבה ענינים, ועל כרחך דנקטינן שאין החלום ע"י שד ואינו מדבר שוא, ובגמ' חגיגה (ה) אמרי: אעפ"י שהסתרתי פני מהם, בחלום אדבר בו, ונמצא שעם כל ההסתר יש רצון ה' להתגלות ע"י חלום, ולמה נאמר כאן לענין נבואה שנטלה מן הנביאים ונתנה לשוטים שלא יהיה ע"י מלאך וכח הקדושה (ואמנם לפי' מהרש"א בחגיגה שם הענין מדבר